# THE HOUSE OF MOSS

By

Damon V. Defrein

Copyright 2025 by Damon V. Defrein. All rights reserved. No part of this book may be reproduced in any form without permission from the publisher, except for the use of brief quotations in a book review.

## Chapter One: The Pink Envelope, 1993

"For the love of God, Moss!" squeaked Dr. Rosen while not removing his eyes from the microscope, "Could you at least try to correctly pronounce the organism we are observing on this slide that you so haphazardly prepared for our review. The stains are a mess!"

Phillip Moss, a fourth-year medical student, kept his face glued to the oculars of his microscope as well, to shield the rolling of his eyes from others in the room and especially from Dr. Rosen. The table at which they were seated had six interconnected microscopes for viewing a single slide simultaneously. Today, those six seats were occupied by Dr. Rosen- the attending pathologist, two pathology residents, and three medical students. The condescending nature and irritating tones of Dr. Rosen's voice had worn Phil down over the past 4 weeks of his clinical pathology elective. He did not know if Dr. Rosen hated just him, hated medical students in general, or simply harbored a collective hate of mankind. With those thoughts floating through his consciousness, he took a deep breath, and repeated in his best booming stage voice, "the methylene blue stain of this specimen, when viewed through the 40x objective shows two Enta-MEEB-a Hist-O-LIT-IKA." The other students and two residents could not completely stifle their laughter, though they desperately tried. Dr. Rosen's eyes hovered over his microscope's oculars and glanced at the more senior resident to his left, rapidly quelling any sense of mirth developing at the table.

Dr. Rosen let out a single word, "Agree", with all the energy of the last bit of air leaving a deflating birthday balloon. He then promptly stood, adjusted his eyeglasses, inspected the alignment of his bowtie in the reflection of a glass cabinet containing jars of floating body parts and left the room.

Since it was now five p.m. on a Friday, and a rotation for which there was no direct patient responsibility, the three medical students all looked at one another and mouthed "Happy Hour." Smiles broke out all around the table. Book bags were retrieved from beneath chairs, notebooks stowed, and winter jackets adorned and zipped tightly. It was late January, and they were in Chicago. The walk back to their respective apartments, though brief, would not be comfortable. Lisa, Kamal, and Phil rounded the corner exiting the clinical laboratory area toward the building exit. They had been friends since the first week of medical school. Not surprisingly, it was dark, and the city lights seemed to magnify the intensity of the snow falling.

After several Chicago winters, Phil was accustomed to the temperatures, the wind, and the winter snow. He had attended college at Northwestern University and was more than willing to stay for medical school. He had made many friends in college who planned to either stay and work in the city or attend some form of graduate school there as well. He was thrilled four years prior when his acceptance letter came from the School of Medicine at Northwestern University. His friends Lisa and Kamal, while from Chicago had been away for their undergraduate education. He loved Chicago, and all it offered, but he would have moments of jealousy when Kamal or Lisa would decide on a Friday to spend a weekend with their respective families, or when one of their parents would just drop by with a food gift, or tickets to a show or Cubs game. He felt the tug deep within; it was time to go home, if he could.

    Many people do not realize that graduating medical students do not necessarily choose where they will spend the next three to eight years of their lives training as resident physicians. New graduates of military academies have more influence on their first assignment compared to freshly minted "M.D.'s." Professional athletes have agents behind the scenes wheeling and dealing to get the athlete where they want to be. The process for fourth year medical students is somewhat of a computerized lottery referred to as "The Match." Those students with the strongest applications have an advantage, and rightfully so. The students submit applications to as many training programs as they wish in the specialty of their choosing. The programs in turn then offer interviews to those applicants they wish to consider. After the interview "season" is complete, the programs list in order their favorite applicants, from perceived best to the last student they would be willing to train. Likewise, the students list in order their number one choice, and subsequent programs at which they would be willing to train. It is verboten to have independent discussions between applicant and program, such as "if you rank me first, I'll rank you first." On "Match Day" which is in the middle of March for most specialties, students learn if and where they have a job. Medical school auditoriums around the country on Match Day are filled with fourth-year students and sometimes their friends and families. The dean then beckons in alphabetical order each student to come forward and receive an envelope containing the name of the place at which they matched. These are emotionally charged situations, that for the most part are joyful. Likewise, the day before, the programs learn who they "matched", or if they had positions go "unmatched." But some specialties had their own "Match Day", referred to as an "Early Match." For neurosurgery, in 1993, the year Phil Moss was to graduate with his Doctorate in Medicine, this early match happened in late January. Phil had strived throughout medical school toward a career in neurosurgery. He wanted to go home for that next seven-year stage of his professional education. If he did a one-year fellowship afterward, he would chuckle to himself realizing that he would finally finish "school" after the 28th grade. His father was a neurosurgeon, internationally renowned, and had done the same. His father, Dr. Phillip Moss, Sr., had been chairman of the department of neurosurgery for over 20 years and built the program into one of the most respected training programs in the country. Phil adored and worshipped his father. The thought of returning home after eight years and working under the tutelage of his father to become a "brain surgeon" seemed surreal. He would do anything for that reality and for his father.

 As medical students arrived for happy hour alone, in pairs, or in groups the vibe in their favorite Streeterville haunt grew stronger. The beers were cheap, and the queso decent enough. Soon a contest of students imitating various professors and attending physicians created the cat calling antics and energy of a bachelor party at a strip club. A coffee table was requisitioned as the stage and the drunker students took turns atop the table imitating their professorial targets while the less drunk tried to guess who they were imitating. Phil enjoyed the good-natured fun and was sorely tempted to go up and do his best Dr. Rosen when he felt a head and shoulder lean into the side of his arm almost spilling his beer. He looked down to see Lisa, swaying to the music blaring Duran Duran overhead and holding what was clearly not her first beer. Lisa was much shorter than Phil, but he never really took notice often of that physical difference given her towering personality and powerful intelligence. They met during medical school orientation, were anatomy lab partners, drew each other's blood in histology lab, and quizzed each other before each test. Outside of the academic world though, they rarely crossed paths or ventured together. Her mother was Puerto Rican and her father unknown, but likely Caucasian given her appearance. Her last name was Mercado, and hence next to Moss alphabetically in the class roster. It was that twist of fate that had them assigned together in anatomy lab. She was attractive, but Phil always viewed her as a medical school sister, and never as a potential romantic partner. She pulled his arm down so she could speak into his ear over the music, "Someone said Roy Gillette received his pink envelope today in the mail." A string of cuss words streamed from the recesses of Phil's brain, but fortunately only one made it through to be spoken, "Shit! I need to get out of here!"

For some unexplained reason, the entity that oversaw the early matches would send correspondence in pink envelopes with information typed on pink stationery. Whether it was to differentiate such important information from other mail, or simply the economics of using paper products no other company would buy was unclear. Though the proximity in time to Valentine's Day was not lost on some, and the more cynical students entertained that the Match Overlords considered the pink color a form of comedic cruelty. The letters were to be mailed from San Francisco today, Friday, and so nobody was expecting them until next week.

Roy Gillette was the one other student in the class of '93 vying for a neurosurgical residency position. He wanted to stay at Northwestern and boasted he was ranking Northwestern first. Phil had ranked Northwestern second, behind his dad's program. There were three neurosurgical openings at Northwestern each year. Roy came from a very wealthy family in Chicago. His family had a multigenerational lineage of holding the controlling interest in the Chicago Mercantile Exchange. Roy would never hold a door open for anybody, never help cover another student's responsibilities on clinical rotations, participate in any sort of functional manner within a group, or acknowledge the thoughts or opinions of others. Roy would come to class wearing French cuffed dress shirts closed with cufflinks made of apparently rare gems and precious metals. In the first year he adorned the shirt with expensive silk ties from Paris fashion houses. The class knew all these details because Roy stated such, repeatedly. He did eventually lose the tie as the months went by, but then something worse evolved. He started leaving his dress shirt unbuttoned lower and lower and seemingly wearing pants much tighter than good taste would dictate. His dark hair was always perfectly quaffed, but shiny and "slicked back." He always wore a heavy chain necklace and a large class ring from H-AH-VAD. By the end of the second year of medical school he had gained considerable weight. He had all the appearance of the stereotypical sleaze ball. To his credit, he was very intelligent and an extremely hard worker, but nobody liked him. Every time the next round of clinical rotations was assigned to the class, every other class member would scour the list to see if Roy was within their assigned group. Early attempts by students to run to the dean's office for various reasons to switch out of a rotation shared with Roy were initially successful. The dean was no fool though, and he quickly appreciated the pattern and put a moratorium on rotation switching after assignments were distributed. The nicely funded Gillette Center for Biomedical Research at Northwestern University visible from the dean's office was somewhere Phil walked by every day on his way to clinical rotations. Suddenly the possibility of being a co-resident for seven years with possibly the biggest dick in Chicago made Phil want to vomit his beer. To say Roy was a pompous asshole would be an understatement. If the class had a vote for "Most Despised" student, Roy would win. In fact, Roy would probably vote for himself. He was that kind of asshole.

Lisa was snapped out of her party mode by the look of pure anxiety in Phil's eyes. "Jesus!" Lisa blurted as she guiltily made the sign of the cross, "Phil are you okay?" She got no response as he numbly walked toward the exit. "I'm going with you!", she yelled over the music as mercifully U-2 now was being pumped through the aging speaker system. She dashed away for a moment, but then quickly emerged with both their coats. "Damn it Phil, I'm the drunk one. Can't you remember your own coat! It's zero degrees outside!"

The realization of his own stupidity made him regain focus. Damn, he was about to find out where he was going to spend the next seven years of his life. But more importantly, was he going home, was he possibly going to match with Roy Gillette and stay in Chicago or was he going to end up at any of the other six programs he visited and ranked. The possibility of matching nowhere at all suddenly flashed in his mind. What would his dad think of him? His older sister was already finishing a residency in radiology at Washington University and headed to a prestigious fellowship at The Mayo Clinic. His younger sister was in law school at the University of Virginia and being considered to clerk for the Supreme Court. The shame would be unbearable if he did not match. He felt like he would be disappointing his father infinitely more than himself. His stomach churned, his throat was dry, and despite the snow, wind, and zero-degree temperature he had the overwhelming need to unzip his coat.

As they began shuffling through the fresh snow on the sidewalk, Lisa hooked her arm around his. Phil appreciated the affection she was showing, but then quite possibly she was using him to steady herself after one too many beers. Suddenly from behind them came a yell, "Where are you assholes going? Are you leaving me behind on purpose?" Kamal was doing his best to navigate the snow covered and slippery sidewalks. He wore penny loafers practically everywhere. The smooth soles afforded no traction in such conditions, and the low height allowed snow and slush to collect within his shoes. Between trying not to fall, failing, and removing snow building up in his shoes, he was a spectacle. He had not drunk any alcohol, as he never did, but a bystander watching the three from afar would swear in court that Kamal was clearly the most inebriated. To add to the irony of his clumsiness was that Kamal played varsity tennis at the University of Texas and was an excellent athlete. He said his Hindu upbringing required him to attend a school that worshipped cattle. When he caught up with them, he was somewhat breathless and said, "Roy Dick-illete just showed up and announced he matched at Northwestern." Then as if speaking out loud to himself, "I need to rethink my rank list for general surgery. I do not know if I could complete my internship and not kill the guy if I had to work with that douche. Maybe I'll just drop Northwestern off my list entirely. Damn, my parents would hate that. I know they are hoping I stay in Chicago. I can still rank the other Chicago programs though."

A smile of satisfaction broke out on Kamal's face, as though he had suddenly thought of something clever, while Phil and Lisa looked at each other rolling their eyes and simultaneously stated, "No shit Sherlock."

Then Phil looked at Kamal and flatly stated, "I'd take one year working with him over seven."

Kamal, though brilliant academically, and one of the nicest people either Phil or Lisa had ever met, was often clueless regarding other people's current state of mind. In a way his cluelessness became almost endearing over time and provided much more amusement than angst for them both. The realization of the matter at hand finally swept across Kamal's face, "Holy Lakshmi! Phil, we need to get to your mailbox."

Then all three looked at each other and then shouted up into the falling snow, "No shit Sherlock!!!", and collapsed laughing until tears were landing on their winter coats and quickly freezing.

The mailroom on the first floor of Phil's apartment was accessed by going through the locked front entrance and veering behind a desk that once served as the post for the "doorman" in a past life of this apartment building. Phil had spent all four years of medical school here. It was convenient, seemingly safe, and affordable. Nobody of any means lived here though. But since it was mostly graduate students and junior faculty, the place did have a lot of intellectual firepower. He considered it somewhat of a dormitory for smart adults.

Phil dug his keys from his pocket and found the small brass mailbox key. Lisa and Kamal stood back as though Phil were opening the Arc of the Covenant. He reached in and with great effort extracted a large wad of envelopes and flyers. Kamal's transfixed gaze was broken as he remarked, "Geez Phil, when is the last time you checked your mail?" Phil just grunted. Kamal turned to Lisa and whispered, "Maybe he is trying to manufacture diamonds." She gave Kamal a stern look and punched him in the arm, hard. Phil started throwing flyers down from local grocers, WorldCom and Circuit City; there was a phone bill, a flyer from IBM for discounted personal computers for students, and then the pink envelope.

"Upstairs," was Phil's only word.

Lisa looked concerned, "Phil, do you want us with you, or would you rather be alone?"

Phil closed the mailbox, gathered the other mail items, and then they hurried to the elevator. The old elevator could be heard but the light indicator showed it going between the 8th and 11th floors. Phil couldn't stand it and his second word since seeing the pink envelope was, "Stairs."

Phil's apartment was on the fourth floor. They bounded up the three flights despite their heavy coats. Phil unlocked the door, and they dropped their coats on the floor and kicked their shoes off within the entrance. A loveseat and chair were around a small coffee table. All three squeezed on the loveseat with Phil in the middle. Lisa repeated her question, "Phil do you want us here?"

Phil without removing his eyes from the pink envelope said, "You guys are my best friends, damn right I want you here." Lisa and Kamal leaned back and exchanged smiles behind Phil, and each put a hand on Phil's shoulders as he opened the envelope.

Phil unfolded the pink paper to read the one line that mattered under "Matched Program." He let out a huge breath, fell back into the love seat, looked up at the ceiling with tears forming in his eyes, and in a raspy whisper said, "I'm going home."

Lisa and Kamal leaned forward, each grabbing one side of the paper and read under Matched Program: "The University of Pittsburgh Medical Center."

### Chapter Two: Battle of Hue, 1968

    Major Moss slept on a stretcher outside a tent that served as a makeshift operating room. The tent had space for six operating tables, though the Mobile Army Surgical Hospital (MASH) unit had only five surgeons when fully staffed. The Tet Offensive was in full swing. The forces of South Vietnam and the United States were fighting against North Vietnam and the Viet Cong in a deadly urban slugfest. The USA was doing the heavy lifting and painstakingly regaining control over the city of Hue and its surroundings, or at least regaining control over what was left of the city. While theoretically "safe" from live fire at this MASH unit, the sounds of artillery and gunfire were frequent. The loudest sounds though, came from the air support of helicopters and jets roaring overhead toward the frontline. For 6 weeks the noise never stopped, the wounded, dead, and dying kept coming, and the evil of mankind was on full display as civilians butchered by the Viet Cong were anonymously delivered at night to the perimeter of the MASH compound. The addition of the heat, humidity, insects, and paucity of sleep made it Hell on earth. What made it tolerable was knowing it was worse for those fighting on the frontlines and for the families caught in the crossfire of this so called "conflict."

    Dr. Phillip Moss, now wore fatigues with a gold leaf adorning the collar identifying him as a Major in the United

States Army medical corp. A few years ago, he had completed his training at Washington University under a chairman who treated each resident so poorly, precious few would remain to finish training. These young doctors were very intelligent, motivated, and some technically gifted. In the end, many had their will to continue in the discipline of neurological surgery crushed by this chairman. Major Moss thought of how many of those young colleagues he would love to have working with him now under these trying circumstances.

After leaving St. Louis, he spent a fellowship year in Ontario, Canada learning the nuances of the burgeoning field of cerebrovascular surgery. His mentor in London, Ontario was not only smart and gifted, but a kind soul who was very appreciative of those around him. That year provided the affirmation that he indeed had done the right thing by sticking with neurosurgery as a career. The mountain of regret he had compiled with his career choice was washed away. He also met a beautiful woman with striking blue eyes and raven black hair at one of his mentor's many home gatherings. Dr. Moss had a nearly perpetual smile on his face as he now had a life where he could leave the hospital before dark on occasion and above all, was respected and valued. He was able to start running and rowing during the warmer months and felt his physical condition returning to how he remembered himself as a medical student. When this young lady accepted an offer to dinner with him, he was beyond ecstatic. For him, it was love at first sight. He hoped she felt the same, but then again, she was quite intelligent and probably not prone to such whimsical thinking. Finally, life was falling into place. They dated throughout his year in Ontario. Camelus Bouchard was the daughter of the chair of radiology and worked within the department as a medical physicist. She held a master's degree from McMaster University. Despite her intelligence and work ethic, she always felt others, whether real or imagined, believed she had her position because of "Daddy." She was desperate for an opportunity to prove to herself as well as others that she had what it took to succeed in her profession, and that nepotism played no role in her successes.

In the spring of that fellowship year the University of Pittsburgh needed to recruit a neurosurgeon with expertise in cerebrovascular surgery. Phillip's mentor informed him of the opportunity. He called Pittsburgh that day and was in his Oldsmobile the next morning to drive to Pittsburgh for an interview. In his mind, he was accepting the job regardless of pay amount or conditions. He was impressed with the faculty and institution. He sensed real potential for both him and the program. Before he left Pittsburgh two days later, the chairman offered him the position of Assistant Professor and Head of Cerebrovascular Surgery. Holding back the urge to kiss the top of the chairman's bald head, he asked if he might have a small signing bonus of $250. While taken aback by such a request, the chairman chuckled and said, "I'll give you $500, but it is coming out of your first paycheck!" They shook hands and the chair directed his secretary to cut a check for $500 to Dr. Moss. Dr. Moss went to the first jeweler he could find, endorsed the check, took off his watch his father had given him, and said, "Give me the best diamond ring these will buy."

Phillip and Cammie were married in July of that year. They bought an old Victorian home in the Shadyside district of Pittsburgh. It was way too big for just the two of them, but both hoped for children, parties, and all that life would throw at them. It was not long before Cammie was pregnant. By the next summer they were parents to a healthy baby girl, and Cammie made the decision to leave her position as a medical physicist at the university. She had transformed the safety and efficacy of the radiology department in such a brief time, and all those around her pleaded for her to return one day. She struggled with the concept of returning to work holding her baby girl at the kitchen table, when Phillip came home one evening as somber as he ever had been in her presence. Her initial thought was a medical tragedy had occurred, but the paper he held in his hand told otherwise. He dismissively tossed the sheet of paper on the kitchen table before her. He had been drafted into the army medical corps. He was to report to Walter Reed in Washington, D.C. in two weeks. His chairman had called his connections at Walter Reed and learned that Dr. Phillip Moss would be stationed "forward" in the very near term. Cammie asked, "What does 'stationed forward' mean?"

He looked up from the letter they were both staring at resting on the kitchen table, and said, "Nam, Vietnam." He pulled up a chair and embraced them both. As mother and father wept, while ironically their baby daughter cooed and smiled. Thank God she is too young to comprehend is all both parents could think.

He awoke with a startle as a corpsman shuck his shoulder, "Sir, casualties are inbound. Most are described as belly and leg wounds, but one soldier took a through and through to his neck and is bleeding badly as soon as they release pressure. A platoon was ambushed trying to evacuate civilians."

"Damn, I was at my kitchen table looking at my...," Major Moss's voice trailed off.

"Sir?" the corpsman respectfully replied.

"Never mind," Major Moss stated as he shook the cobwebs from his brain, "Let's get to work."

While all the surgeons at the MASH unit, regardless of specialty could treat, or at least attempt to treat any combat wound, Major Moss was the only neurosurgeon. The surgery within the canvas walls of the makeshift hospital did not involve the finesse of removing a tumor from eloquent brain, clipping an aneurysm, or carefully decompressing a threatened spinal cord. The surgery done here was to stop bleeding, stop death, or at least delay it.

Within minutes the roar of the transport ambulances could be heard, and corpsmen unloaded stretcher after stretcher. Major Moss saw the head nurse stop one stretcher from entering the tent. The soldier's face was ashen white, and his bowels were hanging off the stretcher. He was beyond help. The next stretcher came with three corpsmen though, as one was applying pressure to the left side of the soldier's neck. They hurriedly were directed to the OR table where Major Moss and his team were assembled. Blood was everywhere. The anesthesiologist cleaned the soldier's face so he could secure the endotracheal tube once placed. God, this soldier looked so young. He had a small entrance wound just to the left of his Adam's Apple and a larger exit wound directly behind on the back side of his neck. The bullet path fortunately had missed the spine and airway but clearly had injured the left carotid artery. Anytime the corpsman released pressure on either the entrance or exit wound arterial blood shot out. The corpsman looked in agony. "How long have you been holding pressure?" asked Major Moss.

"From when he went down to here, sir," croaked the corpsman. "This soldier was providing cover fire for me as I tried to get to his buddy, who was already down. He's on the next table over. Then we both got shot, only he got it worse." The corpsman rotated his back to show where a bullet had traversed and filleted the flesh and muscle of his back, without hitting anything vital. All Major Moss could think was how painful that must be to endure, especially as he had to contort himself to continually apply pressure to the soldier's neck wounds in the field, in the ambulance, and now on the operating table. The corpsman finished by saying, "But this corporal plugged that Viet Cong right between the eyes just as he fired at us again. He took a bullet for me. Save him doc."

Major Moss was overwhelmed by the heroism laid before him, wondering what purpose this all serves in God's Grand Plan, if there is one. The dog tags resting on the chest of the soldier identified him as "John Moretti." Corporal Moretti was about to be the 15th person for Dr. Moss to operate on this week, and it was only Tuesday morning.

After securing more intravenous (IV) access, and a stable airway, the anesthesiologist gave the go ahead to Dr. Moss to proceed. They found another corpsman to be under the surgical drapes and hold pressure on the exit wound, while Dr. Moss quickly exposed the injured carotid artery through the entrance wound that he lengthened significantly with a scalpel.

Most people are right-handed, and hence the left hemisphere of the brain is the dominant side. To the lay person that means a right-handed person uses the left side of the brain to move the dominant (right) side of the body, and probably more importantly to understand and generate speech. It is a tragedy to be left paralyzed on one side, but a double tragedy to be paralyzed and unable to comprehend and communicate. Also, if there were a large enough stroke, the brain can swell and generate so much pressure within the skull that the patient dies. For all these reasons, it was not just a task of stopping bleeding to save Corporal Moretti, but to also repair the carotid artery and restore proper blood flow to the left side of the brain. This would be the first operation requiring any "finesse" that Major Moss would need to perform in Vietnam. Back in

Pittsburgh, this would still be a daunting situation, but with teams of experts, skilled residents, near infinite supplies, and not needing to worry about an artillery shell landing on you, such a case should go smoothly.

After gaining exposure of the injury, he quickly saw that he could not simply sew the hole closed, as a chunk of the artery was missing. A patch was necessary. He instructed the nurse to prep out (clean with sterile solution) the Corporal's left lower leg. He had her then hold pressure on the injured carotid while he quickly harvested a length of saphenous vein from the lower leg to serve as the patch. He was then able to fashion a piece of the harvested vein to match the section of artery missing and skillfully sew it in place. He released the clamps, and blood began pulsing through the left carotid without bleeding. It had taken some time, however, and he may have been too late. The brain can only go so long without appropriate blood flow. All he could do now was close the wounds and wait for the anesthesia to wear off.

He then went looking for the corpsman who had held pressure for so long and was himself shot. It did not take long as another team was taking care of him while the injured corpsman remained seated on a chair leaning forward on a table, letting out very forgivable cuss words for the pain he was enduring. "Just a flesh wound", the most senior general surgeon in the unit said as he cleansed the raw flesh and passed some large sutures that looked like hooks used to reel in a shark. Maybe just flesh, but hell, didn't Jesus just have "flesh wounds" Major Moss thought to himself. He noted the corpsman's name, Luther Robinson. He was going to report to the CO (Commanding Officer) these two soldiers who merited recognition for bravery. He only hoped Corporal Moretti would live to receive any award.

More injured soldiers arrived later, but thankfully nothing as gruesome as the morning. The surgical teams finally had an opportunity to eat and did so voraciously despite the low quality of the food. He shared his meal with the anesthesiologist with whom he worked today. Anderson was an excellent "gas passer." He trained at UCLA and was practicing in Orange County when his notice came. Moss enjoyed working with him because he was efficient, unflappable, and hysterical at the right time. Anderson assured Moss that all the anesthetics would be out of Moretti's system by now. Calories were calories, they would say to each other. After subjecting his stomach to as much "nutrition" as he could bear, Major Moss walked over to the convalescence tent. The nurse in charge directed him to the cot where Corporal John Moretti was. Major Moss leaned over and whispered, "John." After no response he increased his volume with each spoken "John." There was no response. Medical training teaches the next step is to inflict pain to try and arouse the patient. This is an important and necessary part of the neurological examination. Moss simply could not bring himself to "inflict" anymore pain on this poor soul who had done so much. He stood at the foot of the cot and bit his upper lip and just said, "Godspeed John", and turned away.

"I'm fucking Jack. My dad is John", croaked Moretti, "What the hell happened?"

Moss's eyes went wide as he spun around. "Then Jack it is!", Moss gleefully yelled. Moss quickly had Moretti raise both arms, both legs, repeat words, identify objects, and do simple math. Other than an exceedingly hoarse voice his neurological examination was excellent. Jack quickly apologized for his language when he saw the gold leaves pinned on Moss's fatigues. Moss assured him, he could cuss in front of him any time he wanted. Moss explained Moretti's injury to him and what was surgically done, but for the "what happened", he needed to retrieve the eyewitness.

Luther Robinson, while assigned a convalescence cot (he was shot after all), was up and walking around the unit as he heard a rumor somebody had ice cream available. Major Moss had him summoned over the speaker system that happened to be working that evening. He introduced the two enlisted men to each other, or more correctly reintroduced them. Luther Robinson was as animated and happy as Moss to see how well Moretti seemed to be doing. After Luther finished telling Jack the full story from the battlefield, the reality of how serious everything was hit Jack like a bulldozer. He had two people to which he owed his life and countless others he would never know the names of who drove the ambulance, coordinated their safe rival dodging mortar rounds, and played crucial roles in the operating room. Luther Robinson was from Bessemer, Alabama and as black as the night is dark with a smile and laugh that melted hearts. Jack Moretti was built like a fireplug, from Uniontown, Pennsylvania, and offended when called Italian, as he was Sicilian! They became best friends instantly, and shared an unbreakable bond forged in the throes of battle that only those similarly cursed with experiencing could ever understand.

That night, like many nights, Phillip Moss got in his cot with pen and paper to write his wife, "Dear Cammie, Today we had…" and fell asleep.

As the Vietnamese summer weather of 1968 intensified, the intensity of battle waned. Moss was called to the CO's office one July morning. "Phil, I hate your guts," the CO loudly proclaimed, "You are going home. They are rotating your crew stateside. I suspect they'll keep you at Walter Reed for a bit, but hopefully by the new year you can be back in Pittsburgh."

Moss replied, "Sir, if this is why you hate my guts, I am honored to have my guts hated by you as well as any other organ systems."

"Phil, you can be such a sarcastic prick. But then again, I expect that from my surgeons. You should be proud of the work you've done here. You will be missed," the CO stated frankly as he looked down at his desk.

And for the first time since arriving, Major Moss stood ramrod stiff, saluted the CO and returned to rounding in the convalescent tent. In addition to his daughter, he had an infant son, Phil Jr., at home he had only been able to see for two days when granted leave for the birth. He was now a happy man in such a miserable place.

## Chapter Three: Graduation, 1993

    Graduation at Northwestern University threatened to be upended by the last arctic blast of the season whipping across Lake Michigan. Whereas earlier in the week students had been sunning on the beach, and throwing frisbees in the parks, they now could look out their windows and see dark grey skies spitting a mix of snow and sleet. Phil thought out loud, "Pittsburgh weather doesn't win any awards, but it doesn't snow in May there!" His parents were driving from Pittsburgh the next day, a Saturday, and graduation was Monday. His sisters had called with congratulatory messages, but also with apologies that they would not be able to make the ceremony. That was a little bit of a kick in the gut for him, as he attended his older sister's college and medical school graduations, and his younger sister's college graduation. He loved them dearly and was really hoping to see them. The closeness he felt with his sisters was hard for him to explain to others. They both were practically his best friends growing up. He wanted his entire family, including his sisters, to meet his med school best friends, Lisa and Kamal. He was going to miss them. Lisa had matched in Emergency Medicine at Case Western in Cleveland, her first choice, and Kamal likewise matched there in General Surgery. Phil was beginning to think that Lisa and Kamal may be more than friends. While all three would be quite busy as residents, at least Cleveland and Pittsburgh were not that far apart.

Although it was a Friday, happy hour did not materialize. There existed little stress to blow off now that school had finished. Many students were either out of town or out to dinner with visiting family. Lisa and Kamal were spending the night at their respective family homes in the Chicago suburbs. Phil used the time to clean up his apartment so as to not have to explain the untidiness to his parents tomorrow. His parents were staying at The Drake Hotel nearby but would certainly visit his apartment at some point. Also, his lease was up in two weeks, and the thought of moving his belongings to Pittsburgh suddenly became a real task at hand. He did not even own a car, as he walked or took the "T" everywhere in Chicago. He decided to label everything in the apartment as "move", "sell", or "trash." He looked in the refrigerator and was horrified with what remained hidden behind and within cartons and containers. He found salsa and packages of shredded cheese used for making nachos when they had a party at his apartment after Part I of the national board exam; the exam was two years ago. He wondered what Dr. Rosen would see if he made a slide from the fuzzy Monterey Jack he now held in his hand. The refrigerator seemed like a good place to start as he began filling trash bags with food orphaned from what seemed like another era of his life.

At the end of each hallway in the building was a trap door to a chute that went directly to a dumpster in the underground garage area. Phil loaded the first bag to what he hoped was just short of the breaking point and headed down the hall in his boxers and a Northwestern crew jersey. Since the same chute served all eleven floors, Phil always listened for any sounds of a trap door opening on another floor before placing his bag of trash in the chute. He had probably an unreasonable fear of being struck by a descending bag of two-year-old mold laden Monterey Jack cheese launched from 75 feet above on the 11$^{th}$ floor. He opened the trap door listened, placed the bag in the chute and then heard a door open. He quickly let go and slammed the trap door shut. The sound of the trap door slamming reverberated down the hallway. What he had heard was a fellow apartment resident coming out of his apartment with his trash. Trey was a law student that Phil had seen around occasionally. Trey had a muscular build but did not dress to flaunt it. The muscles made him easy to remember though for Phil. Trey approached with a serious and almost angry look on his face, "Did you dispose of a body or something illegal doc?" Phil was mildly embarrassed and began to stumble over a reply that had something to do with moldy cheese bombs when a smile broke out on Trey's face, "I'm just jaggin' yunz doc, but that was one hell of a door slam an nat."

"Jaggin' yunz? Jaggin' me? An nat?" were the first words Phil was able to coherently spit out looking bewildered.

"I'm sorry, your friends told me you were from Pittsburgh. I thought I'd throw out a little Pittsburghese; you seemed nervous. I'm Trey by the way", said Trey as his face that was alive with amusement went to a face of regret as Phil remained flustered.

"Damn Kamal and Lisa," Phil muttered as he gathered his wits, and he began to chuckle. He stuck his hand out and said, "Nice to meet you, Trey. I'm Phil, and I'm not a doc yet. Monday, I receive my degree. So, are you from Pittsburgh too?"

"Hell no. I'm from Minne-SO-TA," Trey emphatically stated as a smile returned," I'm stuck here as well until Monday when I get that cherished law degree. Soon I can be out fighting for the little guy who has been wronged by 'The Man' or being a corporate whore billing by the minute as I sit on the toilet thinking about some profound brief or contract to compose. The truth is my dad is a big shot attorney in St. Paul and is expecting me to join his firm. He paid for all my education, so I owe it to him to give it a go for a while. But more importantly, the Pens are playing the Islanders in the playoffs at 7:30 tonight. Want to come over and watch? We can order a pizza and grab some beers. The neighborhood seems sort of dead tonight for a Friday."

Phil was not much of a sports fan, but how could he turn down such an offer. He said, "I'll bring the beer and dessert. You get the pizza, just no pineapple please. See you at seven-thirty. Apartment 312, right?"

"You got it Phil, 312, 7:30, and no pineapple. See you then", Trey clicked off his reply with a military tone and headed to the trash chute with a big grin breaking out.

Phil felt a mixed rush of excitement, anxiety, dread, and something that seemed joyful as he headed back down the hall. His brain was spinning as he thought to himself, "Is this guy just some studly bro who happens to be incredibly gracious and looking for camaraderie, or was he hitting on me? Why would he have either asked or been told about me being from Pittsburgh? Do gay guys like ice hockey? Pizza and beer? I like pizza and beer." As Phil turned to open his apartment door, he saw Trey standing near his apartment looking in his direction. Trey gave a sheepish wave, followed by a thumbs up, and a wink?

Phil hurried inside as his brain seemed to be spinning faster and now his pounding heart joined in. He sat in the chair across from the loveseat and put his head in his hands, reasoning with his sympathetic nervous system to calm the hell down. After a few minutes of convincing himself, he was overreacting, he put on some sweatpants, grabbed his jacket and headed down the street to the local market. He knew they had Rolling Rock beer at the market, might as well make it a western Pennsylvania themed night with the Penguins playing. He also grabbed a quart of ice cream in addition to the six-pack. The snow and sleet had stopped. He even saw a patch of blue sky. He started thinking about graduation as he headed back to his apartment building.

Phil, freshly showered with a clean polo shirt, knocked on the door of 312 at exactly 7:29. Trey yelled to just come in as the door was unlocked. The place smelled of popcorn, and the reason was obvious as Trey rounded out of the studio apartment kitchen with a large bowl of microwaved popcorn toward the couch that had a small coffee table between it and a widescreen TV sitting atop a bureau. "It took me three bags of microwave popcorn to fill this baby up", Trey proudly stated. Trey wore jeans and a Notre Dame sweatshirt. "A couple of classmates are coming over too. But be warned Sheila is from Long Island, and a serious Islanders fan," Trey said with a smile and a smirk.

Phil could only say, "That's cool," as he tried to hide any dejected look trying to form on his face. "So, who else is coming," Phil managed saying, while trying to sound upbeat.

"Angelo will be with Sheila," Trey said, "He is my best friend from law school. He's older and from here, or more precisely south Chicago. So don't be put off by the neck tattoo. The dude had a rough past and let's just say his introduction to "law" did not involve 'Hill Street Blues', textbooks, or auditorium lectures. He and I lift together, and he puts me to shame. He is an absolute beast in the gym, but the sweetest person you could ever meet."

Phil realized that the evening was not going to unfold as he had either consciously or subconsciously hoped. In a way, knowing he would not be alone with Trey took away a lot of anxiety. It would seem the only thing he had to fear now was Sheila talking smack about Pittsburgh. Still, he felt somewhat crestfallen. To keep the conversation going and his mood elevated he remarked about Trey's sweatshirt, "My younger sister, Sarah, was a Golden Domer. Did you go there undergrad too?"

Trey, who had been in a jovial mood energetically bouncing around the apartment preparing for the evening's get together froze at the question, and glanced sideways at Phil asking, "Your last name isn't 'Moss' is it?"

"Sure is. Did you know Sarah in South Bend?" said Phil with his face lighting up.

"But your crew jersey said 'Newsome' on the front," a bewildered Trey replied.

"Ha! I never rowed crew. One of my college roommates did though, and he gave me the jersey when he transferred to Champaign after sophomore year of undergrad. We were close friends," Phil stated, as he suddenly seemed more somber as memories of Bill Newsome replayed in his brain. "But did you know Sarah?" Phil pressed on.

"Know her? Shit, we dated for almost a year, before…" Trey's voice halted at the pounding on the apartment door, Angelo and Sheila had arrived carrying more beer. "Later," is all Trey said with an almost stern look as he then greeted Angelo and Shiela, and introduced them to Phil.

Trey was not joking about Angelo. The man filled the doorway and appeared to not have an ounce of fat on him. Sheila by contrast was short and somewhat pudgy and would not stop talking to Trey about the weather, her family, the Islanders, the Mets, Chicago, New York, law firms, a past boyfriend, all in the span of about 90 seconds. Her presence, at least initially, was exhausting. Angelo popped open two beers, handed one to Phil, gave the biggest smile saying, "Nice to meet you Phil," and then shook Phil's hand with what Phil equated with shaking the paw of an adult Grizzly bear. This guy was a beast. "Let's get the TV on. They'll be dropping the puck soon," Angelo said as he beckoned Phil towards the TV. Angelo pulled a chair from the kitchen table and sat on it backwards. Phil thought the entire chair was going to collapse as he was convinced that he could hear wood cracking as Angelo sat down. Now Phil understood why Trey made so much popcorn, as Angelo finished half the large bowl before Trey and Sheila made it over. Trey grabbed another kitchen chair leaving the small couch for Sheila and Phil. Everyone had beers, the pizza soon arrived, they all were talking and laughing, and the Penguins were getting annihilated by the Islanders. Sheila seemed to be the only one who really cared about the score.

After the game, everyone pitched in and helped clean up. Other than two pizza boxes and a bag of empty beer bottles, the place looked just like when Phil arrived. Either the beer had a calming effect, or there were quite frankly no other topics known to Sheila upon which to espouse, but she mercifully left quietly with Angelo as they carried the boxes and bottles down the hall to the trash chute on the way out.

Soon as the door closed behind them Trey asked, "Is she coming to graduation?" For a moment Phil was confused and before he could respond, Trey said, "Sarah."

Phil had so truly enjoyed himself, that the pre-game angst over Trey's "orientation" and the talk of Sarah had been wiped from his consciousness. Now those topics all came roaring back. He stumbled over his words explaining that she wanted to be here but could not get away as law school exams for the second years in Charlottesville were the same day as Phil's Monday graduation. Trey looked disappointed. "You seem bummed," Phil said with concern as he approached Trey. "What happened? Sarah always shared a lot with me, but I am quite honestly drawing a blank concerning a boyfriend from Minnesota," Phil said respectfully. "I'm especially surprised given how smart you must be, and don't take this the wrong way, but how good looking you are too," Phil rambled on and blushed, "You'd seem like a 'keeper', uh, for Sarah." Phil developed the uneasiness of someone realizing he had stated, asked, or revealed too much.

Trey straightened up from picking up a renegade beer bottle that had rolled under the couch, and said, "Phil, buddy, I considered your sister the most incredible woman I had ever met and still do. I loved her. Damn it, I still love her. I said some things that I wish I could take back. I was such an asshole. The worst part was I had no idea I was even being an asshole. In her mind though, what I said was unforgivable and she broke up with me on the spot. She never spoke to me again. That was over three years ago. I've come to learn that she was correct and why."

"Thanks for sharing, Trey, but Sarah is tough as hell. I cannot imagine that anyone insulting her, especially unwittingly, would result in such an over-the-top response from her," Phil replied quizzically.

"Well, um, my words were not directed at her," Trey spoke softly as his gaze transfixed on his toes.

"She does have a strong protective streak in her. She will be a great defense attorney but never a prosecutor," Phil said smiling hoping he might have pulled off a joke to make Trey feel better, "I know some of her friends can come off as bitchy and aloof, but the ones I've got to know are all really good human beings. I know I was tempted to say some not nice things to some of her friends before I got to know them better."

"Oh, I know what you are saying. I've met them many times. But in this case what I said, um, was, um, kind of about you," Trey stated as shame swept across his face.

"Now you are jaggin' me! You did not even know me until today! You are making no sense," Phil stated with a quizzical smile.

Trey now had tears in his eyes. He spoke with all the willpower he could muster to not let his voice crack, "Phil, thanks for coming over. I had a blast tonight. When you speak to Sarah again, please tell her where I'll be and what I told you. She knows the name of my dad's firm."

"Trey, you are leaving me hanging here. What's the scoop?" Phil pleaded.

"Not tonight, my friend, not tonight," Trey stated as he ushered Phil to the door.

Phil somewhat reluctantly exited and returned to his apartment down the hall. After getting inside he was tempted to immediately call Sarah. It was after eleven p.m. in Chicago, hence, it would be after midnight in Charlottesville. Sarah would not seem upset if he called her and woke her up, but she would get revenge at a time of her choosing for having her slumber interrupted. "Revenge is a dish best served cold," she would say with a cackle after having served it. Phil had learned that lesson many times over as a teen. He promised himself to call her tomorrow before his parents arrived.

The next morning was sunny, but frigid. Phil could see patches of fresh snow piled up in shady spots atop the lower buildings. Fortunately, the sun quickly melted all of it by 10 am. He would get laundry done today as he had an embarrassingly large pile escaping from his bedroom closet. He would clean his bathroom and kitchen too. That way, all should look tidy and clean for the inevitable, "Let's see your apartment!" visit that his mother would insist upon. After getting the first load of laundry going in the basement common area, he returned to his apartment to call Sarah. Her phone rang five times, then went to voicemail. He hung up. He tried again an hour later, same response, so he left a message to call him. Sarah typically studied at her apartment, so it was a little unusual, but he was not that worried. He tried again an hour later, and still no answer. At that point he called his older sister Anne in St. Louis. She lived with her fiancé, Josh, who was an orthopedic surgery resident, and not particularly liked by Phil or Sarah. Josh picked up the call, and mumbled, "Hello," with what clearly was a mouth full of food. Phil rolled his eyes thinking what a neanderthal this guy was, but grateful someone answered. "Josh, this is Phil," Phil said, followed by a long pause and no reply, "Anne's brother."

"Ooohhhh! Hey Phil," came a garbled reply, followed by the sound of a Mastif swallowing a large bolus of food.

"Can I speak with Anne please," said Phil.

"Oh, um, she's not here. She's um, on call. Yea, she's on call today. Yea, in the hospital," Josh said with slightly clearer speech.

"Please have her call me if you speak with her," Phil requested and wondering where the hell else a doctor takes call other than a hospital.

"You got it dude! Hey, and congrats on finishing college," Josh blurted.

"That was four years…never mind. Please have her call me. Thanks Josh. Bye," Phil said, realizing Anne would probably get the message in a few days from her fiancé.

Back at his apartment, the phone rang. He dove for it ready to find out from Sarah what the heck was the deal with Trey. Instead, he heard his mother, "Phil, It's mom! We just stopped to fuel up. We ran into some traffic and are behind schedule. Dad made reservations at Moretti's near your apartment. We will plan to meet you there for dinner at seven o'clock. Oh Sweetie, we are so proud of you and can't wait to see you!"

"Mom, have you talked to Sarah recently? I've tried calling her all day," asked Phil.

His mother replied, "Yes, we spoke yesterday. She and her mock trial group are at somebody's apartment all day studying for their big test on Monday."

Relief replaced concern on Phil's face, and he replied, "Super. Love ya Mom. I've even cleaned the place up for once! See you for dinner at seven!"

Laundry was done. The bathroom and kitchen were passably clean. What served as a "living room" was uncluttered as he could make it. He took a shower and was dressed and ready at six thirty. It was only a ten-minute walk to Moretti's. Phil was tempted to march down the hall to apartment 312 and demand an explanation from Trey, but the last thing he wanted was to get all emotional or upset immediately before seeing his parents. After taking a few minutes sorting through his mountain of textbooks and trying to decide which of them were worth keeping and hauling to Pittsburgh, he set off by foot to the restaurant. As he rounded the corner on to East Chestnut Street, he could look in the window of the restaurant. The best table in the place had a card sitting atop the white tablecloth saying "Reserved, Dr. Moss." When he got inside, the Maitre d' greeted him warmly and sent a waiter scurrying to fetch someone. A strikingly solid man with thick dark hair who looked about fifty years old came out from what appeared to be an office. "Phillip, it is an honor to meet you. I am Jack Moretti," the distinguished man said with an unusually raspy voice, "Let me show you to your table. Your parents should be here shortly."

In just a few steps Phil saw the round table he had seen through the window. What he did not appreciate was that it was a table for five. As Mr. Moretti pulled a chair out for Phil, he turned to ask Mr. Moretti if this was indeed the correct table when he heard his name yelled by multiple women. He turned to see Anne and Sarah coming toward him as fast as their high heels allowed, behind which were his beaming parents. It was all too much. He collapsed in the chair and wept. He could not have been happier.

After a minute or two of hugs among them all, Sarah and Anne crying, and dad's hand on Phil's shoulder, the family properly seated themselves. Mr. Moretti returned with the head waiter as water was poured. Mr. Moretti produced a bottle of Prosecco announcing, "For my friend and his family, this is on the house!"

Dr. Phillip Moss said, "Jack that is so kind but completely unnecessary."

"Doc, I respectfully disagree. It is necessary. I owe you everything," Moretti stated as he touched the left side of his neck, "This entire meal is on the house tonight, and anytime you or any of your beautiful family eat here."

All three Moss children were wide-eyed. They had heard fragments of stories of their father's experience in Vietnam but chalked anything heroic or noble up to either their father's ego out of control, as it was prone to do, or simply tales embellished to impress. It was their mother who had provided details to all of them though about Jack Moretti. The children, when old enough to start asking questions, would ask her who that man was standing with them all dressed for Easter Mass in the photo that still rested on the fireplace mantle in their Pittsburgh home. Jack had visited the Moss family often when he was in Uniontown, but then a family connection brought him to Chicago and into a very successful restaurant business more than twenty years ago.

The meal was amazing, and everyone ate too much, but with zero regrets. The only tense moment was when Dr. Phillip Moss queried his son innocently between bites of Tiramisu about any romantic prospects he would be leaving behind in Chicago. Sarah and Anne caught each other's glances and quickly changed the subject to Josh back in St. Louis. Josh bashing was an activity that Anne despised, but knew that Sarah and Phil reveled in the opportunity. It was understood between Sarah and Anne that such banter was tolerated if it served a greater purpose. In this case, the greater purpose was to protect Phil from any interrogation, no matter how innocent, about his love life or lack of one.

Jack saw them all to the door. Handshakes were not enough for any of the Moss clan. The children hugged him goodbye like a long-lost uncle, the man on the mantle they thought was a myth had come to life before their eyes. Camelus and Dr. Phillip Moss embraced him heartedly as well and encouraged him to open a restaurant in Pittsburgh so they could see him more and be able to eat so well. Hearing this, the children chimed in, "and for free!" They all laughed.

It was a short walk to The Drake Hotel. The sisters were sharing a room adjoining their parents' room. The Drake is one of those big city iconic hotels, a place visited by presidents, famous actors, and not too many years prior Lady Di. The thought of returning alone to his apartment at this time was too depressing a thought for Phil so he joined them on their walk back to the hotel. He also began to wrestle with the timing and appropriateness of discussing Trey with Sarah. As the family climbed the carpeted steps toward the elevators, Phil beckoned for his sisters to stay behind and chat. The Moss children bid good evening to their parents and went strolling behind the lobby to find a place to sit. Sarah proclaimed, "I need to pee!" at the unexpected sight of a woman's restroom door and disappeared.

"Okay, little brother, what's going on?" Anne stated more than asked, "It's obvious you have not told dad yet. Damn it Phil, you're his son, twenty-five years old, and soon you are going to be his resident too, for seven frickin'years! We can't keep running interference for you."

"Do you think Mom knows?" Phil asked with the eyes of a puppy who had disappointed its master.

"Mom is oblivious as she keeps asking Sarah and me to set you up with girls we know from home upon your 'triumphant return' to Pitt," Anne replied somewhat sarcastically. "She has been oblivious to dad's extracurricular activities for the past few years, so your 'circumstances' are not going to ping her radar. Remember you've been pretty much gone for 8 years."

"Geez, I just wanted to talk to Sarah about...What do you mean extracurricular activities?" Phil asked, realizing he was about to change the subject.

"I thought it would be juicy gossip on neurosurgical interview trips. It is certainly well known even in St. Louis, but maybe that's because dad trained there," said Anne. "You did do a rotation at Pitt last summer, right?"

"You know I did," Phil defensively replied.

"Didn't you work with Ava, or see her around? Dad's N.P.?" Anne asked.

"Well yea, I remember her," replied Phil.

"Jesus Phil, maybe because you are gay it blinds you, but straight guys' jaws drop open at the sight of her," Anne informed him impatiently, "Even the Wash U neurosurgery residents who interviewed at Pitt years ago still talk about her, or more accurately talk about her and dad."

"So, dad has a hot nurse practitioner. That's no crime," said Phil as he straightened up, "As I recall she was very good at her job."

Anne simply said, "Yes, the word is she is *very* good at her job," and ceased speaking as Sarah emerged from the restroom.

"You guys look like you were having an intense discussion. What did I miss?" Sarah asked light-heartedly as she had the most Chianti of all of them.

"Phil wanted to talk to you," said Anne.

Phil turned toward Sarah and plainly said, "Tell ma about Trey."

The look of a comfortable buzz quickly left Sarah's face, "What the fu...dge!" she blurted out and recovered as an elderly couple made their way down the hall past them looking for the well-hidden restrooms.

"I met him just yesterday," said Phil.

"Where?" a horrified Sarah asked.

"He lives in my building. On my floor, to be more exact. He's graduating Monday too," said Phil.

Anne looked on with shear amusement and said to both of them, "See where keeping secrets gets you."

"Graduating from law school? Here? Northwestern? But…," Sarah asked no one in particular as she searched for a seat.

Phil replied with a smirk, "Well counselor, if those were three questions, the answers are yes, yes, and yes."

They all found seats crowded together in an awkward nook that had the creepy location of watching over the women's restroom door. Fortunately, the awkwardness was diminished by having two women in the group. Phil explained honestly the entire encounter with Trey to them both. For him the most uncomfortable part was describing his attraction to a man that he then learned not only loved his sister but likely slept with her as well. He also kept his word to Trey and passed along to Sarah the message entrusted to him.

Sarah looked at Anne for guidance. "Tell him the truth," Anne instructed.

Phil spoke first looking at Anne, "So you knew about Trey?"

She nodded affirmatively, raising her chin and said, "Yes."

Sarah spoke next, "Phil, I love you so much. That's why I never shared anything about Trey with you, because I did not know how you'd react, or if it would hurt you."

So far Phil was feeling more confused than enlightened.

Sarah continued, "When Trey and I would be out with his rugby buddies and their dates, the guys would often have 'one too many' as they say. In those situations, the guys would start telling jokes. Some jokes were funny, some skirted the boundaries of good taste, and others were flat out offensive."

Phil nodded along to indicate he was following, but still none the wiser and said, "Ok…."

"One of the guys had a propensity to tell, shall I say, gay jokes," Sarah swallowed hard as she said it, "He was the team captain, and thought he was God's gift to women. He and Trey were buddies. I tolerated it for a while, but then let Trey know how much those so-called jokes that I considered homophobic trash bothered me and why. Trey said he would talk to him. But one night soon after that discussion, I was not going to join the gang at our regular meeting place as I had a paper to write. I ended up finishing the paper more quickly than I anticipated, so I walked over to Newf's and as I'm approaching the table, I hear Trey telling a joke. Let's just say he seemed on a mission to surpass his buddy in degree of offensiveness and homophobic content. I went to the bar, grabbed one of the cardboard coasters and wrote 'We are Done!!!' on the back of it, walked over and slammed it in front of him. He smiled, not even reading my message, and reached to kiss me. I punched him in the nose and would have kicked him in the balls had he been standing. I walked out and refused to speak with him again. He tried to make amends using my friends as couriers, but they had my back and thwarted his attempts."

Anne gasped with a smile breaking out, "You hit him? God, I have the most awesome sister! You never told me that part."

Phil was less amused and asked, "If I weren't….um…who I am, would you have done the same thing?"

All Sarah could respond with were tears welling in her eyes and said, "I don't know Phil, I really don't know."

Anne interjected, "Look you guys, we all love each other. We always have been and always will be there for one another. That's more important than any hypotheticals right now. Let's get some sleep. Call us in the morning Phil so we can make plans for brunch somewhere. I'm sure mom and dad are already asleep." And with that, the Moss sibling meeting was over.

They walked back to the elevators and Phil gave them each long hugs before heading down the lobby stairs and out the revolving door into the night, alone.

Phil awoke and decided to go for a run. Like every other person who was inclined to run that lived nearby, and those numbered in the thousands, there was only one choice, the Lakefront Trail. He would walk to Oak Street Beach, get on the trail and head north. Today he ran as far as Fullerton Beach before turning around. The longest he would run would be to Belmont Harbor and back when he was feeling particularly energetic. Today he just needed to get all of last night's pasta and focaccia moving through his system before even thinking about brunch. When he returned, he called over to The Drake Hotel and asked to be connected to his sisters' room. Sarah picked up, clearly having been awoken by his call. "Hey Bright Eyes, I was told to call you guys this morning to arrange brunch," Phil said with as much cheer as possible.

"Anne is in the shower now. She left a sticky note here that says, 'Café on Oak' at ten forty-five. What time is it?" she asked with a voice consistent with a hangover.

"It's about nine fifteen. I just got back from a run. I'll see you guys there," Phil exclaimed.

"Geez, Anne went for a run too. Don't you doctor types sleep in," she rhetorically stated as her eyes rolled back, and her head collapsed back on to the pillow while simultaneously hanging up the phone.

The Moss family enjoyed a leisurely brunch as all the children took turns talking about their lives. Anne had signed a lease in Rochester without ever seeing the apartment, but it was where the outgoing breast imaging fellow had lived, and she had assured Anne, it was perfect for her and Josh. Anne and Josh had yet to set a wedding date, which had Mrs. Moss perturbed. Dr. Moss and Sarah convinced Mrs. Moss that it was good to wait until Anne knew the lay of the land with her fellowship schedule. Sarah secretly hoped it would provide enough time for the engagement to dissolve. Sarah discussed how difficult law school was, but that Charlottesville was a beautiful place in which to be miserable. Phil said little about his upcoming transition, other than he still needed to find a place to live. The easy answer was to just come home to Shadyside, said his mother. His father made it clear that he was more than welcome to live at home "until" he found another place to live.

Brunch was followed by visiting the shops along Michigan Avenue, and a visit to the aquarium. Dinner plans were to go to Phil's favorite deep dish pizza place, Gino's. As the family was returning from the aquarium to get ready to go to dinner, the inevitable announcement came from Mrs. Moss, "Oh my gosh Phil, this is the perfect time to see your apartment!" From writing holiday and birthday cards to his same address for four years, Mrs. Moss had the address memorized and quickly told the driver to head there.

Sarah and Phil exchanged looks, with Sarah looking horrified, and Phil mouthing the words, "Do not worry."

As they got out of the crowded cab, and Dr. Moss paid the driver, Sarah whispered to Phil, "I better not see him."

"Sarah don't worry. I've barely seen him all year," Phil whispered back, "Anyway, he seems like a really nice guy now, even if he likes women," which forced a smile from Sarah.

Whether they took the elevator, or the stairs they would have to walk past apartment 312 to get to Phil's apartment. Had Phil left the window open, the fire escape could have been an option, though a difficult one to explain. The hallway was quiet, and the Moss family uneventfully made it to Phil's apartment door, though Phil did continuously remind his excited mother to keep her voice down. Once in the apartment the shared secret tension between Phil and Sarah evaporated. Anne was enjoying the quiet show however, and was hoping to see this Trey guy pop out of his door for the pure entertainment of it all.

Phil hurriedly made some coffee but had no milk, cream, or sugar. So, it was black coffee for those that wanted any. His father, Anne, and he each had a mug, while Mrs. Moss and Sarah passed on the opportunity. Phil turned on the local news and they were all pleased to see that graduation day had a weather forecast for seventy degrees and partly cloudy. After a quick apartment tour, as it was a six hundred and fifty square foot apartment, and the coffee finished, his family was ready to return to the hotel before dinner. Phil told them he would meet them at the hotel in about an hour to walk to Gino's for what he promised would be a life-changing experience. He watched his family make their way to the elevator. He stood watching and praying that the door of apartment 312 would stay closed. His parents were surprised by the concern he was showing, watching them until they were safely within the elevator. They began to wonder if the hallways of their son's apartment were a dangerous place. For a second time in about an hour, Sarah was relieved and Anne remained somewhat disappointed.

Soon as the secure front door exiting the building closed behind them, Sarah realized she had left her handbag in Phil's apartment. "We can just call Phil and tell him to bring it in an hour," said Mrs. Moss.

Sarah thought for a moment and imagined Phil carrying her large pink Dooney and Bourke handbag through the streets of Chicago in the evening. She was not going to put that on Phil, even though he would willfully do it. Sarah rang the intercom button after punching in Phil's apartment number code and hearing him pick up she said, "Phil, this is Sarah. I left my handbag in the kitchen. Could you either let me in or better yet bring it down to me?"

"I'll be right down with it," came the cheerful and understanding reply, followed by a click.

"Hey, do you guys need help getting in? Lots of family visiting this weekend for graduation and you look like a trustworthy bunch," said that deep melodic voice with a twinge of a northern accent that Sarah knew all too well.

Sarah kept her back turned away from the street and the voice. Her father politely replied, "Thank you, but our son is coming down with Sarah's purse. She left it upstairs by accident but thank you again so much."

Trey looked directly at Anne, who resembled Sarah on first glance, but certainly not twin like. They were both attractive young ladies, Anne was taller with lighter hair compared to Sarah. Anne smiled, because most importantly she was getting the show for which she had hoped and secondly, because it was impossible to look at Trey's handsome face and not display an emotional response. Trey looked at Anne, raised a finger gently moving it as if tapping slowly on a window pointing at her and said, "But you are not Sarah."

Anne quickly replied, "Oh no, this is my sister Sarah here," as she gestured toward the frozen figure facing the intercom.

Sarah felt every corpuscle rushing to flood every capillary of her face. She felt as if on fire. While Anne knew full well what was unfolding, the parents remained bewildered.

"Honey, you can turn around now, Phil is coming down with your purse," said her mother sweetly. Sarah remained unmoving.

Trey was a changed man in some ways. He now had the emotional intelligence to know the best thing was for him not to speak to or even look at the face of the woman he loved. While every fiber in his body wanted to grab her, tell her how sorry he was, how much he loved her, and to kiss her right there on that Chicago sidewalk in front of her family, he knew that is not what she would want. He simply said, "Well nice to meet… most of you. I hope you have a wonderful time here." He then unlocked the door, retrieved his mail without looking back, took one of the envelopes he had received promoting a carpet cleaning service and wrote his phone number on the back, with the words, "Call me. Please. Love, Trey." He then walked out of sight where the elevator and stairwell were located.

The elevator door opened, and Trey jumped in shocking Phil. "Here, put this in Sarah's handbag," Trey pleaded, "Thanks man, I owe you one."

Phil pushed the envelope under the outer flap and walked out as nonchalantly as possible to deliver the handbag. Anne, in agony from the torture of staying composed, successfully held back laughter. Sarah looked like one wrong word could cause a nuclear explosion to occur. The parents while aware they had encountered a polite handsome young man with their unmarried daughters, did not consider him so Zeus like as to create such emotional turmoil at simply his sight and voice. Hence, they remained appropriately bewildered.

"Here you go sis," Phil said as he gave the handbag to Sarah.

"Thank you," she stated pouting as if she were a child being given a toy back that was taken away from her for punishment. "Did you see him?" Sarah asked.

"The hallway was empty," Phil replied truthfully as the hallway upstairs was otherwise empty.

Sarah shrugged and turned around to confront the stares of two concerned parents and one amused big sister. Phil waved as the foursome headed back toward the hotel.

Gino's did not disappoint. The deep-dish pizza that Phil raved about was indeed exquisite. Sarah seemed to have recovered. She had a small clutch purse, and by her behavior Phil assumed she had not opened her Dooney and Bourke that he had delivered to her. It was also possible that Anne intervened and reminded Sarah why they were here, and that was to celebrate Phil's graduation. He easily could hear Anne admonishing Sarah in his head, "Don't make it about you!"

The evening was uneventful and pleasant. Dr. Moss talked about the neurosurgery department and failed to conceal the excitement he felt to have his son join the training program. Phil asked about the other two students who had matched. Dr. Moss told him one was a lady who was a Pitt medical student and originally from the Philadelphia area, and the other was a gentleman from Duke who had grown up in Alabama. He assured Phil, they were both outstanding by every metric and would be a joy to work with. Phil was grateful for a boring evening. They all walked Phil back to his apartment, then parents and sisters returned to the hotel.

The graduation exercises were executed with the perfect amount of pomp and circumstance fitting of such an occasion. Smiles broke out across the faces of the seated Moss family as Phil's name was called and he received his medical degree. The family now had three doctors. At the reception for the medical school graduates hosted by the dean in a rather austere conference room within the Northwestern medical campus complex, Phil was finally able to introduce Lisa and Kamal to his family. They were sharing stories of the past four years when Roy Gillette approached their group. Roy squeezed himself in between Anne and her father without recognizing anyone else, and turned to Dr. Moss, Sr. extending his hand, "Good to see you again sir."

Phil's father politely shook Roy's hand while asking, "Have we met before?"

"Yes sir. You interviewed me last December at Pitt. I wanted to say hello and apologize for not ranking Pitt higher, but I am staying at Northwestern," Roy proudly stated.

Without missing a beat Dr. Moss, Sr. replied, "Apology accepted. And I owe you an apology as well. Since the match began, I have remembered every student we have placed on our rank list, and I'm afraid I do not remember ranking you at all."

With the velvet dagger expertly piercing Roy's inflated ego, Roy walked away with his mouth agape and speechless.

Phil did his best to turn and politely stifle his laugh. Kamal and Lisa spent no effort to conceal their enjoyment of what they just witnessed. It represented their first truly good laugh as physicians.

A faint alarm sound could be heard and Dr. Moss, Sr. reached into his suit jacket breast pocket. He withdrew his Nokia cellular phone and extended the antenna as he walked away from the group suddenly becoming quite animated with a smile on his face. The three new physicians thought how cool it would be to be able to answer pages like that as residents rather than needing to find a regular phone in the hospital or to use a payphone outside the hospital. While they looked on with a small amount of wonder and envy in their eyes, Mrs. Moss looked on with disgust in her eyes. Was it because the call took Dr. Moss, Sr. away from the celebratory group, or was it because she knew who was calling him, or both?

## Chapter Four: Pittsburgh, 1983

    After a long day in the operating room Dr. Phillip Moss returned to his office. The staff had left for the evening, and it was dark within the cramped labyrinth of halls, offices, and nooks created to accommodate the various faculty, staff, and residents. He made his way to his desk and clicked on his desk lamp. His secretary had left a note atop his desk calendar, "Breakfast with the Dean, six thirty a.m. tomorrow, Faculty Club." In his tenure at Pitt after returning from Vietnam he had been promoted to Associate Professor more than ten years prior, and a few years ago he had been promoted to Professor. He had maintained leadership over the cerebrovascular program and grown it tremendously in volume and prestige. He also had been program director for the residency training program for the past five years. He had poured his heart and soul into the department. He was regarded as an expert in his field of cerebrovascular surgery both nationally and internationally. The dean was regarded as somewhat of a tyrant and asshole, so trepidation crept into Dr. Moss's consciousness as he began rescheduling his morning responsibilities in his head. Many colleagues that Dr. Moss had considered excellent academic physicians as well as friends had their careers at Pitt end abruptly for unclear reasons at the behest of the dean. Some were notified through their department chairs, and others notified personally by the dean over a meal. The latter gave the impression that firing physicians was something the dean enjoyed doing. This last thought caused Dr. Moss to consider the risks and benefits of punching the dean in his fat face if indeed he were to be "let go."

Dr. Moss rarely visited the Faculty Club for breakfast. He primarily would eat lunches there with prospective faculty members his department was recruiting. The Faculty Club was located on the highest floor of Presbyterian University Hospital, that everyone simply called "Presby." He had checked in with his chief resident early that morning to make sure the patients they had operated upon yesterday were doing well. He then got on the elevator at six twenty-five a.m. and punched the button to the 14$^{th}$ floor.

Dean Detrick was seated at a small table with his back to a window and facing the entrance to the Faculty Club. Dr. Moss and the dean made eye contact as the dean was shoveling a forkful of scrambled eggs into his mouth. Dean Detrick made no attempt to stand to greet Dr. Moss. Moss considered that a good thing as the portly dean was squeezed behind the small table and probably would have upended the table along with his breakfast and a craft of coffee. "Have a seat Phil," the dean mumbled though a full mouth of eggs. No hand was extended to shake by either gentleman. The scent in the air held a blend of eggs, cheap cologne, and a fart as best Dr. Moss could tell. His appetite vanished.

Phil indicated to the waiter that he would be satisfied with black coffee only. "So, dean, to what do I owe the pleasure for this impromptu breakfast?" Phil asked.

The dean swallowed an incompletely chewed sausage and struggled for a moment to get it down and asked," Phil, do you know what a 'Dean's Tax' is?"

"Sure. I am not one to ask about financial details as the Chair handles that aspect of the department though," Dr. Moss replied.

"Well then what is your definition of the tax?" Dean Detrick replied slightly irritated with a more pointed question.

"The tax is a percentage of clinical revenue a department generates that is paid to the school of medicine ostensibly to contribute to the educational mission of the institution," Dr. Moss answered.

"Not simply 'a percentage', but eight and a half percent to be exact," responded the dean.

"Okay, Eight and a half percent. I'm not sure why you are quizzing me on this topic though. I'm happy to talk about the cerebrovascular institute we would like to establish or the training program. Fitzpatrick and the department business manager are the best people to discuss finances with," Dr. Moss countered with rising impatience in his voice.

"Well, Dr. Fitzpatrick was the chair of neurosurgery here for a long time, well before you were recruited. A large part thanks to you, your department has become one of the largest revenue generators in the health system, or so we think," the dean stated ending with an accusatory tone to his voice.

"I am not following you Dr. Detrick," Dr. Moss bluntly stated.

"From whom does your paycheck come?" asked the dean.

"I assume the University of Pittsburgh. It's all done by direct deposit, so I don't see an actual check," responded Dr. Moss.

"Your department pays you directly. Your department does its own billing and keeps its own books. Your department informs my office quarterly of the revenue generated when the quarterly 'Dean's Tax' is due," Dean Detrick said coolly.

"We pay the eight and a half per cent tax? Correct?" Dr. Moss asked rhetorically shrugging his shoulders.

"Yes, the department pays the eight and a half per cent tax to my office on the revenue *reported*," said the dean. "It's difficult for the School of Medicine and the Dean's office to confirm those numbers since your department's books and bank account are maintained in the Cayman Islands," the dean paused awaiting a response after that fact was allowed to be processed by Dr. Moss.

"Well, I am learning something new this morning, if what you say is true. But I still don't understand the purpose of us having this conversation. As I said Dr. Fitzpatrick would be the person to provide confirmatory data for you regarding finances," Dr. Moss said hoping to conclude this conversation.

"Don't you think I've made such requests from him a half a dozen times already! I've had the university health system financial office extrapolate the revenue reported to the work being done by you and your department at Presby and Children's. Their conclusions were stark and irrefutable. The department of neurosurgery is generating more than twice the revenue being reported to my office," the dean said with a scary resolve in his eyes.

"That is quite the accusation dean. But again, I have neither knowledge of, nor access to the information you claim exists. I can't help you with this," Dr. Moss firmly stated.

"Phil, I don't want your help on this. I can let the FBI do that work. What I want to know is: Will you be my next chair of neurosurgery, because Fitzpatrick's days are numbered once I go to the Provost and President with this," the dean said without hesitation.

For the first time this morning Dr. Moss's brain was caught off guard. He had been braced for an assault and was playing verbal defense. Suddenly he was being offered the chair of his department. He had thought of one day becoming a chairman, but certainly not under these circumstances. Fitzpatrick was not only a mentor and colleague, but also a friend, even a father figure. "May I get back to you with an answer? This is a big decision to make on rather short notice," Dr. Moss asked.

"By noon," the dean said and continued, "I'm meeting with the Provost, President, and University counsel at two p.m. today. We will still need to do the song and dance, and pony show of a search for an external candidate. But Phil, if I can walk into that meeting knowing you are onboard with this opportunity, then I have a lot more leverage to make it happen. You are my number one pick. Period."

With that Dr. Moss stood and reflexively pulled the table toward him so the dean could extract his rotund torso without fear of knocking something over. The dean finally stood as well. Dr. Moss extended his hand to shake with the dean. The dean simply looked at him and repeated, "By noon."

Dr. Moss had more than an hour before his clinic hours began. He realized Cammie may still be asleep, but he went directly back to his office to call her and discuss what had just transpired. He passed Dr. Fitzpatrick's office on the way to his office. The light was on, but Fitzpatrick was not present. Fitzpatrick usually operated on this day of the week but rarely arrived early as he relied on the residents to get his cases going. Dr. Moss turned the corner and entered his office. Sitting in his desk chair was Dr. Michael Fitzpatrick.

The usual warm smile was missing as Dr. Fitzpatrick spoke, "So what did the dean want?"

"Your head on a platter as best I could tell. Jesus Mike, what the hell is this about the Cayman Islands, under reporting revenue, stonewalling his office? Maybe he was trying to scare me, but it sounded like some serious shit. He mentioned the FBI too," Dr. Moss exclaimed.

"Noted. But what did he want from you?" Dr. Fitzpatrick asked.

"He offered me your chair with a noon ultimatum," Dr. Moss replied.

"Well, I'm in your chair now, so that only seems fair," Dr. Fitzpatrick stated as a subtle but real smile made inroads upon his sullen face. "Take the offer Phil. I'm seventy-one years old, and have smoked way too much, and worked way too hard for probably too long. My body and spirit are exhausted, and my health won't allow me to keep going much longer anyways. I did what was necessary to build this department and reward my team appropriately for all the incredible work accomplished day and night, decade after decade. Why do you think we are so powerful at this institution? It's because we have not allowed ourselves to be neutered by deans and administration. Look at the other departments. All of them neat little trimmed boxwoods in the dean's proverbial front yard. But neurosurgery is the one-hundred-year-old oak tree in his yard. We rain a torrent of acorns upon that yard to feed the health care system, its employees, subsidize many other specialties, and pay for all those fat administrator salaries. And while we may make a mess with acorns, leaves, and branches, we clean up our own messes and provide life to this place," pleased with his clumsy metaphor he continued, "Phil, you are more than ready and capable to be chair. Recruiting you was the singular best thing I did here. For years I have considered you the obvious successor, I simply wish it were not under these circumstances. Please promise me you will not let this department be turned into a boxwood," Dr. Fitzpatrick concluded.

"Mike, I appreciate your words tremendously. And you know I'll preserve your remarkable legacy. What can I do to help protect you though? I need to call Cammie as well," Dr. Moss said.

"Follow your gut. I'll be fine. Shit, I took Detrick's five-one disc out when the fat ass had so much unbearable acute leg pain. He was so grateful, at least verbally back then. He claimed his significant weight was because of the pain. Well, I made him pain free ten years ago and he has only gotten heavier. He clearly doesn't understand cause and effect well. You should have heard what he said when under the effects of anesthesia. I wrote it all down. I fact checked with two of the medical students he named when 'bragging' while he was loopy. The guy is a pervert. I don't think he ever had any idea what he said to me. I took it to the provost's office and later was told they investigated and found nothing. They simply gave me lip service and buried it. Through intermediaries I circled back with those students that were now a fellow and a practicing physician. Both of them said nobody from the provost's office or university contacted them. I'm no choir boy either regarding this Cayman's matter, so I did not pursue it any further, but shit, students? I also tried to get him to see Douglas, the bariatric guy, but that ruffled his feathers, saying those surgeries were for fat people. What could I say. Put him down for lacking self-awareness too. All this rambling is to say the dean, while having a storied academic past can be quite oblivious to reality as well as a pervert. Keep that in mind as you negotiate with him," said Dr. Fitzpatrick with a wink.

"Negotiate? I just need to tell him whether I want the chair…your chair," remarked Dr. Moss.

"Phil, this is the only time when you are going to have the power to ask, hell, demand, what you want as chair. Everything and anything are negotiable. Make your acceptance conditional on those things you want for the department. That's why he gave you such a short time to respond, so that you would not compile a list of conditions. Start thinking right now, put them in writing, and put that paper on his desk by noon. If you need any help with ideas, get a hold of me around 10 am; I'll be done with the first case by then," stated Dr. Fitzpatrick.

"Will do, and thanks. But Mike, how the hell did you know I had breakfast with the Dean this morning?" asked Dr. Moss.

"Lucy may be your secretary, but she was my secretary for ten years before, and she has a good nose for when serious shit is happening. She told me while you were still operating last night. And Phil, this discussion never happened," replied Dr. Fitzpatrick. Dr. Moss nodded in agreement. Both men stood, shook hands, and then hugged. It was eight a.m. and time for the real work of the day to begin.

Dr. Moss reclaimed his desk chair upon Dr. Fitzpatrick's departure and picked up the phone. Cammie quickly picked up. Mornings were a little less hectic in the Moss household now that all three children were teenagers. All three were excellent students academically and capable of awakening, dressing, and eating breakfast before blasting out the door to school. Anne was a senior in high school with plans to attend Swarthmore College in the fall. Phil was a freshman, and Sarah was in middle school. Cammie was thrilled to hear the news and knew her husband deserved that opportunity. She quickly gave her husband her blessing on the matter, then kissed three foreheads goodbye as the children ushered themselves out of the house and readied herself for a morning of tennis.

Between surgical cases and clinic patients Drs. Moss and Fitzpatrick developed a forward-looking and respectable list of conditions that would be put in writing, and one condition that would be delivered verbally.

When the brief pause in patient scheduling occurred before lunchtime, Dr. Moss made his way to the dean's office. This was not going to be an answer delivered or a discussion had over the phone. Dr. Moss was greeted by the secretary and told that Dr. Detrick was expecting him. Dr. Moss went in without knocking. He had not been in the dean's office for years and almost walked into the dean's large desk that had been moved away from the windowed wall toward the door. This afforded the dean the required berth to dock his girth in a large leather chair behind the desk in which he sat eclipsing the daylight trying to gain access through the window. The scent of the room reminded Dr. Moss of the morning's breakfast other than he could not smell eggs.

Dr. Moss began, "Dr. Detrick I've been able to speak with my wife and give this opportunity careful consideration despite the short timeline. I, however, cannot simply jump at this offer and accept. What I can provide you, however, is a conditional acceptance based on this list," Dr. Moss continued as he held up the document, "While Dr. Fitzpatrick has done a spectacular job in developing this department, there are some areas that would benefit from more resources being directed to them. And finally, a topic and names I have chosen not to list in writing currently. I cannot inherit a department only to have the FBI crawling up my ass, Mike's ass, and everyone else's. Whatever this matter, real or imagined, I will not accept the chair position only to endure such a distraction when there is real work to be done. And I'll be damn sure to let any other external candidate know about the topic as well. So, I need a guarantee in writing signed by you and the president of the university that law enforcement will not be involved in any investigation of the past financial practices of the neurosurgery department, or any law enforcement directed at Dr. Fitzpatrick either. I will play a fair game with the school of medicine if chair, and I outlined those game rules in this document as well, so that everyone that needs to know, knows those rules. And as for the names: Sheila Strauss and Matthew Loudon," and Dr. Moss tossed the document in front of the dean and sat down in a leather chair opposite the dean.

 Detrick's typically ruborous complexion went pale as Dr. Moss spoke the names of the two former medical students. The dean collapsed back into his chair and slid his spectacles down his bulbous nose and gazed over them studying Dr. Moss. He then began to peruse the document just given to him with intermittent grunts and scowls. After a few minutes the dean simply said, "I'll try to make this work. You've got me by the balls somehow Phil. I'll call you this afternoon." As Dr. Moss stood so did the dean this time and extricated himself from the large chair that he filled.

The dean extended his hand this time and Dr. Moss simply said, "When I see those signatures," and turned around and left.

The call came at three p.m. from the dean's office down to the clinic where Dr. Moss was seeing patients. A notarized signed document would be delivered agreeing to all the conditions that were delivered, written *and* verbal. This also meant that Dr. Moss's request for a discounted 'Dean's tax' was acceptable to the president and provost. Dr. Fitzpatrick's oak tree would remain; and Dr. Moss intended to plant more.

## Chapter Five: Return to the 'burgh, 1993

Phil, who was now Dr. Moss, Jr., in the eyes of the department in which he was about to begin his residency, rolled into Pittsburgh with Lisa and Kamal. They had borrowed Kamal's family's SUV and rented a U-Haul trailer big enough to bring Kamal's and Lisa's belongings, as well as Phil's. They stopped in Cleveland to drop off Kamal's and Lisa's boxes at their newly leased apartments on June first and then headed to Pittsburgh the next day to deliver both Phil and his belongings to his family home. The Moss's had invited Kamal and Lisa to spend as long as they wanted. With Sarah and Anne away, there was plenty of room for the two friends.

Phil was anxious to show them the quaintness of Walnut Street in Shadyside, Schenley Park, the museums, a Pirate's game, as well as the university medical center. Phil also had to find an apartment. On this task he had procrastinated, given the free and easy comfort of the family home in which he had grown up. They rolled in to Pittsburgh late Wednesday morning. Nobody was home. Phil's mom had left a note that she was playing tennis then going grocery shopping and would be home later in the afternoon. Kamal expertly backed the SUV and attached trailer up the driveway that continued past the house and stopped in front of a carriage house. Lisa and Phil watched in amazement awaiting some disaster to ensue. Kamal hopped out with a big smile. Lisa stammered, "How in the hell did you….," as she gestured her hands up and down the driveway.

"I worked landscape and renovation jobs every summer during college. We pulled trailers all the time loaded with equipment and supplies. It's a bit like flying upside down I guess when you are backing up one of these things, but you get the hang of it after a while. We practiced in an empty field with traffic cones (may they rest in peace) for hours before the bossman would let us drive on a job," Kamal proudly stated. Kamal and Phil unhooked the trailer, unburdening the Chevy Tahoe from the awkwardness of driving around a city with a U-haul. Lisa kept shaking her head in disbelief.

The three of them helped Phil get his belongings inside. It was quick work as Phil had pared down his belongings nicely in Chicago before leaving. Soon as they were done Phil said, "Okay guys, time for the world's best hotdogs, on me. We are headed to The O!" The three of them piled into the Tahoe and were headed down Fifth Avenue to The O, which was short for 'Original', an iconic hotdog and fries joint that was near the medical center and university, so frequented by many. Lunch was fantastic as long as they did not consider the saturated fats and cholesterol being consumed.

Since they were so close, Phil gave them a quick tour from the outside of the medical center. He walked them up from Fifth Avenue through the dark tunnel like driveway that separated the Children's and University hospitals. He then walked them up "Cardiac Hill" past the Pitt football stadium to the VA hospital that sat above the stadium. Kamal kept looking down into the stadium while almost walking into street signs and fire hydrants until Lisa slapped his shoulder hard. "You horn dog! That's a high school cheerleader camp going on down there!" she yelled as she wound up and struck him again.

Kamal replied, "No, I think they are college cheerleaders," and kept looking with no reaction to the physical pain Lisa was trying to inflict upon him. Phil stopped Lisa from striking him again, and that caused Kamal to break his gaze. "Oh sorry," he muttered, "eyes forward." Lisa just shook her head with a mix of disgust and anger.

The trio returned to the Tahoe and headed back to the Moss's. Lisa was in the backseat and not talking to Kamal who was driving after the 'cheerleader camp' incident. She finally broke her silence, "Bhatia, you need to get laid."

Kamal simply replied, "I cannot argue with you on that." Phil started to chuckle, followed by Kamal, and finally Lisa joined in. Soon the trio was laughing uncontrollably as they had done together so many times before. It was a short drive back to the Moss's house. Kamal pulled all the way past the garage doors to the carriage house so he would not block Phil's parents' comings and goings. Mrs. Moss had already arrived with the garage door up and was unloading groceries. Soon she had three helpers and was grateful as she greeted them all. Phil received a long hug.

Phil gave his friends a tour of the house and showed them where they would be staying. Mrs. Moss had Anne's room ready for Lisa, and the guest room for Kamal. Somewhat to Phil's dismay his bedroom had been converted into a "crafts room" by his mother. His bed was still there, but a table, chair and large bins of undefinable stuff occupied almost every other square inch of the floor. His small desk where he studied so diligently as a high school student was barely visible. Regardless, he was glad to be home for a while even if he had to walk sideways just to get to his bed.

Phil remained undecided as to whether anything romantic was happening between his two friends, and decided not to ask, at least for the moment. Phil asked Lisa and Kamal if they wanted any "pop" and was greeted with confused stares. "That would be 'soda or soft drinks' you philistines," he exclaimed.

"When in Rome...," said Kamal looking at Lisa, "grab us some pop!"

The three friends headed out to the screened porch at the back of the house and sank into the cushioned wicker furniture. Before long, all three were asleep. They awoke when a siren from an ambulance headed toward the medical center headed down Fifth Avenue which was only two blocks away. Soon they would learn that sound would create anxiety or dread within their consciousness for the rest of their professional careers, and never the excitement seen on television shows or sensed as medical students. Phil went into the kitchen to ask his mother if he and his friends could help with anything. She was not there. He went to yell for her but then heard her agitated voice as one side of a heated discussion muted by the closed bedroom door. When he no longer heard talking, he knocked on her door, "Mom, can we help you with anything? Mom?"

Eventually Mrs. Moss replied though she sounded upset, "I'm just freshening up. I'll be out in a minute."

When Mrs. Moss returned to the kitchen, Phil was waiting for her while Lisa and Kamal were still relaxing on the porch. Phil could tell his mother had been crying. "Mom what's wrong?" he asked earnestly.

"Nothing new. And nothing we are talking about today. Your father is going to be home around 8 tonight. Can you guys last until then for dinner?" she asked tearfully, as if Phil had a choice in the matter.

"Of course, Mom! We had lunch at The O. We could make it until breakfast, but don't challenge us," Phil stated playfully and gave her a hug. "Promise to ask us for help when it comes time to make dinner," he said as he kissed her forehead.

"I will Sweetie," she replied as she wiped a tear from her eye.

Phil returned to the porch to check on his friends and inform them that he volunteered them for kitchen duty later. They were more than happy to help with anything. Simply doing anything that was neither studying nor hospital work was an unadulterated joy for all of them. "Hey Phil, who plays tennis in your family? They could use a new can of balls," Kamal asked as he held up two very tattered tennis balls.

Phil's eyes popped wide open, and his jaw dropped, "Holy shit! How could I forget!" and Phil went tearing back inside and down the steps yelling, "Charrrrrrlllllllliiieeeeeee!!!"

Moments later the sound of paws and claws on hardwood steps came thundering from the open basement door. Mrs. Moss came out of the kitchen to see what was going on and gasped, "Oh with everything going on I completely forgot I had put him downstairs," as a flash of bronze blasted past her and out onto the screened porch. Charlie was a large Golden Retriever of the darker shade, and though ten years old, behaved like an 85-pound puppy.

Kamal reflexively positioned himself behind Lisa to shield himself from the unknown canine. Charlie had that trademark permanent smile and stood there looking at the two strangers with a "Let's play" look in his eyes before he spun around and headed full speed back toward Phil as Phil emerged from the stairwell. Charlie leapt up almost knocking Phil back down the stairs and began licking his face.

Lisa turned around, looked at Kamal with a sneer and said, "Those cheerleaders would have been real impressed with your bravery there, hot stuff." Despite his complexion, Kamal managed to blush shamefully.

After playing with Charlie outside and Lisa and Phil helping Kamal overcome his fear of dogs, they headed back inside at the request of Mrs. Moss. She put them to work cleaning, peeling, and slicing. After about thirty minutes she told them thank you and to grab beers or pop from the basement refrigerator if they would like. They collectively decided to forego the beer or more pop given the lunch they were still digesting, and to head back outside with Charlie.

It was still light out at eight p.m. as the summer solstice approached. Charlie had gone comatose and was serving as a pillow for Lisa in the warm June grass, when something unseen caught the retriever's attention. For half a second his head popped up, and then he was gone. Lisa was grateful they were not on the sidewalk as her head hit the soft turf. Dr. Moss, Sr., had arrived home, and Charlie was going to be the first to greet him.

The three friends clambered inside to greet Dr. Moss, Sr., and to get ready for dinner. The house now smelled amazing. Dr. Moss, Sr., shook hands with Kamal and gave Lisa a quick hug, followed by a bear hug with his son. He shouted a greeting to his wife, but did not go to the kitchen, instead he retreated to his room to change out of his shirt and tie. Phil took a mental note, only because all his prior memories consisted of his father's arrival home being associated with kissing his mother. No big deal, Phil concluded; that was years ago and suddenly all of us are here. Phil dismissed it from his mind.

Dinner was simple but delicious, with warm garlic bread, a freshly prepared tossed salad, and spaghetti with marinara sauce. Mrs. Moss had smartly put meatballs as a side in case either of Phil's friends were vegetarian. Kamal said he was Hindu and vegetarian until today and began raving about the lunchtime hotdogs and Mrs. Moss's meatballs. That comment provoked smiles and laughs around the table, for which Phil was grateful because his mother seemed to be not her typical relaxed self. The conversations gravitated toward medicine and the three careers that were about to launch. Dr. Moss, Sr., knew the programs at Case Western well having served on the trauma review team that visited Cleveland for the American College of Surgeons. He assured Lisa and Kamal that they would be very well trained, but half-jokingly stated not to expect to have any fun. He also warned them about certain characters they would certainly encounter, as avoiding them would be impossible. Dr. Moss, Sr., also shared some stories from Vietnam that left Lisa and Kamal slack jawed with amazement. His wife unsuccessfully tried to get him to stop talking about such things at the dinner table. Somewhat uncouthly, Dr. Moss, Sr., then asked Lisa and Kamal if they were dating. Lisa and Kamal looked at each other before responding, with Lisa mouthing the word "no" to Kamal with clear concern on her face as to how Kamal would answer. Kamal replied that they were not currently dating but he would strongly consider it, if such an arrangement would help advance his surgical career, and concluded, "Hey, my people are all about arranged marriages." The Moss's realized they had quite the comedian in the house.

After dinner Phil, Lisa, and Kamal headed to the family room and crashed on the big couch with Lisa in the middle to watch Seinfeld and Frasier. Kamal and Lisa both remarked what an impressive and incredibly accomplished father Phil had. Phil replied, "He is amazing. I hear that from everyone that meets him. I've always wanted to grow up and be like him. I am going to kick my ass these next seven years to make that happen and impress him."

Kamal remarked with a coy smile, "Well Phil, you look a lot like him as well, but I don't think you can be *entirely* like him."

Lisa immediately smacked Kamal in the shoulder.

"Yea, very funny KB. I may not marry a woman, but everything *professionally* about him I will strive to emulate," replied Phil maintaining his dignity.

"Dude, you are using SAT words now. My apologies, that's a clear sign I hit a nerve. I want you to be you; simple as that," Kamal said earnestly. Phil nodded in acceptance of the apology.

"Phil, you know I love you, so just tell me to shut up if you want, but do your parents know?" Lisa asked cautiously.

Phil took a deep breath and straightened his back, "I couldn't, I can't, not yet," he said as he exhaled.

Kamal chimed in, "Phil, we understand. Just know we got your back and will support you as friends, always."

Lisa continued, "Yes that is true, but Phil there is going to come a time when you just can't hide who you are."

"Damn it, Lisa, I know, but can you imagine if I were 'out' and trying to match in a neurosurgery residency and how a lot of the other residents would treat me if I did match. Plus, what would my dad think?" Phil ended looking distraught.

"Guys, it's 'Seinfeld'. Let's drop this, enjoy the evening, and get some laughs," commanded Kamal.

"Agreed!" Lisa and Phil responded.

And then Phil softly said, "Thanks guys, I love you both."

They stayed up watching television until David Letterman finished his show and then they went to bed.

They slept in and one by one emerged from their respective rooms about 9 a.m. They each silently realized that the ability to sleep as late as they desired was about to become a remote memory. There was a note on the kitchen table from Phil's mom saying she was playing tennis and for them to eat whatever they liked. Kamal immediately looked to see if any meatballs were left. "Geez, we've created a carnivore!" remarked Lisa.

"No. I am now an omnivore to be exact," said Kamal frankly.

"I stand corrected. We've created a prick," countered Lisa.

"Calm down you two," said Phil. "Kamal, you cannot eat meatballs for breakfast even if we had any left. We will go over the rules of being an omnivore later," stated Phil.

"Rules? Can they be guidelines instead?" Kamal asked pleadingly.

Phil looked at Lisa and just said, "You were right."

After breakfast and showers, they went for a walk around Shadyside and popped into the quirky shops along Walnut Street. Phil wrote down several phone numbers attached to 'For Rent' signs planted in front of numerous places as they explored the tree lined streets. For the most part these were turn of the century multistory houses that had been turned into apartments, with one apartment encompassing each floor of the house. Many were grand structures that instead of housing the well-to-do families of the past now housed tenants consisting of graduate students, medical trainees, and other young professionals. They went back to the Moss's and Phil made some calls. The trio went back out again by foot and met with various landlords or their agents to look at some of the available places. Phil remained underwhelmed despite Lisa and Kamal providing encouragement and highlighting the positives of every apartment Phil visited. By the time they returned it was late in the afternoon and Lisa and Kamal could sense Phil's frustration. As they walked up the driveway to the Moss's home Kamal asked, "What's in the carriage house, carriages?"

"I haven't been in there forever," said Phil as he shrugged his shoulders.

"Let's take a look then!" Lisa said excitedly.

Lisa ran forward and pulled one of the two large double doors open. Each door must have been almost twelve feet tall and six feet wide. Kamal and Phil stood back expecting a cloud of disturbed bats to erupt and escape with the opening of the large door. Then they heard Lisa say, "This is so cool." Kamal and Phil joined her inside. There were old leather bridles, horseshoes, and wooden wheels hanging from the walls. Along the back wall was a staircase that went up to an enclosed upper level. "The staircase looks like it was built after World War Two at least," said Lisa assuring herself it was safe to ascend before she headed up the stairs. The door did not open easily but was not locked. Lisa was able to get it open with her shoulder though, as Kamal and Phil waited yet again anticipating bats or wasps or something pissed off. "Oh, this is even better," they heard Lisa say.

Kamal and Phil, feeling a bit ashamed that Lisa boldly explored the carriage house with no help from them, reluctantly climbed the stairs. There was a stair rail built from two by fours that was no architectural wonder but sturdy enough to serve its purpose. When they entered the room Lisa was opening more doors and wiping grime from the window interior. "Look," she said, "you can see straight down the driveway and out to the street."

The room had a desk, an old twin sized bed frame, and a sink with a two-burner electric range and small counter at the far end of the room. There looked to be a space for a small table and chairs between the bed and "kitchen." Kamal turned the tap, but no water was forthcoming. Inside one door was a closet with empty hangers and some old leather shoes, and inside another was an old toilet of an uncertain color and a rusty shower head. Very distant memories were starting to float through Phil's consciousness. Hide and seek with his sisters popped into his mind, then somebody falling and going to the hospital, and then some old guy. He continued thinking and ignoring Lisa and Kamal arguing about what color the toilet originally was. He and his sisters when very young would play hide and seek in the carriage house whenever their mother just needed some quiet in the house. Sarah fell running down the stairs in the carriage house and broke her arm. That put the end to hide and seek. Finally, Uncle Jeff lived here for a while. He was dad's younger brother. Damn he was probably only in his thirties, and I remember him as an old guy, Phil thought and chuckled. There was some argument Phil remembered, and dad threw Uncle Jeff out. As young kids suddenly the carriage house seemed like a bad place when that happened. Phil thought it had probably been at least 15 years since he had been inside those big doors.

Kamal and Lisa were now counting light switches and outlets which was pretty easy because there were only two of each. There were light bulb sockets with burned out light bulbs in the ceiling of the toilet room and the main room. There also was a radiator near the window that looked not down at the driveway but out the side of the carriage house. They headed down the stairs and followed pipes down that lead to a water heater tucked in the corner on the lower level. How it worked, or if it worked, they had no idea.

That night at dinner the carriage house became a topic of discussion. Dr. Moss, Sr., remained evasive regarding Uncle Jeff, but happily discussed the carriage house and the history he knew concerning it from before they bought the property. Lisa mentioned that they should fix it up and rent it out. Both parents stated they had no desire to have a stranger living there. Then Kamal said, "What about Phil?"

Mrs. Moss's face lit up, Phil's face indicated he was processing the concept, and Dr. Moss, Sr.'s face showed skepticism as he said, "It requires a fair amount of renovation. A lot of stuff would need to be replaced, refurbished, upgraded, painted. I don't have the time to make that happen."

"Piece of cake," said Kamal.

Everyone looked at him curiously with Lisa asking, "What's a piece of cake?"

"The carriage house," said Kamal, "we would knock out renovations like that in a couple days. But I would not recommend doing anything unless we know the status of the hot water and plumbing. The heat comes from a hot water radiator, so you need hot water for winter heating and showers. You could also use an electric heater, but you definitely need hot water for showering and washing dishes."

Lisa looked on in amazement as common sense spewed forth from Kamal's lips. Who is this guy, she thought to herself.

Dr. Moss, Sr., chimed in, "The water heater currently there is electric. I installed that when Phil's uncle lived there. It's old. Even if it works now, it should be replaced. If you guys want to make this a project, then give us a proposal. If it is a feasible undertaking, then I'll get our plumber to install a new water heater and toilet. The water supply to the carriage house is controlled by a valve in the basement below us. It's been off for many years. You guys can open the valve and see what happens. For everything else you guys figure it out."

"Wait a minute," said Phil, "I never said I wanted to live there, or here, or anywhere. You know what I mean." Phil noticed the excited smile on his mother's face disappear as he spoke.

Dr. Moss, Sr., noticed his wife's reaction as well and said, "Phil, where you live is your decision. But that carriage house could use some attention, and it would be something for you to work on with or without your friends until orientation starts in a couple weeks while you consider where to live. Being an intern or resident and living in the main house would frankly be too disruptive. And as you've seen, your bedroom has been pirated for a so-called higher purpose. Anyone living in the carriage house would be like someone living down the street as far as I'm concerned. Think about it. We are willing to fund the project if you three can give us a solid plan by this time tomorrow. Plus, I suspect whatever rent we charged would be very competitive. You are a young single man as well and need your own space for many reasons." Dr. Moss, Sr., delivered that final comment with a poorly disguised wink.

Secretly Phil was thrilled. He was also thrilled his dad did not start asking questions about his love life. But now the opportunity to not only work under and be trained by his father, but to also live so close to his parents was more than he could have ever imagined. His friends were really coming through for him whether they knew it or not. While Lisa and Kamal had planned to head back to Cleveland by the weekend, it now seemed like they might stay longer.

After dinner the three new doctors headed to the family room and switched on the television. The Pirates were home. They started talking about the carriage house and Kamal took the lead and muted the television. He outlined everything. He said they would go back in the morning and inspect the carriage house apartment, that they now referred to as the CHA. They would turn the water on, check electricity from outlets, assess circuit breaker status for handling the load of a microwave and space heater, remove a chunk of drywall and assess insulation and any infestation. Gross is all Phil and Lisa could think at Kamal's last reason. They would look for any evidence of water damage or leaks. He said the lower level had a 220-volt outlet that apparently had been used for some woodworking tools by somebody in the past that Phil could now plug a dryer into. After they had addressed the "guts and bones" of the place, then they would address the "skin"-the walls, flooring, fixtures, etc. Phil and Lisa began to wonder if Kamal had missed his true calling. The guy was going to be a great general surgeon though. He really could frame the whole concept of the task at hand and still be detailed oriented. It was impressive.

As they talked more about it, Kamal and Lisa fully realized how excited Phil was to be able to live in the CHA. He finally came out and told them so, thanking them profusely for all their ideas and help. That is when Lisa said, "I guess we are staying a while longer. Cleveland must wait."

Kamal, who soon was called "The Foreman" by Phil and Lisa, and then eventually Phil's parents as well, orchestrated a smooth and efficient renovation. The plumber that the Moss's had called saved the trio a lot of time and effort. Dr. Moss, Sr., had an electrician come by and make sure all was up to code and had a few more outlets installed. They also had a phone line connected that was separate from the main house phone line. They spent the final day of renovation painting. Following that they were off to IKEA with the Chevy Tahoe. They hooked the trailer back up and had room to spare as they returned with everything Phil needed for his new home.

    On their last night together in Pittsburgh, Dr. Moss, Sr., gave Phil and his friends the department season tickets along the first base line at Three Rivers Stadium. He said he would try and join them with the fourth ticket later but had an important meeting that may run late. Phil kept the empty seat next to him hoping to see his father headed down the steps to join them at the end of each inning, but his father never showed up.

## Chapter Six: Ava, 1988

As chairman, Dr. Moss established a policy that each faculty member would have either a Physician's Assistant or Nurse Practitioner assigned to them to help with clinical care, communicating with the residents, and just as importantly dealing with families. These health care professionals were incredibly helpful in an academic neurosurgical practice where the surgeons could not be reached routinely because of either being in the operating room for hours on end or traveling to various conferences around the country or world. They served as the eyes, ears, and mouth of each attending. Those that had been in the department for several years often knew more about neurosurgery than the junior residents, and even sometimes the senior residents. Because these P.A.s and N.P.s were so valuable and integral to the running of a surgeon's practice, each was chosen with careful consideration. Likewise, it was more than an inconvenience should one of these "physician extenders," as they were sometimes labeled, decide to leave the department.

Margaret Dabrowski, who preferred to be called "Dab", looked to be no more than five feet tall, and almost as wide. When amongst themselves, the residents referred to her as "Five Squared." She was a battle hardened former military nurse who after serving in the navy and then experiencing a failed childless marriage, returned to school to obtain her Master of Science in Nursing. She was Dr. Moss's N.P., "The Chairman's," she would often say, and she used that leverage to both the advantage of his patients as well as to make her life easier. Because she was smart, experienced, unflappable, and a hard worker, Dr. Moss overlooked some of her misgivings. Most patients loved her, but if she had just returned from one of her frequent cigarette breaks and not chewed gum long enough there would be the occasional complaint, "She smells like an ashtray," or something similar. Her voice was coarse, which fit her demeanor. She would cuss out just about anybody that screwed something up, whether a scheduler in radiology, a resident, a floor nurse, or even attending physicians other than Dr. Moss. More often than not the recipient of her tirade deserved it, so she was often forgiven with those at the receiving end rolling their eyes and thinking to themselves I have been Dabbed. Those not familiar with her method of communicating her displeasure could be found curled up in a corner crying. While the neurosurgical residents were a tight crew, part of the initiation for a second-year resident was to be unknowingly placed in a situation that would attract Dab's ire. All attempts were made to maximize the number of resident witnesses for when Dab unleashed her nicotine fueled spittle upon the uninitiated. Once the attack was over the more senior residents would quickly provide reassurance and the back story to the new junior resident. If they did not particularly like the new junior resident, however, then they would let that resident wallow in misery. To Dr. Moss, however, Dab was indispensable. She got things done and made things happen. He cared mostly about results and not the means to achieve them. So, when she came into his office after he had just returned from the operating room and squeezed herself into one of the wooden chairs opposite him to give her four weeks' notice that she would be retiring, Dr. Moss felt the air leave his lungs. He knew there would be no changing her mind. This was Dab.

The next week, Dr. Moss directed his secretary, Lucy, to begin the process of recruitment for a nurse practitioner or physician assistant. He thought about just taking one of the N.P.s or P.A.s from one of his partners. He was chairman after all. He thought about some of the other N.P.s within the department that were much "easier on the eyes" compared to Dab but decided it would be unfair to exercise that power for those reasons.

Dr. Moss was a solidly built man, about six foot and one inch with thick cropped greying hair and chestnut brown eyes. He had the appearance of someone who may have played tight end or offensive lineman in high school, but not Division one college football. He was neither attractive nor ugly. He had gained some weight but would not be considered obese or fat. Any "je ne sais quoi" that he broadcasted was secondary to his station in life and his professional accomplishments. He was quick witted enough to be funny, but also curious and nerdy enough to be awkward when speaking. He was not deaf to the comments he would hear in public from what were probably medical or nursing students, or residents from other specialties talking to each other, "I think that's the neurosurgery chair, Moss. He's like world famous." He was not accustomed though to being the target of infatuation or lust, because he simply was not such a target. He was married and too busy for "that" anyway. But at times he would think he deserved more attention or any attention from the "fairer sex."

Within a day of the job opening being posted a knock came on Dr. Moss's office door. He bid to whomever knocked to enter. To his surprise the N.P. who worked with Dr. Nilsson, the director of the Gamma Knife radiosurgery program entered. Ella was a tall slender blonde who always seemed to have a perpetual frown on her face. She said, "Sorry to bother you Dr. Moss, but in regard to the job opening," as Dr. Moss's pulse suddenly quickened, "there is somebody who may be a good fit for your team that I know," and then his pulse slowed.

It took only a moment for him to reorient to reality and Dr. Moss said, "Please, sit down."

"Well," Ella continued, "a year or so ago we had an N.P. student rotate with us in Gamma Knife and interventional radiology. Both teams thought she was fantastic. The IR folks had an opening for her, but she turned it down. Evidently, she had a boyfriend or fiancé in D.C., so went to work at Georgetown. I've heard through the grapevine that she is unhappy there and really misses Pittsburgh. We all thought she would be a great addition to neurosurgery, but of course at the time there were no positions open. I can get her name for you if you like, and Lucy can track her down."

"I like that idea," Dr. Moss responded, "Please do get that contact information to Lucy. She can find anybody. Thank you for stopping by."

"Oh. Her name is Ava. I'll get her last name from IR and tell Lucy," Ella concluded and wryly smiled.

Ella turned around and left, and Dr. Moss savored every moment he could, watching her walk away. He then took a deep breath, released a sigh, and returned to the paperwork on his desk.

Dr. Moss felt obligated to have a farewell party for Dab. The problem was that few other people did. Most members of the department were quietly thrilled she was retiring. Dab was not the type to befriend colleagues. She tended to function using a scorched earth policy to achieve her goals. Dr. Moss was insulated from and ignorant of many of these battles in the trenches of health care, but the other N.P.s, P.A.s, residents, floor nurses, ICU nurses, and radiology and OR schedulers endured her wrath almost daily. But free food was free food, and so when the Friday, three p.m. celebration occurred any resident not in the OR was present along with office staff that primarily did not have to deal with Dab. Only one other N.P. was present and that was Ella. The other six "physician extenders" were said to be too busy to be able to attend. A smattering of other faculty quickly dropped by to snatch a piece of cake and to make sure Dr. Moss saw their faces before retreating to their offices. They were simply trying to be good soldiers by being present, but for the absolute shortest amount of time. Dr. Moss at times did envy the lesser responsibilities of the other faculty. The residents brought the three medical students who were rotating on the neurosurgery service, one was a fourth-year student, Ricki Bouba, who was very interested in a career in neurosurgery.

Ricki, while raised and schooled in New Jersey, was born in Cameroon. His parents emigrated to the United States when he was only two years old. His parents spoke primarily French; hence he was fluent in English and French. His English had an accent that was hard to define. If speaking with him by phone and not knowing him, you could only ascertain that he was not from the United States originally, although the USA was the only country of which he had any memories. Some astute listeners would note a lisp in his speech as well. The lisp, along with delicate features and mild mannerisms, earned him the name "Twinkle Toes" from Dab. He knew he was "different" and tolerated her branding and ignorance with class. She was not the only person to poke fun at who he was during his medical school experience, but within the neurosurgery department she was the only one who put her bigotry on full display around him. He was glad to see her leave the department, though practically, he only had one more week left in the rotation, then he was going to do an Infectious Disease rotation. He did take solace in knowing however, that if he matched in the neurosurgery residency in Pittsburgh, which was his current dream, he would not have to continue to tolerate Dab.

By four p.m. most of those who attended Dab's farewell celebration had either politely wished her well through gritted teeth or quietly left. Dr. Moss did his best to stay for the entire hour and keep an artificial smile plastered on his face. He was truly sad that Dab was retiring, but more for the selfish reasons that she kept his professional life more organized and less stressful and not that he enjoyed her as a person. He gave her a framed commemorative plaque for all her years with the department. Nobody could think of a viable gift for her, though many among themselves suggested a broom or cauldron. He attached an envelope to the plaque containing a handwritten note and a check for two hundred and fifty dollars. They exchanged an awkward hug and Dab left.

His mind was in an entirely different place watching Dab waddle away compared to wistfully watching Ella leave his office when he felt a tap on his shoulder. Lucy, his secretary, was there to remind him of a four p.m. meeting with the neurology chair, and that he would be interviewing Ava Chelidon Monday for the N.P. position. Ava would be the third candidate to interview for the opening. The first two candidates, while seemingly capable, just did not click with his personality. They were simply too girlish and bubbly is what he told himself. Maybe all those years of having Dab as his N.P. had warped his expectations. He prided himself on having an N.P. that was tough, even scary. When he got back to his office and surveyed the application on his desk from Ava Chelidon, he once again looked at the birthdate, another applicant thirty years younger than himself, Penn nursing school, Pitt Master's degree, strong letters regarding clinical skills and work ethic. He looked at her passport-like photo stapled in the upper left corner in black and white. Ava's appearance was emotionless reminding him of a mugshot seen at a post office bulletin board, but she was certainly attractive. He just did not want to suffer through another interview with a woman as young as his daughters as they smiled and giggled and told him how dedicated they were to easing human suffering and how wonderful they were working as part of a "team" with others. He thought seriously about calling Dab at that moment and begging her to return, but he knew he would sound pathetic, and she would tell him so.

That weekend he and Cammie attended the matinee showing of the musical, "Funny Girl", and dined at the Pittsburgh Golf Club. Cammie played tennis there often. Neither of the couple golfed though. Dr. Moss used the membership primarily for dinner dates with his wife, family holiday meals, and for departmental functions. As the years passed, the meal itself became the main event of the evening. In the years prior, the meal had often served as a prelude to what Dr. Moss considered the main event of the evening. If only he could turn back time. Dates with his wife now instilled in him a degree of melancholy even while he truly enjoyed her company and loved her dearly. He often thought how two clocks made by different watchmakers, at different times and in different places could stay synchronized for as long as they did. Eventually though, the clocks will show different times, or one will break, or one will need to be rewound before the other. It was the inevitable entropy of shared lives.

Monday morning arrived quickly. The weekends seemed to provide just enough respite to provide the energy and drive for another week as chairman of a top tier neurosurgical department. When the weekend involved being on call, however, the subsequent weekend became all that more critical to restore those same qualities. Even the weekends Dr. Moss was not "on call", there were always either clinical or administrative issues where his input as chairman was needed. It was an exhausting but rewarding job. He had one daughter in medical school and a son in college planning to attend medical school. He had a second daughter who was going to be "finding her way" at Notre Dame. He and Cammie were extremely proud of their children. He interpreted the fact that two of his children were entering the medical field as evidence that he had been a good father and set a good example. Cammie quietly held a different opinion.

    The first Monday of each month there was a breakfast meeting between all department chairs and the dean. Any real business with the dean he addressed privately with the dean. He found these breakfast meetings useful to learn about the hospital and medical school challenges, but some mornings they were a painful waste of his time. This Monday was one of those mornings. He was to help one of his younger faculty that day with the resection of an arteriovenous malformation, or AVM, of the cerebellum. Dr. Sharma was highly skilled and competent. An AVM however can be an unforgiving beast in the OR at times and having experienced back up or assistance can be imperative in achieving a successful outcome. Dr. Moss was rehearsing in his mind the steps appropriate to resect that AVM as he imagined the angiogram he had reviewed last night, how the patient should be positioned, and so on. He was deep in thought as he rounded the open door of his office and was taken by surprise as he entered. A young lady with long red hair and athletic calves visible below her hemline had her back turned to the door and had a framed Moss family photo in her hand seemingly studying it. Dr. Moss cleared his throat to get her attention. She turned toward him, and he then recognized that same unsmiling almost emotionless face. He extended his hand in introduction, "Good morning, I'm Dr. Moss. You must be Ava."

She turned back and took what seemed an inordinate amount of time to reposition the photo exactly as it had been. She then turned back toward him and flatly said, "Yes. I know both of those things."

Dr. Moss was already trying to think how to end this interview that had not yet begun as quickly as possible. Ava wore flat bottomed shoes, a light linen skirt, a blouse that was contoured to her proportions tastefully and unbuttoned to her mid sternum, with a dark green jacket over top. While most men would look at a photograph of her and think only of her physical beauty, the only judgment invading Dr. Moss's consciousness is that this woman is weird. "Please, sit down," he beckoned while gesturing toward one of the chairs opposite his desk.

Dr. Moss began by asking about her experience in Pittsburgh with radiology and the Gamma Knife team. She answered with striking clarity and insight. He then asked about her past year at Georgetown. She implied that she was bored with a lack of responsibility and frustrated with the paralyzing creep of political correctness at that institution. He asked about any other connections or experiences she had in D.C. She quickly and bluntly stated that her ex-fiancé became a "wimp that did to know what he was doing with his life." Dr. Moss then gave her hypothetical after hypothetical clinical scenarios ranging from the straightforward to the complex. He remained amazed at the almost robotic nature of her replies that outlined how she would handle such circumstances, and when she would involve the residents or directly bypass the residents and contact the faculty. His opinion of her had changed completely; so much for first impressions, he thought.

Dr. Moss asked, "So Ava, did you ever consider medical school?" as he braced for her robotic reply.

"No, why pay all that money to create a knowledge base of which ninety percent I would never use," she stated plainly and continued, "I use just about everything I've learned in nursing and graduate school."

Dr. Moss had no reply but simply thought that she made a good point and said, "Well I hope you enjoy the rest of the day visiting here. I see your agenda has you meeting with the nursing director, our clinic manager, and some of our N.P.s and P.A.s. Ella, who serves as our de facto "lead N.P." will be taking you to lunch." And seemingly with the mention of Ella's name a smile cracked across the heretofore austerity that had occupied her face. Dr. Moss's next thought was if she would only smile more, people would eat out her hand.

Ava stood and now awkwardly extended her hand, and as they shook, she confidently stated, "I look forward to working with you, Phillip." She turned ninety degrees with almost military precision and exited his office.

Dr. Moss collapsed into his office chair uncertain whether he would be thrilled to hire her, or in peril if he did not. Her competency was beyond question. Her sense of professional boundaries or decorum, at least with him, was in question though. Ava was stiff, a bit odd, and even physically intimidating though she was a svelte 5 and a half feet. At one of the recent combined neurology and neurosurgery grand rounds, one of the neurology faculty, Frank Walsh, spoke about "autism." It was a concept or condition not taught during Dr. Moss's medical school tenure or training. Now he was wishing he had paid more attention during that very non-surgical presentation rather than spending the hour mentally undressing one of the junior neurology faculty and Ella, who was seated next to the new neurologist. He did remember from the presentation that some individuals labeled as "autistic" could function at a very high level, and in fact could be considered brilliant or even geniuses. At the end of the talk Dr. Walsh listed several "geniuses" suspected to be autistic: Charles Darwin, Bobby Fischer, Isaac Newton were a few mentioned. Who the hell would not hire Isaac Newton is all Dr. Moss could think as he picked up the phone to tell Lucy to generate a job offer for Ava Chelidon as soon as possible.

## Chapter Seven: General Surgery Internship, 1993-1994

"Get the fuck up Moss," Giana now screamed for the second time shaking Phil's shoulder. She was another surgery intern doing her one-month emergency room rotation. Giana, like all the interns, was smart and hard working. She had a shoot and ask questions later mentality and cussed as her preferred means of communication. This quality made her problematic to work with though. She and Phil had been pulling every-other-day coverage over the Thanksgiving holiday week, so that other interns could get away. All the surgical services functioned similarly, ignore any work hour limits, provide the coverage, do the work and you too will be granted a long weekend at some point during the year while teetering on the verge of collapse from stress and exhaustion. It was considered the ideal method of surgical training. They both, however, partly were glad not to be traveling that holiday. There had been an early winter storm. The downside of remaining was that the iced over Pennsylvania turnpike was a demolition derby of holiday travelers. The amount of severe blunt trauma stressed the resources of the level one trauma center, and much of that stress fell on the resident staff. There were no medical students over the holiday, so all the proverbial shit rolling downhill piled up on the surgery interns and junior residents. After a particularly ghastly head on collision, Phil had to zip up three deceased souls in body bags after unsuccessful trauma resuscitations, a mother, father, and a young child. The worst part was they rapidly had to clear the trauma bay for another accident. There were no gurneys available, nobody to help him move the bodies. He ended up dragging the black bags containing freshly mangled corpses one by one down the hall and around a corner out of sight. Though the child's bag was by far the easiest to physically manage, it was also by far the most painful. He carried that bag and was balling by the time he reunited it with the child's parents' remains. That was at five a.m.

Giana had arrived shortly before seven a.m. for the beginning of her 24-hour shift. For a surgery intern to arrive at seven a.m. to start the day seemed like an all expenses paid trip to Disney World initially. When covering the various surgical services within the hospital they were often hungry for lunch by seven a.m. The change to 24-hour shifts versus 12-hour shifts prior to the holiday coupled with the gruesome barrage of trauma cleared all similes to anything Disney out of their minds rapidly.

Phil's bloodshot eyes cracked open to identify the person assaulting him after less than two hours sleep. "Holy shit Moss, you look like crap," blurted Giana. "Get the fuck out of here before I have to take care of you."

"Your compassion is overwhelming Giana," Phil said with a scratchy throat as he struggled to sit upright.

"Fuck you Moss, I'm going into orthopedics. I just need to measure, drill, and hammer," she replied half-jokingly.

Phil began to give her a summary of the events of the past 24 hours, not out of any patient quality of care needs, but more as therapy for him. As he was about to describe the horrific family deaths, they both saw Nancy D. in full surgical garb walk swiftly by the door. Dr. Nancy Delgado was the general surgery chief resident, for unknown reasons, everyone called her "Nancy D." Even though there were no other Nancies to the residents' knowledge in need of differentiation. She was well liked and respected. An informal evaluation would read that she has her shit together. Seeing her walking quickly past their door toward the emergency room was not a good sign. Giana and Phil realized this, and Giana emphasized to Phil again to leave. As Phil was tying his sneakers' laces Nancy D. Popped her head in the doorway and pulled her surgical mask down, "Sorry guys, I need all hands-on deck. Some asshole must have been upset with the Cowboys losing last night, because EMS is bringing in four gunshot victims still alive from up near Oil City. Mostly torso shots except one with a shot to the head."

A collective "Fuck" is all that escaped Giana's and Phil's lips.

"My sentiments exactly," Nancy D. responded as she popped her mask back up and headed toward the trauma bay.

Trauma codes had become a routine for the surgery interns. They were relegated to specific tasks. The intern on the surgery service would be responsible for placing a femoral vein catheter, a large IV, and the emergency room surgery intern had the glorious job of placing a Foley catheter into the bladder. The Foley placement consisted of a quick cleaning of the appropriate anatomy, and with men of grabbing the penis with the left hand and inserting the catheter with the right hand, assuming one was right-handed. Hence, it was advantageous to be standing on the patient's right side to perform this task. If a woman was receiving a Foley catheter, more finesse was needed to find the urethra and the legs may need to be parted while spreading the labia with the left hand and placing the Foley catheter in the correct orifice with the right hand. After a few experiences most interns had little trouble regarding Foley catheters with either sex whether the intern harbored a Y chromosome or not. Likewise, it was advantageous for a right-handed intern to be on the patient's right side to place a femoral venous catheter. Hence, there was competition when both interns were right-handed, and they often were, to capture the position on the right side of the patient first. While this competition was often collegial, it was not unheard of for the penis holding intern relegated to the left side of the patient to "weaponize" the to-be-catheterized penis and "accidentally" soak the other intern. Chest tubes to drain blood or trapped air, and peritoneal taps to sample the abdomen for internal injuries were the purview of more senior residents. Trauma thoracotomy or "cracking the chest" to manually squeeze the dying heart was the purview of chief residents and attending staff. Severe head injuries were the realm of neurosurgery, but not until the patient could be stabilized by assuring an airway, oxygenation, and an appropriate blood pressure. While neurosurgery was critical in the care of the severely head-injured, neurosurgery residents often arrived after the resuscitation and lifesaving maneuvers were underway.

The ambulances arrived shortly. Two stretchers were left outside indicating two victims died en route. The other two were whisked into the trauma bay that housed space and equipment for two full trauma resuscitations. One of the survivors was a man who looked to be about forty years old with the gunshot wound to his head. He had short hair, but longer than a crew cut. He was unconscious and a breathing tube was in place. The emergency room attending was compressing the Ambu bag to provide oxygen and ventilation to the patient. Phil took his position on the right to place the venous catheter. Despite his exhaustion both physical and emotional, he robotically went through the steps and deftly placed the venous catheter. Thank God is all he thought, maybe now I can go home. Suddenly the patient's left leg flexed upward at the hip and the knee bent keeping the foot dragging up the stretcher. Phil looked down at the foot of the bed to see a wide-eyed Giana. "Shit, I didn't expect that. All I did was pinch his toe," she apologetically stated. She gestured toward the now abandoned patient on the other stretcher saying, "He didn't make it. At least we are one for four."

"Don't get too excited," said a voice. Phil looked up and recognized one of the neurosurgery residents. He often wondered how the cardiovascular surgery fellows and the neurosurgery residents could look simultaneously so young, and yet so old. It was as if their youth, or some part of their spirit had simply been robbed from them, and something undefinable filled that space like some chemical preservative that allowed them to endure what many considered impossible. "Moss, come up here with me. You gotta know this shit," Ricki Bouba commanded succinctly. "See this pasty shit in his hair above his left ear, that's brain that has squirted out the exit wound. Give me a gauze. See this neat round hole above his right ear," he rhetorically asked as he wiped away brain and blood from the right side, "that's the entrance wound. It even has the powder burn. Now look at his pupils."

Phil elevated each eyelid. Phil could not even see the color of the man's eyes as the pupils were as big as saucers. "What the...but he was just moving?" Phil asked, perplexed.

"His leg flexion was just a spinal reflex. His spinal cord is not dead yet. His brain is though or will be shortly. Bastard probably shot himself after shooting the others," said Ricki. Then looking up to the others in the room, "you can get a CT for kicks if you like, but this guy is dead. I'm surprised the transplant vultures are not already here." Ricki turned around and headed to exit the trauma bay as all the excitement in the room was sucked out with his words. Before leaving he turned back to Phil and said, "Looking forward to having you on service next year," and smiled.

Phil felt like he had been punched in the gut. Did Phil suddenly see his future as a neurosurgery resident? Was he going to walk into a room someday and cast a pall with such certainty, removing all sense of hope from a desperate family praying for survival or other docs and nurses doing their best to save someone? How could someone so young nonchalantly stroll in, tell everybody the man is dead they are striving to save, and walk out smiling. What the hell is wrong with that guy is all Phil could think. But it only took moments to prove the neurosurgery resident correct or simply prophetic. Pink froth filled the endotracheal tube from the reflex outpouring of fluid into the lungs caused by an unsurvivable increased level of intracranial pressure as more brain oozed like toothpaste from the head wounds and the trauma team could no longer oxygenate the patient or maintain a blood pressure. At that moment Giana came up and gave Phil an affectionate squeeze of his biceps, batted her thick eyelashes, sympathetically looked into his eyes, and told him to, "go the fuck home."

Phil headed to the OR locker room and changed into jeans and a sweatshirt, grabbed his heavy jacket and backpack containing the textbook he would read during any brief downtime. Instead of going directly to the parking garage he decided to go to the cafeteria and use his meal voucher for a plate of sad pancakes, rubbery sausage, and a Yoplait yogurt. After having eaten enough to assure himself that hunger would not wake him from his upcoming sleep he headed outside and down the icy sidewalk to the garage. He easily spotted his car, a beige '73 Plymouth Valiant, as the usual sardine can packing of vehicles in the garage had not occurred due to the reduced holiday staffing at the hospital. After many a long day, or long day and long night and another long day, he would wander floor to floor in the parking garage as he simply could not remember where he parked. The sea of other vehicles made it all the more difficult. He could name every major arterial branch in the human body, describe the embryology of the human fetal nervous system, and name origin and insertion of every muscle in the body. Knowing he knew these things made him feel like an idiot when he could not even remember where he parked. When he reached the driver's side door, he had to scrape ice out of the keyhole to be able to unlock the car. He threw his backpack on the passenger side, put the key in the steering column ignition, turned the key, and heard two clunks and a buzz. He turned the key again and pumped the gas pedal. That maneuver earned him one clunk and a buzz. The third try provided a single clunk, and the fourth nothing at all. "Shit, the battery is dead," he said aloud to himself. His apartment in the carriage house was only a two mile walk from the hospital. Everything was half coated in ice and snow, but he calculated his Nikes would be up to the task. Numb from lack of sleep, numb from the early morning horrors, and about to be numbed by the early winter weather he started his shuffling walk toward Shadyside.

It was not long before the towering structures of the university medical center gave way to a mix of old apartment buildings and modest homes. At that point, a car slowed down and pulled up along Phil as it moved in the same direction as Phil. Phil did not see anyone else around other than a pair of headlights about three blocks away stopped at a traffic light. Phil could hear muffled music beating from within the Honda Civic that suddenly became clearer and louder as the passenger side window was lowered. "Shit, I figured the son of the chairman would have his own car," yelled Ricki Bouba with his unique dialect, "Want a ride home? I know exactly where your parents live."

Phil turned toward the Honda as Ricki leaned across toward the passenger side. Phil's face had not yet replaced his apprehension with the relief that he was now experiencing. An hour ago, he was close to labeling Ricki as the Devil's Spawn, now he was considering him a savior. "Geez Moss, I guess you don't see many black guys in Shadyside. Don't look so scared. Come on, hop in!" beckoned Ricki.

Phil shuffled through the wet snow accumulated on the grass between the sidewalk and curb, opened the passenger door, slid into the seat, and plopped his backpack between his snow caked Nikes. "A million thanks Dr. Bouba. My car's battery is dead," Phil sheepishly said.

"You look awful," commented Ricki, "Get some sleep. It's Friday, and most places should be open today. I'll write down my number for you when I drop you off. Call me before three p.m. and we will go get a battery for your car. I promised to back up the junior resident tonight, so let's just get your car ready by five p.m. And call me Ricki!"

"Uh, Ricki, I really appreciate it, but I can get my sister to drive me, or maybe my dad. I don't want to trouble you when you have a few hours off," said Phil.

"Trouble! Ha! Moss, you are one of us now. We take care of our own," Ricki exclaimed with a smile. "Nothing is troublesome that one does willingly," stated Ricki.

"That was profound," said Phil.

"I cannot take credit. But those are words to live by as a resident. And make sure you know who I am quoting or maybe paraphrasing. You will need to know when on service," Ricki explained as they pulled into the Moss family's driveway.

"You can stop here. I don't want you getting stuck in this slop," Phil said as went to get out, "And many thanks for the lift." Phil extended his arm for a handshake. Ricki, likewise, extended his arm. Phil was surprised at the unexpected, pleasant softness of Ricki's grasp, and the sensation of Ricki's fingertip trailing across Phil's palm as they released hands. He found himself looking into Ricki's eyes for just a moment. There was something there he did not anticipate.

"Remember, call me by three," said Ricki, as he smiled and handed Phil his phone number scribbled on the back of a Taco Bell receipt. Phil gave him a thumbs up, smiled somewhat bashfully, grabbed his backpack and headed toward the carriage house. Ricki wondered why Phil didn't head into the main house through the front but then dismissed it from his mind.

There was a crust of ice sealing the side door that shattered as Phil opened the door to the carriage house. He trudged up the stairs, stripped, turned on the heat, took a shower, set his alarm for two fifty p.m. and collapsed. He had not seen anyone from his family since Wednesday night. Thanksgiving had come and gone. His last thoughts as he fell asleep were of that handshake. He was hoping this was not going to be another Trey fiasco. That would be an embarrassment difficult to hide from for the next seven years, he realized.

## Chapter Eight: The Holiday Inn, 1990

    Dr. Astrid Nilsson was the first woman to be on the neurosurgical faculty at Pittsburgh. Dr. Moss encouraged her recruitment before he became chair and closed the deal as soon as he became chair. She was an internationally renowned neurosurgeon for her expertise with radiosurgery. She had come from the birthplace of radiosurgery in Stockholm, the Karolinska Institute. It took a lot to leave her home country. Her husband, a university physicist, was recruited along with her. They were the perfect stereotypical Swedish couple in appearance. Both were tall, athletic, blond, with high cheek bones. Not that they tried, but they could pass as Scandinavian royalty. When dressed for a formal social event they turned heads, and they were both in their mid-fifties.

    Radiosurgery is a discipline where hundreds of small individual doses of radiation are all aimed at the same target within the head. Each wave of energy begins from a different location scattered across a virtual or real hemispheric dome that encompasses the head so that as each wave heads towards the target very little energy is transferred to the brain, hence avoiding injury. When these hundreds of individual "energy waves" of radiation meet at the calculated precise target, however, there is a tremendous amount of energy delivered. Enough energy to destroy tumor cells or shrivel up vascular malformations. It is considered a means of delivering a surgical effect through the use of a single dose of radiation without making an incision. The name, "Radiosurgery" was therefore given to this discipline, and Dr. Nilsson was one of the best. For the past eighteen months she had been president of the World Radiosurgical Society and was hosting the society's annual meeting in Pittsburgh.

The society at the time was relatively small with fewer than one hundred members. Such an intimate group, at least by medical conference standards, allowed the lectures, presentations, and social events to occur in smaller venues. For that reason, Dr. Nilsson was able to secure and reserve one of the recently modernized university lecture halls for the scientific presentations. While conference attendees were free to stay wherever they wished in the city, the society did secure a block of rooms at the university Holiday Inn. While not luxurious, it was new, conveniently located, and very economical for those traveling on small or no budgets at all. The hotel served as the conference headquarters where attendees picked up program books, ID badges, and registered for any special events. Because of this, Dr. Nilsson reserved a room for herself and her husband, as well as another room for Ella, Dr. Nilsson's N.P., who helped tremendously in the planning and execution of this conference. It was no perk even if it had been a Four Seasons, as they would both be busy making sure everything ran smoothly twenty-four/seven for the three-day conference.

Ella seemed to be the only peer among the department's growing group of N.P.s and P.A.s with whom Ava had a connection. Because they were each single, attractive, and somewhat disconnected socially from others in the department, many rumors swirled around, particularly among the resident staff. Ella was older than Ava by about a decade, which seemed to only add more energy to the rumor mill. It was probably because of this urban legend of a lesbian relationship between two hot single neurosurgical N.P.s that nobody took notice of Ava's understated yet growing affection for Dr. Moss. It can be human nature at times for people to see what they want to see, and this facet of human nature was currently rampant among the resident staff and many others simply connected to neurosurgery in some fashion. Anyone aware of this rumored relationship was on high alert watching for "confirmatory evidence" of such between Ella and Ava. Hence, every touch to Dr. Moss's arm, every positive remark made concerning his surgical prowess, every criticism leveled at Mrs. Moss for any perceived shortcoming by Ava were either unnoticed, discounted, or attributed to her generally accepted oddness as a person.

The one person who had not missed these cues and at times when they were alone, explicit flirtations was Dr. Moss. He was very much enjoying the attention whether authentic, false, or imagined from this attractive yet odd young lady, almost thirty years his junior. He started swimming in the morning to drop some weight, and getting his hair trimmed every other week versus the every three-month decades long routine. He consciously wanted to look better for Ava. When Cammie innocently inquired about his new routines, he snapped at her, "You play tennis all the time and are constantly getting your hair done!" His wife was about to provide a follow up remark on how she very much approved of her husband taking better care of his health and appearance, but his stinging response left her aghast, and she walked away shaking her head bewildered and wondering.

Dr. Nilsson had asked Dr. Moss to provide some welcoming remarks at the opening reception scheduled at the Carnegie Museum of Natural History the evening before the scientific portion of the conference began the next day. This was customary for a department chair or dean to provide some type of formal or informal welcome to a conference hosted by a university, even though that particular chair or dean may have no academic interest or even knowledge of the subjects to be discussed. In this case, however, Dr. Moss was knowledgeable about radiosurgery. His recruitment of Dr. Nilsson while openly and truthfully was about program development and department growth, also included selfish prerogatives, as he adored her as a woman and thought her expertise as a radiosurgeon could help with the clinical care of the dozens of poor souls with vascular malformations of the brain that were referred to him each year. For all those reasons he was more than eager to provide opening remarks for her conference. When he learned her husband would also be attending the reception, and in fact was a speaker at the conference, his eagerness was somewhat blunted. He was having too many schoolboy fantasies, he told himself.

Dr. Moss paid from the departmental coffers the registration fees for any resident or clinical member of the department that wished to attend the meeting. For any resident not currently doing dedicated research time, however, it would be impossible to attend much of the meeting. The reception was another story, as it was in the evening, and more importantly had free food and drink. So, it was not surprising that about a dozen residents made plans to attend, Ricki Bouba, now a second-year resident was one of them. Dr. Moss liked Ricki and was glad to have kept him in Pittsburgh for residency. The chairman, however, was bothered by numerous comments and much innuendo concerning Ricki's sexuality. Neurosurgery was no place for queers he thought to himself. When one of his more senior partners, Dr. Kleinwurst, who had been at the university before Dr. Moss was recruited came into Moss's office last month and said, "I don't want any faggots scrubbing on my cases." Dr. Moss quietly shared the same sentiment but asked who and what he was talking about. Dr. Moss then got an earful of comments and secondhand stories ending with, "just listen to him talk!" Dr. Moss had made a mental note to sit down with his chief residents to discuss the topic. The clinical flow of the service could not be disrupted, even if it required his department to tolerate a "queer" on the team. Men loving men, the thought disgusted him. Real men fucked women he told himself.

As the reception commenced and the night progressed, he made his rounds saying hi to everyone and keeping an eye on most. Many of the European attendees really enjoyed the California wines selected for the reception. Several enjoyed the wine too much. One French medical physicist kept saying how much better the French wines were yet continued to drink glass after glass of the Stag's Leap Cabernet being poured. The residents present stayed huddled together for the most part. Dr. Moss did take note that Ricki independently was speaking with one of the radiation oncology fellows that shared similar mannerisms with Ricki. Dr. Kleinwurst sidled up to Dr. Moss and gestured toward Ricki and the rad onc fellow, and simply said with a sneer, "Two peas in a pod," and walked away.

Another pair trying and failing to keep to themselves was Ella and Ava. The problem was that they were both outfitted in snugly contoured dresses with plunging necklines and open backs and wearing high heels along with more makeup than usual. They had the attention of many men, mostly overweight attendees that probably could not see their dicks anymore beneath their bellies when they pulled them out to urinate. The two N.P.s appeared to be having an intense discussion when not being interrupted. Those in the department had already formed their conclusions about the two and hence they garnered little attention from the home team that evening, despite looking no less than stunning. Dr. Nilsson ran a little interference for them initially but found herself similarly in peril, so retreated to the safety of her husband's side. Had she not been the host of the conference, she would have dealt with any perceived lechery herself expeditiously and severely. As for now, she decided to remain warm and inviting.

Dr. Moss was returning from the bar having just been poured a glass of Cakebread Cellars Chardonnay as he had heard a very drunk Frenchman saying the Cakebread may be the best wine he had ever tasted in his life. Dr. Moss was passing a small crowd of attendees when he felt a hand on his bicep and that familiar voice saying, "Oh Phillip, there you are." Ava locked her arm around his and used him to extricate herself from the latest group of now drunk attendees to descend upon Ella and herself. She mouthed the word, "Sorry," to Ella. Ella replied with a wink and a smile.

"I didn't know you were attending this evening," stated Dr. Moss as Ava continued to keep her arm locked around his.

"Ella pleaded with me to come so that she would have someone to talk to," said Ava, "I had no idea it was going to be like that," she gestured back to where Ella remained surrounded.

"So sorry. Had I noticed I would have told the bunch of pervs you were both my dates," said Dr. Moss with half a laugh.

"You'd like that, wouldn't you," responded Ava as she raised her eyebrows and licked her upper lip.

Dr. Moss was caught off guard by her comment as he awkwardly replied thinking he was joking, "Ella is not my type, too old for me."

"Well then, what about me?" Ava asked as she pulled the side of her head against his shoulder now embracing his biceps with both hands.

"Have you been drinking this evening?" asked Dr. Moss.

"Not a drop," Ava quickly replied looking straight ahead, "Take me back to the Holiday Inn now. My car is there. Ella gave me a ride here," then Ava whispered up into his ear, "she also gave me her room key," and gently bit his ear lobe.

Dr. Moss had only taken a sip of the Chardonnay and thought the world record for speed of seduction had just been set, and said, "We can't be seen leaving together. I'll pick you up outside the main entrance in fifteen minutes."

Ava responded with a pout and said, "Okay," before blowing him a kiss.

Dr. Moss's mind was reeling. Was this really happening? They had flirted many times before, but it was all just harmless fun. Maybe she was just teasing him, albeit mercilessly at this point. He made his way over to Dr. Nilsson and congratulated her on a tremendous opening reception and told her he knew the conference would be a grand success. Then he felt for his keys to his '88 Jaguar XJ, that now shared a new companion in his suit pants pocket. Good God he thought, had anybody noticed his current state of arousal? He hurriedly left and walked to the adjoined underground garage. He got in his Jag, pulled out onto the street where he could call with his cellular phone. He called home and it went to voicemail. He left a message for Cammie that he needed to check on one of his aneurysm patients that was not doing well, so he may be a little late getting home. He pulled up into the circular driveway of the main entrance. He saw both Ella and Ava at the exit doors. His mind quickly considered the possibility both were coming with him, and what that could lead to. After about thirty seconds he saw just Ava coming down the steps, and his mouth went dry, and his body felt numb. He had never truly grasped how physically appealing Ava was until that moment.

Ava opened the passenger door herself and when he saw her legs begin to slide in, he half expected to start having chest pain. She closed the door, leaned toward him with her left hand resting well up his inner thigh and matter-of-factly said, "Ella is giving us two hours. We get the queen bed closer to the door. Let's get out of here." The car was already reaching the speed limit as she finished speaking.

The hotel lobby was deserted other than the clerk, probably a student working a night shift, at the desk who paid no attention to them since they did not approach the desk but turned straight down the hall to room 113. Once inside the room they embraced in an awkward open-mouthed kiss and then Ava said, "Phillip, make love to me as many times as you can in the next two hours." They were both naked in thirty seconds.

Two hours later, Dr. Moss was up, showered, and dressed; Ava, however, remained naked in bed. Damn she looked good simply spent just lying there he thought, but their proverbial stagecoach was about to turn into a proverbial pumpkin. Dr. Moss asked, "I thought we only had two hours?"

"Actually, *you* only had two hours. Good night, Phillip, and thank you, three times," stated Ava flatly before she pulled up the sheets and rolled away from him. He kissed the back of her shoulder and left.

As Dr. Moss walked back out to the Jag, his mind was reeling almost as fast as before. The experience in the moment was incredible; now he was not so sure. He perceived she was enjoying the sex as much as he was, but what a cool sendoff. Did he say something or do something that turned her off. Was he not a good lover? Was he "ill equipped"? Shit, he thought, he should be walking on cloud nine after making love to a gorgeous young woman multiple times who had clearly wanted him, seduced him. With each passing thought he was feeling worse and worse. And then there was the foolishness of Ella being aware of Ava and him being in her room. What was wrong with him that he just let this all happen, that he made it all happen? For all he knew it was some set up to blackmail him or extort something from him. How could he be so stupid? He pulled the Jag into the driveway and into the garage. As he entered the house Cammie was at the kitchen table and asked, "So how is your patient?"

"What? Oh, fine," he curtly replied.

"Daniel called here looking for you. I told him you were at the hospital or in your car and to call your cellular phone," Cammie calmly stated, "Did he find you?"

His Nokia. He knew exactly where it was. Damn, now he was feeling even more ignorant. He feigned looking for his phone in his suit jacket and said, "Darn, I left it at the hospital. I'll give him a call from my office." Phillip Moss briskly walked down the hall to his office and closed the door. He thought about calling his cell phone to see if Ava would answer, but it would be better to call Danny Harrison, the chief resident, first. Danny responded to Dr. Moss's page immediately. Fortunately, all was good with Mrs. Klinefelter. She had a short seizure from her sodium being too low, but the residents had already instituted the appropriate medical management to correct the problem. He then called his cell phone, a woman's voice answered, "Hello, Dr. Moss's phone, may I help you?" The voice was

Ella's. His heart seemed to stop, and he remained speechless. Ella sensed his silent panic and simply said, "I will have Ava bring this to you tomorrow. I trust you had fun. Good night, Dr. Moss."

As he fell asleep that evening, he told himself he would never do anything so stupid again. As soon as he was about to sign that internal pact with himself, his brain would replay the vision of Ava's naked body rocking to the rhythm of his thrusts, the carnal sounds she made, and how she made him feel so alive and how she electrified every sensation in his body. He wanted more. He needed more. He deserved it after all he had done and accomplished. He was a world-famous neurosurgeon. He could have what he wanted, he told himself. His conscious ended up signing an entirely different internal pact that night.

## Chapter Nine: Junior Resident, 1994-1995

With Dab gone the neurosurgical residents had yet to reinstate their initiation prank for the incoming junior residents who had just finished their general surgery internships. The chief residents were far too concerned with the daunting task of running the neurosurgical service at either the university or children's hospitals than to give any thought to concocting pranks. Similarly, the senior residents who now had more responsibility and expectations to perform in the operating room at a much higher level than the prior year could not mount the mental inertia to concern themselves with pranks. Therefore, if any pranksters were to emerge from the resident staff to create a new tradition, they would need to come from residents currently on research rotations who had some semblance of normal lives. Hence, those not actually working on the clinical team with the new junior residents allowed the senior and chief residents on the clinical service to have an ironclad alibi of having nothing to do with any pranks sprung on their new colleagues.

Ricki Bouba was in his sixth year of residency and finishing the calendar year working in the lab of a neurologist. Following his research time, he would serve as a senior resident on the university service before his seventh and final year as chief resident. Ricki was working with a rodent model of creating targeted small brain injuries and tracking dopamine levels within discrete parts of the brain. The general aim of this research was to further the understanding of surgical treatments for

Parkinson's disease. Throughout his residency he had become quite interested in what was considered "functional neurosurgery," a sub-discipline of neurosurgery that dealt with modulating brain and spinal cord functions by either providing stimulation or destruction of very discreet areas of the central nervous system. He hoped to make this his career after he completed his residency. Ricki was not a prankster.

The medical training "New Year" is July first, exactly one hundred and eighty degrees out of phase with the actual new year. As of July 1, 1994, there were three fifth-year residents beginning their 18 months of research time, and three sixth-year residents starting their final six months of research time. So, a pool of six highly intelligent young physicians dedicated to the pursuit of knowledge through research, and more importantly for the chief residents they were a resource for concocting pranks to be utilized as a "welcome to the jungle" tradition for the new junior residents. Of these six residents, all were male, and half were white. There was only one of these six, however, who was the clear choice, Bart Wozniak. Bart was a high-testosterone smart-ass who grew up in one of the rougher neighborhoods in Baltimore. He attended college on a lacrosse scholarship and never looked back. He could take it as good as he could dish it out; and he could dish it out. When he was a junior resident Dr. Kleinwurst quickly realized that Dr. Wozniak needed a little humility despite his rough and very humble upbringing. Dr. Kleinwurst had reluctantly admitted a young man from clinic who required a stereotactic biopsy of a brain mass. The young man was homosexual, almost certainly was going to be diagnosed with AIDS, and had multiple intracranial lesions affecting his speech and movement of his right side.

A stereotactic biopsy refers to a technique where a target is located within a frame around the skull by Cartesian coordinates, the X, Y, and Z planes of high school geometry to put it most simply. The frame is fixated under local anesthetic with four pins to the skull, and a CT scan repeated with the frame in place and calculations made. An attached arc then serves as the guiding arm to fix on the planned trajectory and entry point. The surgeon makes a small incision after numbing the scalp, drills a small hole in the skull, and then advances a biopsy needle to the calculated target depth and then aspirates a sample. Yes, the patient is often awake for this procedure.

Dr. Kleinwurst took this opportunity to test the young Dr. Wozniak's physical and neurological examination skills. He also made sure that every medical student rotating on the service, and all other available neurosurgical residents were present to observe Dr. Wozniak's examination being performed under his highly critical eye.

Bart Wozniak entered the hospital room along with Dr. Kleinwurst's entourage of "learners." Dr. Kleinwurst introduced the young man to Dr. Wozniak and explained that Dr. Wozniak would be performing his admission physical examination as a teaching exercise for the others present. The helpless look in the young man's hallowed eyes would haunt many of the students and residents present that day for months to come, but not Dr. Kleinwurst. With surprising indifference, he quickly gave the history and plan to the students and residents. For him the main event was the physical examination, and he wanted to get Dr. Wozniak on stage as soon as possible.

Bart began with a general physical examination of the head and neck, followed by auscultating the heart and lungs, followed by palpating of the emaciated abdomen, and feeling for pulses in the arms and legs. Dr. Kleinwurst was expressing impatience and encouraged Bart to get to the neurological portion of the examination. Bart, unsure of why he was being made to do this, continued on. He examined the cranial nerves with the exception of olfaction, the sense of smell; he checked motor strength, sensation, coordination, and reflexes. He had the young man repeat words, show specific fingers on command, do simple math, and answer questions as to where he was and when it was. When Bart thought he was finished, he turned to Dr. Kleinwurst, intending to summarize his findings.

"You are not done yet," Dr. Kleinwurst stated coldly, "What about the bulbocavernosus reflex?"

Bart had been somewhat uncomfortable with this entire spectacle, but now he knew Dr. Kleinwurst's intent. "Do you think that is a necessary part of this gentleman's examination, sir?" asked Bart.

"Yes, I do Dr. Wozniak. And for the education of our students please explain that reflex and how it is performed," a puffed-up Dr. Kleinwurst said raising the volume of his voice.

"Well, sir, it is a reflex to assess the integrity of the lower sacral spinal cord and nerve roots. When examining a male, one inserts a finger in the anus, and squeezes upfront," said Bart.

"Upfront! What the hell does that mean? And what is the reflex you are trying to elicit?" a slightly irritated Dr. Kleinwurst scolded.

"Yes, sir. With the finger inserted, one then…," Bart said and was interrupted again by Dr. Kleinwurst.

"Inserted where? How deeeeep?" Dr. Kleinwurst cruelly asked, ignoring the impact on the patient who had a front row seat to the attack. "Step-by-step, Wozniak. Every detail. You are teaching students here, remember," Dr. Kleinwurst continued.

"Yes, sir. With the finger inserted past the external and internal anal sphincters, the examiner then reaches with the other hand and squeezes the glans of the penis. An intact reflex is manifested by a contraction of the anal sphincters," Bart said with a look in his eyes praying for no further questions.

"Very good Wozniak. Now show the students how it is done, and go slowly, explain each step aloud as you perform them," said Dr. Kleinwurst almost cackling.

One of the other residents present had retrieved lubricant and examination gloves for Bart and handed them to him with an apologetic look. Bart took the gloves, donned them, and asked the young man to roll on his side away from him and to pull his knees halfway up to his chest. He liberally lubricated his gloved right index finger talking all the while to the students regarding patient positioning and the need for gloves and lubrication. He spoke out loud explaining every nuance of the examination he was performing, "Begin with the pad of the distal phalanx, not the tip. If the sphincter has too much resistance, ask the patient to bare down as if trying to fart. Feel for the muscular ring of the internal sphincter to know you are past it."

"Very good Wozniak. Now what?" chided Dr. Kleinwurst.

"Next you reach with the other hand and," stammered Bart.

"Slowly Wozniak. This is the critical part. I would hate for me to make you repeat it," Dr. Kleinwurst said with false concern.

"Yes, sir. You reach and grasp the glans of the penis and squeeze it," said Bart as he squeezed the head of the young man's penis.

"So, do you lovingly squeeze it? Do you milk him like a cow? How do you squeeze it Wozniak?" Dr. Kleinwurst relentlessly went on.

"A quick firm squeeze and release sir," said Bart.

"Good. Now all the students are not able to see. Please keep repeating this technique for them as they can file to the other side of the bed," said Kleinwurst with an evil grin.

While the residents knew full well what was happening, the medical students simply surmised this was just another day of clinical learning. One student even produced a pen and note pad to write down the specifics. He received some awkward glances from his fellow students with looks expressing thoughts of how could you *not* remember this?

When it was all over, Bart had a new seething hatred for Dr. Kleinwurst. He asked the patient if there was anything he could get for him or do for him. The dying young man simply said no and vacantly stared toward the wall. Dr. Kleinwurst left without even asking whether the bulbocavernosus reflex was present or not.

After the chief residents had approached Bart about devising a new method of indoctrination for the junior residents, he initially developed a mischievous gleam in his eyes, only to have that gleam replaced with a more sullen appearance. He still loved mischief but had matured to value fair play and respect more. As he remembered that poor soul being examined by him under Dr. Kleinwurst's direction and how it made him feel. He could only imagine how the patient felt. He let the chief residents know he was just too busy in the lab, and maybe such pranks were not a good idea.

Dr. Phil Moss, Jr.'s first year as a neurosurgery resident was difficult enough. The lack of an indoctrination tradition was not a loss as far as he and the other two junior residents were concerned as the rumor spread through the resident grapevine that the tradition of pranking the junior residents had died. He felt a pressure beyond that of having one of the more trying jobs of all the residents out of all of the possible specialties. He desperately wanted to be the neurosurgeon his father was. He wanted his father's approval and admiration. He wanted to be validated for who he was. At times he was consumed by the anxiety of not ever gaining that paternal stamp of approval. Pranks or no pranks, he was going to make his father proud.

One July Friday, he made it back to his apartment in the carriage house well before dark. He could see out a side window into the backyard of his neighbors. The Corchran's had an in-ground pool. They had two daughters who were roughly the same age as he and his sisters. He spent many a prepubertal day playing at that house. He remembered it fondly. He almost liked that house more than the home he grew up in. It had lighter colors, more windows, and of course, a pool. It just seemed like such a happy place. He was dismayed to learn that the Corchran's had recently divorced. Phil liked both Mr. and Mrs. C very much. He considered them almost family, like a favorite aunt and uncle. Mrs. C had remained in the house despite her daughters now married and both with children out of state somewhere. He realized what a shitty job he had done of keeping in touch with that family. So, when he looked out and saw who he was convinced was Becky Corchran, who was the older of the two sisters with two toddlers out at the pool, his heart leapt. He headed over immediately still in the scrubs he had put on yesterday morning.

"Becky?" he said as he unlatched the gate to enter the backyard pool area.

Becky turned toward the voice and did a double take as she saw someone or something that made no sense. Why was Dr. Moss calling her name, why was he walking toward her, and what Time Machine had one of them entered. There is no way he could look this young, but it was him, right? The bewilderment remained on her face and Phil sensed it, "Becky, it's Phil from next door. Remember?"

"Holy shi…zam! Phil?" she exclaimed as she quickly edited her colorful response in front of her twins and their grandmother. She ran toward him and gave him a sunscreen lathered hug. "My God, I haven't seen you for ten years, at least! You look just like your father from a distance, but up close your blue eyes gave you away!"

Phil responded in kind with a reciprocating bear hug and lifted her off her feet. "So, you are a mom now!" Phil exclaimed.

"Yup, two adorable Tasmanian devil twins. They just turned two and are wearing me out," she stated with a proud smile as she looked at her twins with their grandmother.

"I heard from mom that you are in Dallas. How's Texas?" asked Phil.

"Julio, my husband, has family near there. It's a great area for young kids. We really enjoy being there, but I do miss the quirky quaintness of Shadyside," Becky replied and continued, "How 'bout you? Any serious love in your life?"

Phil cast his eyes toward the pool and replied, "Not really."

"Well, what the heck are you doing, DOCTOR?" she jokingly asked as she looked at his ID badge clipped to his scrub shirt breast pocket.

"Too busy being a neurosurgery resident right now I guess," Phil replied.

"Double Holy shi...zam! You are working with your dad!?!? Phil, that is amazing. He must be so proud," Becky said while beaming.

"He certainly is proud. Sometimes I get the feeling he is prouder *of* himself having a son in neurosurgery than he is actually proud *of* me though," Phil said plainly, "But I'm doing my best to make him proud of me."

"Oh, I'm sure he is proud of you. Darn it Phil, you are a D-O-C-T-O-R!" She said smiling and putting her hand on his arm, "Now come meet my twins."

Becky and Phil walked over to the other end of the pool where the little boys were splashing in the shallow end and being watched by Mrs. Corchran. After a few minutes Phil excused himself to return home, as he walked back toward the gate he marveled at the home and yard as the memories of all the hide and seek, and kick-the-can games played here fifteen to twenty years ago washed through his brain. When he reached the sidewalk, he looked back at the house with nostalgic tears welling up as he reminisced about how much he loved those times.

Phil did his best to hide from others outside his inner circle that he technically still lived with his parents. When explaining to somebody where he lived, the description had such a great young professional vibe, 'newly renovated apartment in the top floor of a carriage house in a swanky section of Shadyside...,' until the inevitable question anyone interested would ask, 'So who lives in the main house?' Having to then state that his parents lived there often resulted in eye rolling, a polite 'oh cool' or the worst...complete silence. Privately he loved remaining at home though the vast majority of his waking hours were spent at the hospital, hence, where he slept really did not matter much. Every Sunday though, when he was not on call, he was expected for dinner by his mother. This custom started early in the summer of his intern year, and as far as Phil was concerned, he would keep the custom alive forever. As the seasons of the first year passed and the summer of his second year began, he did sense growing frustration or maybe concern from his father at these Sunday dinners. Phil would be peppered with questions from his father regarding his social life (or lack of one), relationships, and many oblique references to still residing in the carriage house apartment. The questions from his father regarding anything to do with finding love, a girlfriend, or even just going on a date were the most uneasy for Phil to handle. He would explain to his father that he was simply too busy (and he was very busy) as a neurosurgical resident to have time for a relationship. His father would express gratitude for his son's dedication to his training but would then point out how almost all the other residents enjoyed having a significant other or at least enjoyed or took the time in the pursuit of one. His father became convinced that Phil's living 'at home' had stunted his social development and prevented him from finding the "girl of your dreams," his father would say while looking at Cammie with a conjured smile. It was a father's method of telling his son to go find somewhere else to live so he would grow up. Cammie was somewhat torn, as she shared the sentiments somewhat of her husband, but relished having her 'baby boy' so close and would become furious, despondent, or melancholy when the Sunday dinner was complete, and Phil had returned to his apartment behind them. She failed to be able to put into words the sadness she felt every time her son left the house those evenings. Phil noticed the tenor of the Sunday dinners had changed. No longer were they sharing stories, new and old, and laughing together. Now the dinners seemed to be an event to endure, and simply complete, as terse glances were exchanged between his mother and father. He knew what the right thing to do was, though he cried himself to sleep the night he made that decision. First, he really needed someone trustworthy who would understand his predicament, so he could share all he was feeling. He wanted to answer all those questions his father asked of him, but to provide those honest replies to somebody else. He needed a catharsis with a peer. He could find somewhere else to live. The mechanics of that would be easy for him. What would be difficult is the emotional toll of removing himself from his childhood home again. When he left for college nine years ago, it was tough, but exciting. He had always dreamed of returning to Pittsburgh and returning home as well. Now he realized that part of his dream would need to end.

Ricki Bouba was on the clinical team at the university hospital for the week. He was covering for the chief resident who had taken one of his two weeks of vacation allotted for the year to interview for faculty positions down south in North Carolina and Alabama. Phil had immediately realized that Ricki was different from the other residents, and not because he was from Cameroon. Ricki smiled more and had an energy about him. He was more optimistic and less cynical than the others. He had his dark times too, like all the residents, but he never lashed out at those below him as the others were prone to do. Phil felt as though he had formed a connection with Ricki that Thanksgiving week last year. It was not a friendship, at least not yet, but an unspoken contract that they understood each other. For that reason, after evening rounds had concluded Phil approached Ricki with the hopes of confiding in him. "Hey chief, can I bother you for a second?" Phil cheerfully asked as Ricki sat at the desk in the call room which also served as the resident meeting space. The other residents had departed the room to carry out assigned tasks before either heading home or dealing with being on call and up all night. Phil had been on call the night before and was spared any more work as it was now eight p.m. If he could be home by nine p.m., eat dinner quickly, and read about the next day's cases he might be able to capture five or even six hours of sleep. Six hours, he thought, that would be Nirvana.

"Of course you can! Let me call your father first to let him know how all his patients are doing," said Ricki. Ricki pulled an index card from his scrub shirt breast pocket and plopped it on the desk next to the phone. Phil could see the card listed all the attending surgeons' names and phone numbers. In red felt tip pen he saw 'Boss Man' written with his dad's cellular phone number, and a note reading 'never call home phone' below it. Ricki punched in the numbers as he kept the phone receiver cradled loosely against his ear with his shoulder. Phil actually had never been around when the chief resident called his father from this end of the conversation. Probably precious few residents ever had. By this time of the night residents were either scooting home as quickly as possible or busy doing tasks so they could go home or were bearing the brunt of call. There was no reason for a resident to sit in the call room with the chief resident when the chief resident called faculty. He certainly had been at home more times than he can remember as his father fielded calls from residents throughout the years. He kept thinking how cool it will be to call his dad when *he* is chief resident. Phil was rocked out of his exhausted daydreaming when he heard a familiar woman's voice answer Ricki's call. Ricki replied, "Hi Ava, this is Ricki. Can I speak to Dr. Moss please." A few seconds later Phil heard his father's voice querying Ricki whether certain patients had had a bowel movement, were scheduled for an angiogram, had physical therapy working with them, and so on and so on.

When Ricki hung up the phone, Phil asked, "Is dad still in the hospital?"

Ricki just shrugged his shoulders and answered, "He never tells the chief resident where they are."

They? What the hell does he mean by "they"? Phil was losing focus as to why he was in the call room, or what he should even say. Ricki sensed Phil's confusion and asked in an effort to reorient as well as redirect Phil, "So what did you want to talk about? I'm only chief through Sunday. I'm not going to be able to make any resident's life easier. Not that I could anyways."

"Remember last year when you gave me a ride home?" asked Phil.

"Yes man, of course I do. You looked rather pathetic walking in the snow. It was an act of charity," Ricki stated as he struck an exaggerated righteous look and posture before breaking into his trademark smile.

"Well, you were the first resident in the department to know where I lived, and that it was with my parents. I was actually embarrassed for the first time, that I am a damn doctor, and I lived with my parents. But you never gave me a hard time about it, and best I can tell you didn't tell the other residents. I told the other residents on my own accord at a time of my choosing. I wanted to thank you for that," said Phil.

"My dear Phil, it is not my place to tell people where my colleagues or future colleagues live. In Cameroon I thought everybody lived with their parents and their grandparents, or so it seemed until the grandparents died. And my grandma would tell me from her perspective everyone lives with their children and grandchildren. My mother would say everyone lives with their parents and children. Life is perceived from where you stand and where you find yourself along the timeline of life. You living with your parents is normal to me, but I have been here long enough to understand your perspective and concerns *from where you stand*," said Ricki empathetically.

"Thanks Dr. Bouba," said Phil sincerely.

"Remember, call me Ricki! If in two years I am faculty here, then you can call me Dr. Bouba while you are still a resident," said Ricki before breaking into a laugh.

"Ricki, do your parents ask you about having a girlfriend?" asked Phil seriously.

Ricki's face lost its inviting look, and he matter-of-factly replied, "My mother does quite often, but not my dad. Why do you ask?"

"I have the feeling that you and I may have some things in common," Phil swallowed hard as the words came out, "and my parents, particularly my dad pressures me every week about women, dating, girlfriends, and finding the woman of my dreams."

"I get that too Phil, but what's your point. We are busy neurosurgery residents," said Ricki with an impatient tone.

"I don't dream about women Ricki. Never have," Phil said while looking at the ground and holding back tears.

"Phil, I hear you. I respect you. I like you. I've got less than two years until I am done with this residency. I am not going to say what you want me to say. Jesus said the truth will set you free. Around here the truth may end your career or worse. We can talk more later, but my advice is to keep your secrets secret, especially being who you are. I've got your back and always will. Now go home and get some rest," concluded Ricki.

"Thanks Ricki," said Phil as they both stood up. After an awkward moment of whether they should shake hands, they embraced in a hug, and Ricki kissed Phil's forehead. They looked into each other's eyes for a few seconds with a silent agreement that enough affection had been expressed, before Phil pivoted to leave. Phil turned back before opening the door and asked, "Does Ava answer my dad's phone for him often?"

"Your dad is not as good at keeping secrets as you are," answered Ricki before he turned back to the handwritten operating room schedule for the next day on the desk for which he needed to make assignments.

Phil muttered, "Shit, no way," under his breath and headed home.

Phil quickly went through his routine of necessary nutrition and reading. He had heard other residents joke about placing a feeding tube in themselves so they could just drip dinner into their stomachs while they slept so they could get every precious minute of sleep possible. A year ago, he considered such banter either humorous or disgusting. He was now beginning to think the concept had real traction. As he was brushing his teeth, he saw the headlights of the Jag pull into the driveway. It was after ten p.m. He knew his dad was neither operating nor on call that evening. For the first time he had a desire to live somewhere else before exhaustion overcame his ability to ponder what was going on between his father and Ava. He fell asleep in time to rack almost six hours of slumber, not quite Nirvana.

The brutal pace of his life as a junior resident slowed his ability to look for an apartment. He was able to get the rental classifieds from the Sunday Post-Gazette each weekend and start looking for an apartment that he thought would work for him. He was hoping to stay in or near Shadyside as a consolation prize to himself. Ideally, he would have a garage for his car at his new apartment. Car theft was rampant in Pittsburgh and scraping snow and ice off a windshield at four o'clock in the morning was no fun. He found a third-floor unit in an old building on Kentucky Avenue. He would have more stairs to climb, but it had a garage and was in good condition. It was now September, and the lease would not begin until January first. A doctoral student was currently leasing the unit. She was defending her thesis before Thanksgiving, and if successful, then heading to Durham, North Carolina for a faculty position in Duke's English department. The property manager told Phil that he could move in before the new year if the unit became vacant in time. Phil signed the lease. While Phil loved autumn in western Pennsylvania and despised the winters; he could not wait for winter this year.

As the fall progressed Phil completed his four months at the university hospital. The next four months would be at the children's hospital. While at the university hospital he was on call every third night, allowing him to sleep two out of three nights at his apartment. With the children's hospital schedule he would be on call every other night, so he would be at his apartment half of the nights. The junior resident preceding him at the children's hospital gave Phil a quick tour in the late afternoon of Halloween. Nurses and doctors were dressed in costumes. The rooms where children had likely been inpatients for a protracted time were decorated. She warned him about first impressions and said, "Phil, to be clear this is not Disney World or the land of lollipops and candy. The nurses will bite your head off for the sheer joy of it. And by all means, stay out of the NICU unless absolutely necessary. Evil does not even begin to describe the older nurses there." She did continue to tell Phil she had enjoyed her time on the pediatric neurosurgery service despite the above warnings, though one attending she described as a misogynistic raging asshole. The sixth- and seventh-year residents each covered the children's hospital for two months to share in the every-other-night call coverage. One of the seventh-year residents would be with Phil for November and December, while the word was that Ricki Bouba would be the chief at the children's hospital January and February. The prospect of working in tandem with Ricki for two months lifted Phil's spirits tremendously.

After transitioning to his pediatric neurosurgery rotation Phil found he had more time to read. The faculty neurosurgeons and nurse practitioners did much of the clinical work more commonly performed by the residents at the university hospital. The chief of the division made it very clear that the residents were there to learn and help provide care, and not to make the faculty's lives easier. Phil quickly realized that these were going to be a very different four months. Phil even visited Ricki across the street at the lab Ricki was working in once or twice a week. Once or twice a month they would meet for lunch at either the university or children's hospital cafeteria as workloads allowed. They became good friends and began talking about doing something together outside of the medical center one of the nights Phil was not on call. Come January, one of the two of them would always be on call until the end of February, before they both transitioned back to the university hospital March first.

For Thanksgiving everyone was returning to the House of Moss. Anne and Josh would be flying into Pittsburgh Thursday morning, and Sarah would be driving up from Virginia Wednesday. The Sunday before Sarah dropped the big news that she and Trey had rekindled a long-distance relationship. She had called during dinner time asking if Trey could visit over Thanksgiving. Phil laughed aloud as he overheard the conversation. He was so happy for his sister and Trey, and equally surprised. Good for Trey he thought to himself; that is an example of not giving up. Sarah was going to pick him up at the airport Wednesday night. His happiness for Sarah and Trey along with his looking forward to seeing Anne was abruptly erased when both parents stumbled over their words interrupting each other to ask Phil if he had anyone that he would like to invite for Thanksgiving dinner. He initially said no, but his mother pressed on telling him anyone was welcome, as she envisioned the awkwardness of her son being the only one at the holiday table without a partner or friend of some type. After his mother's third, "are you sure?" he blurted out that he would ask Ricki. In retrospect he immediately wished he could take his words back. His mother's face broke out with a smile of satisfaction, while she asked, "Ricky who?" his father's face appeared quite stern as he answered for his son, "Bouba."

Phil nodded in the affirmative and his mother, recognizing the last name as one of the residents she knew was even happier. "Oh, I like him. He is so nice and handsome. I've not seen him since graduation in June. I hope he can come," she gleefully stated. Dr. Phillip Moss, Sr., abruptly excused himself stating he was going to check in with the chief resident regarding one of his patients while muttering to himself, "peas in a pod, peas in a pod," as he made his way down the hall to his office.

The next day after Phil was done assisting in the operating room, he made his way over to visit Ricki in the research lab. He told Ricki his parents had *insisted* that he invite a friend for Thanksgiving dinner. When Ricki asked if Phil thought it was wise to invite him, Phil explained he had already told his parents that he would be inviting him.

Ricki had become fond of Phil and would thoroughly enjoy sharing a holiday meal with him. As Phil explained who else would be at the table, Ricki became hesitant to accept the invitation. "Phil, everyone else at the table is a 'couple'. Remember what I told you about *secrets*, about survival, about finishing this residency!" Ricki stated more emphatically with each word.

"Ricki, you are the only true friend I have here. When my parents kept badgering me, your name was the only one I could think of," said Phil as though asking for forgiveness. They quickly switched their conversation to the intricacies of caring for someone with a ruptured aneurysm when a lab technician came into the room.

Ricki straightened up his posture after the lab technician had left and said, "Phil, you are very special to me. Thank you so much for the invitation, but I really think it would be a bad idea for me to share this holiday meal with you and your family. I am certain your father knows about me. He treats me differently than the other residents. He pokes fun at my interest in doing functional neurosurgery. He makes remarks about it not being real surgery, that it's for 'pussies'. His old NP called me all sorts of names. I can't imagine she did not share that vitriol for me with your father. Phil, if I show up at your house as your *friend*, your father will label you and persecute you. I am certain of it. I've worked under him for half a decade. I may know him in some respects better than you do. He has many qualities and is an amazing individual but tolerating and working with people like…us is not something he is capable of. Bide your time my friend. Lay low or find another career."

"Damn it Ricki, I understand, but shit, my mom was so happy when I said I was inviting someone. I'm not looking forward to telling her you are not coming. There is nobody else and especially no girl I know who would come over on such short notice," Phil said.

"Oh yes there is," Ricki said slyly.

"No there isn't!" replied Phil.

"Ask Ava," Ricki said with a wink and a wry smile.

Phil pondered what Ricki said. Initially he thought Ricki was crazy, but then after a moment or two he considered Ricki's suggestion may be pure genius. He would not be without a friend or date, and that would make his mother happy. His dad clearly liked Ava, a lot, and she was a *she*! As he left the lab, he headed straight to the neurosurgery clinic at the university hospital where he knew he would find the peculiar and beautiful Ava Chelidon.

It may have been the first time of what would be very few times over the next year that Phil ever saw Ava reveal a smile. She without hesitation accepted the invitation. Despite her multiple years of working with Dr. Moss, Sr., she had never been invited to dinner at the Moss's home. There had been the occasional social backyard barbecue for the department, but never anything as intimate as a family meal.

Ava grew up never knowing her father. In fact, Ava's mother did not know who specifically the father was. She could list two or three possible men that could be Ava's father, but only by their faces somewhat. She had no idea what their names were, though she was certain each had told her his name at some point. She was simply too strung out on heroine to remember or care. Ava remained an only child, at least as far as Ava knew. Her mother cleaned her act up enough to be a parent to Ava until Ava was fifteen years old. When Ava returned to their fifth-floor apartment in Philadelphia after her first week as a sophomore in high school, she found her mother's lifeless body naked on the couch with a tourniquet on the left arm and an empty syringe and needle on the floor. The neighbors remarked to the paramedics how Ava did not scream, cry, or seem upset. She simply knocked on doors politely until someone answered. She flatly told them her mother was dead and that she needed to use their phone, as Ava and her mother could not afford one.

Ava was sucked into the vortex of the Philadelphia foster care system. Any so-called family she was placed with seemed more like a puppy mill to her. Houses with several children to a room and adults that seemed not to be married to each other, and even if they were, showed no love toward each other or the children. Never did she experience anything close to the June and Ward Cleaver parenting of stereotypical middle-class America. Most of her did not care, but a small part of her did yearn for attention and affection if only once in a while. Even with no money to buy clothes or make up or get her hair cut, she was an attractive teenaged girl. With one foster family headed by an alcoholic "father" she needed to protect herself repeatedly. She kept one half of a pair of scissors under her pillow. In one standoff with him as he stood before her naked and drunk laughing at her "weapon" she kicked him so hard in the testicles he collapsed allowing her to drive her scissor blade deep into his buttocks. As she ground the blade into the whimpering pile of putrid flesh, she told him next time she would run the blade in one ear and out the other if he even looked at her again. She said it with calm conviction, and even in his drunken stupor, he did not forget those words.

While Ava had developed street smarts, her emotional intelligence was lacking. What was not lacking though was her academic prowess. She did well enough in high school and standardized tests to garner the attention of leading area universities keen on enrolling the downtrodden and underprivileged who had the academic chops to succeed. While her college application essay read with the aesthetic of a police report, the sheer power of the facts describing her experiences concerning her mother and foster care drove many who read it to tears. When she received notice from her high school counselor that Penn had offered her a full scholarship she accepted immediately. The counselor, a matronly older woman smiled warmly and opened her arms to dispense a congratulatory hug after delivering the good news, but Ava simply stepped back and walked away holding the envelope and letter in hand.

In college she showed an aptitude for a broad range of disciplines. Those who knew her were surprised to hear that she chose to pursue nursing, a profession almost by definition associated with compassion and empathy, traits that were not apparent in Ava. What attracted her to nursing was the control it gave her over other human beings. She was not sadistic in the sense that she had no desire to inflict pain on someone for her pleasure. She simply wanted control over others, maybe to compensate for the seemingly sadistic control institutions and individuals had over her until she was an adult.

In nursing school, she strongly considered a career in the military, but everyone she spoke to was flummoxed because she was already on a full scholarship. Nobody wants to be a military nurse, she was told. Nursing students join the military only for financial reasons, others would say. She found the rigidity of a military system and hierarchy attractive. When she spoke to a navy nurse in charge of recruiting though, she thought the lieutenant was an idiot and so immediately dropped any thoughts of a military career.

When real clinical rotations began, she was star struck by surgery. The processes were very regimented and military-like, and the surgeons she worked with were not idiots. Her enthusiasm went beyond the professional and academic in the field of surgery. She found herself physically attracted to surgeons of either gender and slept with half a dozen male and female surgeons in her final year of nursing school. She never really dated anyone to the point of having a significant other. Ava simply enjoyed the physical aspects of intimacy as long as she was in control or being controlled in a way she liked.

After a few years of working as a trauma surgery floor nurse, trauma ICU nurse, and scrub nurse in the OR she went back to school for her master's degree to become a nurse practitioner. Her exposure to neurosurgery was the most exhilarating for her. Once again, her enthusiasm spilled beyond the professional. The more accomplished, stern, powerful, and inflexible the neurosurgeon, the more she was turned on. When she crossed paths with the chairman, Dr. Phillip Moss, there was no doubt who and what she wanted.

For her this Thanksgiving dinner was an opportunity, not to connect with others and celebrate, but to observe and study. She was comfortable being an integral part in the life of a powerful neurosurgical chairman. Her professional and private roles gave her purpose, satisfaction, and stability. She also immensely enjoyed the sex. She continued to sleep with other men and women, unbeknownst to Dr. Phillip Moss, but he remained the lover she most repeatedly returned to. Now she had the opportunity to see the inner circle of Phillip Sr.'s family life. She wanted more of him. What better way to learn how. Ava never gave a thought as to how her lover would react to her being his son's "date" or if Mrs. Moss was suspicious of her ongoing affair with her husband. If these thoughts had registered in her mind, she would have dismissed them as inconsequential. Any hypothetical reactions by others would not influence her goals for the evening and for the future.

The Thanksgiving morning weather was atypically glorious for Pittsburgh, clear blue skies with temperatures quickly climbing out of the thirties into the upper fifties. Phil had been on call Wednesday night and made it home by ten o'clock that morning. After showering and changing he walked across the back courtyard and entered the main house through the screen porch. He was caught completely off guard when he saw Trey sitting on the couch watching ESPN and conversing with his father. Trey caught Phil, Jr.'s eye, quickly stood up with a big smile and open arms saying, "My favorite apartment hall buddy!" Phil could not resist the unexpectedly warm welcome and the two exchanged a big bear hug. Phil, Sr., remained seated, feeling somewhat out of place and simply wished his son good morning as he reached for his coffee on the table beside him.

Upon releasing from Trey's hug, Phil sat down next to his dad and gave his dad a one-handed hug around the opposite shoulder and said, "Happy Thanksgiving Dad!"

"Glad you are not on call today. Your mom is thrilled to have everyone home. So is Ricki joining us as well?" his father asked with a reluctant tone.

"Ricki already had plans. I asked Ava to join us," Phil, Jr., nonchalantly stated as his father was emptying the last gulp of coffee from his mug.

His father choked, coughed, and sputtered for a moment before regaining his composure, "Does your mother know she is coming instead of Ricki?" he asked with a look of concern on his face.

"I haven't seen her yet to tell her. Why? I know Ava is a bit odd, but she will eat half of what Ricki would," replied

Phil, Jr., "Plus you seem to get along with her fine at the hospital, better than with Ricki, or with any of the residents for that matter."

"Well, she is not a resident. I treat her differently. You should have cleared all this with me first," Phil, Sr., sternly said.

"Cleared with you? Did Sarah clear inviting Trey?" Phil, Jr., defiantly asked, pointing at Trey who sat on the opposite couch and found himself with the sudden need to go to the kitchen for another cup of coffee.

"In fact, she did call and ask, and she is not even my resident," his father replied with an air of superiority to his voice, and he stood up, "I need to make a call."

"You can't uninvite her," muttered Phil, Jr., as his father walked away.

"The hell I can't," replied his father as he strode purposefully down the hall to his office.

Much to Dr. Phillip Moss's chagrin, despite his best cajoling and even flat-out bribery, Ava Chelidon was going to be present for the Moss family Thanksgiving dinner. She had never experienced a true family holiday dinner. But her reason for insisting she would be there and her not retreating from the opportunity were not so that some empty portion of her heart and soul could be filled with the warmth and love of a holiday family gathering. This Thanksgiving dinner would be a reconnaissance mission. She would scout the life of the man with whom she wanted to more deeply intwine herself.

Dr. Phillip Moss, Sr., emerged from the hallway to see Trey and his son trying to talk about college football. They both looked up at him, and he said to his son, "Tell your mom, Ava will be joining us tonight," and he spun to return to his office.

Phil sat there confused before standing and leaving. He had wanted Ricki to join them tonight, but Ricki declined mostly from fear of how the chairman would react and assume there was more than friendship between Ricki and him. Phil in turn invited Ava, knowing his dad was quite friendly with her, and all the concerns Ricki had would not be an issue with Ava. Inviting a lady guest allowed him to keep the appropriate boy-girl balance at the Thanksgiving table as well, thinking that would please his mother. So, when he went into the kitchen where Sarah and his mother were drinking coffee, chatting, and preparing a turkey for the oven, he imagined himself the bearer of good news. He had a guest coming, which is what his mother wanted. His guest was female which would not create tension regarding perceptions of his lifelong sexual orientation for any at the table who would be made uncomfortable otherwise. Ava was odd, but not outspoken or rude. She was highly intelligent. Even he could appreciate that she was an attractive woman. He knew very little about her otherwise and frankly was not curious to learn more. He had invited her to play a role and check a box to keep his parents happy, or so he thought. He had little excitement about chatting with Ava, but very much looked forward to seeing his sisters and hearing about their lives.

As he walked into the kitchen, Sarah lifted flour covered hands and beamed as she shuffled quickly over to hug her brother keeping her hands in the air. Happy Thanksgiving greetings were shared among them and Phil gave his mom a peck on the cheek. When Phil joyously announced who his guest was going to be it was as if all oxygen left the room. "That's nice honey," were the only words muttered by his mother as she no longer made eye contact with Phil and returned to preparing the turkey. Sarah gave him a

'How stupid are you' look and gestured to him to leave the kitchen. As she walked out behind him, she announced to the house that Trey, Phil, and she were going to the local Giant Eagle grocery store before it closed at noon to buy more paprika.

All three piled into Sarah's pea green Toyota Corolla hatchback that was parked in front of the house. "Jesus Phil! You have managed to drop the biggest turd possible," Sarah yelled at him once all the doors were closed, and the engine started. Trey remained bewildered as to what was going on. Every time he would begin to ask a question for clarification, Sarah would just glare at him to restore silence.

Phil was despondent and becoming more troubled than confused after they had driven a couple blocks. "What the hell is going on Sarah? Why does everybody lose their shit at the mention of Ava's name in this house? I see her every day. She is different, but she's not on the FBI's most wanted list, or is she?" he satirically asked.

"No, dipshit, she is not. Mom and I talk… a lot. She's convinced that dad and Ava…" said Sarah unable to complete the sentence.

"Oh, come on Sarah, I'm there. Those are just rumors. The word in the department is that she likes girls anyways," responded Phil.

Trey finally chimed in trying to lighten the mood, "She sounds like an interesting person to meet," he said with a smile.

"Shut the hell up Trey," snapped Sarah. Trey quickly assumed the pose of a scolded puppy in the passenger seat. "So, Phillip, can you uninvite her?" said Sarah with an analytical tone to her voice implying the storm for now, had passed.

"I believe dad already tried to," responded Phil, "And I don't know her phone number. Shall I ask dad?"

"Smart ass," muttered Sarah, "so much for the idyllic Thanksgiving. Still want to date me, Trey?"

"Even more so now. You guys are not boring. I'll hand you that," Trey replied as the three of them shared a brief chuckle.

"I think we are good on paprika," said Sarah, "Let's go to the airport and pick up Anne and Josh. It will be a nice surprise for them."

"Please don't make me sit next to Josh," pleaded Phil.

Fortunately, Josh and Anne had packed lightly as all five plus luggage barely fit into the small hatchback. Trey offered Phil the passenger seat, which Phil in turn offered to Josh who readily accepted. The ride back to Shadyside comprised of Sarah delivering a tutorial to Anne and Josh on what had transpired this morning regarding Ava, and how they should all behave and address certain topics if they arose. As they pulled into the driveway Trey asked if they should synchronize watches and choose a safe word. For that he received a sharp punch to the shoulder from Sarah when they exited the car.

The sight of all three of her children coming into the house erased much of the pain Mrs. Moss was feeling. She told herself this was going to be a great Thanksgiving after all. The house already smelled delicious with aromas from the kitchen. Anne made sure to give her mother an extra-long embrace. Dr. Moss emerged from his office upon hearing the commotion and received unbeknownst to him, a more tepid response from Anne, but a warm handshake from Josh, as Josh remained oblivious to the angst having kept his Sony Discman playing with the headset in place the entire ride from the airport. Six of the seven were now ensconced within the main home. Since they were engaged, Mrs. Moss had told Anne that she and Josh could use Anne's old bedroom. Trey was assigned to Phil's old room, while Sarah had her own bedroom for childhood. Phil, of course, had his carriage house apartment that he was less than eager to show to his sisters. He knew inevitably that a tour would be necessary, so he excused himself after he and Trey transported Anne and Josh's luggage inside with, not surprisingly, no help from Josh.

Phil headed out the back through the screen porch to his apartment. He quickly tidied up the kitchen, picked up dirty clothes, and gave all surfaces a wipe down. He noticed the light flashing on his phone's voicemail machine and hit the play button. It was a message from the property manager at the Kentucky Avenue apartment building. He could move in as early as next Friday, rent free, for what would be the remainder of December. He still had mixed emotions, but after the insanity of the morning he thought maybe it was a good time to move on. His thoughts were interrupted by a knock on his door. Nobody had ever knocked on his door, primarily because he never invited anyone, and you needed to enter the carriage house at ground level before climbing stairs to get to his apartment. When he opened the door, his sisters, Trey, and Josh were all on the small landing outside his door waiting for the tour. Trey and Josh offered polite comments, whereas his sisters screamed with delight reminiscing about what a gross place this had been in the past. After several minutes they all headed back to the main house. Phil sadly realized they were the only guests ever to visit his apartment in almost eighteen months, and now he was about to leave it.

Phil had offered to pick Ava up, but she told him she would drive herself. He had no formal time for her to arrive but said four p.m. would be reasonable as his mother had planned dinner to be ready about five p.m. Everyone but

Mrs. Moss had gathered in the family room where the television was broadcasting the first NFL game of the day. The Lions were playing the Bills, and it was deep into the fourth quarter around three thirty p.m. when the doorbell rang. There was a collective deep breath taken by many of the Moss family. Dr. Moss arose from his seat on the couch and silently went to answer the door. He opened the door not really knowing what to expect. Before him was a squat heavily mustached man about forty years old holding a large box. "Thanksgiving wishes from Mr. Moretti!" the man cheerfully exclaimed, "Where may I place this for you?"

Dr. Moss indicated the floor in the foyer would be a good place to leave the box. Dr. Moss, shouted, "Tell Jack Thank You!" as the man returned to the black Chevrolet Suburban where another man of similar size and appearance sat in the driver's seat. Within the box was a crate. Dr. Moss pulled out his pocketknife and was able to loosen the nailed down lid and pry the top off. Inside was a case of Chianti Classico Reserve from Tuscany and a note from Jack Moretti, "With eternal thanks I wish the Moss Family a wonderful Thanksgiving, Jack." Dr. Moss smiled only for a moment, because as the Suburban drove away, it was quickly replaced by another car he recognized all too well.

Ava stepped out of the driver's side of her Acura Integra on to the street. Dr. Moss glanced sideways through the sidelight glass of the front door as she rounded the front of her vehicle and headed toward the house. She was wearing the same dress she wore four years ago when they first crossed that line from health care professionals working together to weekly lovers. The dress fit her like a glove, and he loved to see her in it as much as he did out of it, but not in the family home in front of his wife. Cammie had met Ava on multiple occasions in the past, but Cammie never gave her a second thought as a threat to her marriage. Ava was just too bizarre in conversation, or more accurately, lack of conversation. Ava said very little, and when she spoke it often led to head scratching and bewilderment for those listening. Despite her physical beauty, her personality was often so off putting that it would be difficult to imagine her in any romantic sense. Dr. Moss had done his best to prevent Cammie's and Ava's paths from crossing at the occasional department social events sprinkled throughout the past couple years as he sensed Cammie's growing anger anytime Ava was mentioned. He had no idea what his wife knew or suspected. All he ever considered was that almost every week, he experienced sexual bliss beyond anything he could have imagined. He had become an addict. While he had no intention of hurting or disappointing anyone, his priority was to get his "fix"; collateral damage be damned. Dr. Moss turned away and headed back toward the television, and said, "Phil, I think your date is arriving."

While heretofore everyone in the house was dressed nicely, Ava was awkwardly overdressed in her Kelly-green form fitting low cut evening gown. As Phil opened the door for her, he was taken aback by her striking appearance. He escorted her into the family room for introductions where everyone was chatting and watching the football game. The chatting immediately stopped and all that could be heard was the voice of John Madden describing the ferocity of the most recent tackle. Anne and Sarah politely stood and shook hands with Ava. Trey stood and offered her his seat on the couch as he had been seated next to Phil, Jr. Josh simply ogled her until Anne smacked his arm, and then he stood to introduce himself. Dr. Moss greeted her warmly with what would have been an innocent appearing light hug, other than his hand landing on the small of her exposed back, which did not go unnoticed by Sarah and

Anne. The entire room was fixated on Ava when they heard Mrs. Moss clearing her throat standing behind them all. "Nice to see you again Cammie," said Ava.

"Thank you, Ava. And very nice dress," replied Cammie with a forced smile.

As Ava took in what those were wearing around her, which appeared as a tasteful sea of khaki, denim, button-downs, and sweaters, besides Josh's stained and torn St. Louis Blue's hockey jersey, she flatly remarked, "My apologies for dressing so. I've never been to a real Thanksgiving dinner before." Everyone other than Mrs. Moss immediately assured her that she looked lovely and that they had not yet dressed for dinner. Sarah and Trey left first and returned with Sarah now wearing a dress, and Trey a blazer. Anne then pulled Josh away from the game, and likewise Anne returned wearing a dress, and Josh remained in his hockey jersey, but now wore one of Dr. Moss's suit jackets over it. Phil, after suppressing his own laughter, sensing the trend, excused himself and shot across the back courtyard and retrieved a blazer.

Anne and Sarah entered the kitchen to help their mother. Before they could say anything, their mother noticing they had changed, asked sarcastically, "Where are you two going?"

Sarah spoke first, "Mom, I know this is difficult for you. You've done all this work and to have *this* happen. You always taught us to make guests comfortable, so…"

Mrs. Moss interrupted her daughter and said pointing toward the family room and holding back tears, "I have no desire to make *her* comfortable."

Anne chimed in, "Mom, we get it. We are on your side. Please remember we have Josh and Trey here too. Josh has already put a ring on my finger, but we don't want to scare

Trey away. You are the Queen of the House of Moss and will always be the most beautiful woman here. You look spectacular. If you want to change though, it's only fair because everyone else has."

Mrs. Moss, looking slightly mortified asked, "Dad too?"

"Okay, not Dad. But Josh is wearing one of Dad's suit jackets…over his hockey jersey," Sarah stated as her final words were almost extinguished by the laughter building inside her.

"Tell us what more needs to be done in here and go freshen up before dinner, Mom," Anne said with a commanding voice.

Mrs. Moss gave them the instructions regarding what was in the oven, what needed to be stirred, and to set the table. Cammie Moss walked out of the kitchen with her head held high and past the four in the family room. She noticed her husband had donned a blazer.

The Thanksgiving meal was spectacular. Dr. Moss uncorked a few bottles of Chianti from Jack Moretti. Dr. And Mrs. Moss sat at the ends of the rectangular dining room table with the three remaining couples filling in all other six seats. Ava was seated in the middle across from Phil. Josh and Trey were on either side of Ava with Josh next to Dr. Moss. As Josh shoveled food from platters to plate and plate to mouth, Dr. Moss observed with suppressed horror as many a dollop of sauce or side splattered down on the sleeves and lapels of his very expensive Italian suit jacket. Conversations of Anne and Josh's wedding plans, Sarah's plans following her clerkship, and general conversation from Trey made for lively discussion. Questions aimed politely at Ava to include her in conversation always seemed to have the opposite effect. Where is your family now? They are dead. Where did you get that dress? I stole it. Do you have any hobbies? No. Do you have any pets? Not anymore.

After the dinner was finished everyone helped clear the table and clean up, including Ava in high heels and an evening gown. Ava began handwashing wine glasses, cutlery, and the large carving knife. The second football game was well underway with the Cowboys hosting the Packers. Everyone with the exception of Mrs. Moss and Ava gravitated to the family room for more football. Charlie, the family Golden Retriever, was busy licking and slobbering all over the suit jacket being worn by Josh. After all were seated in the family room Anne and Sarah looked at each other wondering where Ava was located. Upon realizing Ava and their mother were alone together in the kitchen they shared a look of concern between each other bordering on panic. They both quickly rose, stated they were going to see if mom needed anymore help, and made a beeline for the kitchen. As they approached, they heard Ava's voice saying, "Thank you very much for a wonderful meal, Cammie. I need to be going soon. I do hope we can become friends." Anne and Sarah immediately turned around and made a beeline back to their seats in the family room.

Ava emerged from the kitchen unaware of Anne and Sarah's accidental eavesdropping. She stood behind the couch where Phil, Jr., was seated while Sarah silently with her eyes and face tried to get Phil, Jr.'s attention to stand up and pay attention to his "date." Phil eventually received the hint and stood up to turn around and face Ava. "Phil, thank you so much for inviting me. It was lovely to meet your family. I need to be going now," said Ava. Phil, Jr., walked with Ava back out to her car and shook her hand goodbye. Ava started up the Acura and drove to Ella's house where she spent the night.

Mrs. Moss had joined the others in the family room in front of the television upon Phil's return. Everyone thanked her profusely for an extraordinary meal. She appeared more at ease, whether because the burden of orchestrating, preparing, and serving a holiday meal for eight was behind her, or because Ava had left, or both. Everyone in the room was biting their lips trying not to provide commentary or a question concerning Ava. Trey was aware of Sarah's brother's sexual orientation and had been for years. He simply would have assumed Ava was a friend of Phil's, but the innuendo implied by Sarah during the faux paprika trip was disturbing. While Josh had been informed years ago by Anne when they began dating regarding her brother's sexual orientation, he either did not remember or care. He simply thought Ava was hot. He did not listen to a single thing Sarah said on the way back from the airport, as he had his headset on playing the Ramones. Neither Sarah nor Anne had shared the subject matter concerning Ava with their respective significant others of numerous phone conversations with their mother. There seemed so much to wonder about. Josh was confused as to why Phil, Jr. paid so little attention to her. Trey found it hard to believe that Phil, Jr. was so unaware of rumors concerning Ava and his father that he had the balls to invite her to a family dinner. He did recognize, however, the likely reason why Mrs. Moss never addressed Ava or recognized her presence. Sarah and Anne were still confused as to what their brother's motives were for inviting Ava. Dr. Moss, Sr., was also caught off guard by his son's motives. Did his son know of the affair, and this was a barb directed at him, or was his son also romantically attracted to Ava? Why did Ava accept the invitation? What about Ricki? Was his son gay or not? Mrs. Moss was hoping her son would not be dating that odd woman, whom she despised for whatever relationship existed with her husband. Why was Ava the first girl he had invited over since high school is all she could think.  Phil, Jr., was the only person not wondering. He felt as though he had pleased mother and father, by having a guest for Thanksgiving who was a woman. Everything else that seemed to concern his sisters he considered gossip and rumor. Eventually the remaining seven concentrated on the football game or began talking about random topics. Trey was the only one happy to see the Cowboys win, or more accurately, happy to see the Packers lose.

## Chapter Ten: The Office, 1992

"He looks a lot like you," said Ava as she held the framed photo of the Moss family gathered for Dr. Moss's older daughter's medical school graduation.

Dr. Moss was seated in his departmental office chair and swiveled to look at her, "Yes he does, for better or for worse, half of him is my DNA."

"Oh, definitely for the better, especially if he shares other similarities with you," she said with a satanic grin.

"That, I would not know," he replied trying to sound dignified and failing.

"Well, if I ever had a baby boy, I would want him to look like you... or your son," she flatly stated as she sat the heavily framed photo back on the counter in front of the window.

"Ava, we have a good thing going for both of us. We cannot complicate it. You are in charge of birth control unless you want me to be," said Dr. Moss with a business-like tone.

"I hate condoms. I also love the thought of your sperm swimming inside me after we fuck... despite them having a doomed mission," she plainly stated as she walked over, lifted her plaid skirt revealing no panties, and straddled his lap as he remained seated in his chair wearing only surgical scrubs. After a while she released the drawstring on his scrubs and pulled out what she wanted. Dr. Moss prayed the office door was locked because he was not going to leave his chair to find out.

After Ava took what she wanted the two of them restored a semblance of order to their appearance. It was early evening, and the office staff were gone. They had a "rule" that no such activity occurred during regular hours in the office. Anything earlier in the day required a walk down the street to the Holiday Inn. The evenings were not without risk as other faculty and residents could be around at virtually any time. Despite being both highly intelligent and outwardly professional their strongly suspected affair was a common topic of gossip within the department and medical school. A combination of his shear arrogance and her belle indifference resulted in a shameless display of impropriety. Even third year medical students not interested in neurosurgery who were assigned to rotate on the neurosurgery service would spend as much time talking about Dr. Moss and his N.P. as they would discuss the indications for intracranial pressure monitoring in head trauma. The dean heard these same rumors and could only chuckle to himself knowing that he now had something to hold over the head of that cocky self-righteous neurosurgeon who threatened him years ago when Phillip Moss was negotiating the terms of becoming the next chairman of neurosurgery. Now neither one held a moral advantage over the other should the world of medical school administrative politics draw them into conflict. On the other hand, the situation shared by both men prevented the dean from unilaterally acting on simply rumors, no matter how obvious the affair was between the chairman, and someone considered professionally under his control. If the dean could have solid proof of such an affair, he would destroy Dr. Phillip Moss and remove the neurosurgical chair who somehow knew of the dean's sordid past. Dean Detrick needed this monkey off his back.

Cammie felt the coolness at home. The playful touches, taps, and squeezes she had taken for granted over the years faded away. While older like her husband, she had always been an attractive lady. Her avid tennis playing kept her in striking shape. Many people meeting her for the first time were surprised that she had borne three children. While the libido of her premenopausal years was gone, she still longed for the touch and caress from the man she loved. She initially attributed her husband's fading physical affection toward her to the intensity and stress of his work. One day while playing in a tennis tournament at her club in a doubles match, one of the opposing players, Rachel, who was the wife of a prominent attorney of dubious ethical standards and universally despised by the other club members more for her personality than her husband's reputation began hurling insults at Cammie about Phillip's "girlfriend." Trash talking was not part of the game Cammie had grown to love, and she played pitifully as a result. Fortunately, her doubles partner, Linda, who had played varsity tennis at Penn State and was married to the chair of anesthesiology, carried them to victory. After the match Linda made sure to tell Rachel to go sit on a can of tennis balls and to offer condolences to Rachel's doubles partner for being paired with such a bitch. She then approached Cammie who made no effort to meet at the net at the conclusion of the match and said, "Cammie, I'm so sorry she brought that up. Everyone knows what a ruthless bitch she is. Both she and her husband will do anything to win. Fuck 'em."

Cammie wanted to say thank you but could only ask, "What do you mean, brought *that* up?"

"You know. Medical center gossip. Bunch of rumors people like to talk about when they have no purpose in life," replied Linda trying to sound nonchalant.

"No, I don't know. What rumors?" asked Cammie.

"Oh, sister, I may have just stepped in it. We've been friends for five years since Roger took the job here. He tells me the good, the bad, and the ugly, or at least I think he does," responded Linda, "He has been a witness to nothing, but does say that your husband's N.P. can turn heads. You know that. I'm sure you've met her."

"Well, yes, I suppose so, but she's so young?" pleaded Cammie.

"Cammie, if she were your age would it be a rumor that anyone would care about?" Linda replied rhetorically.

"So, she's attractive and young. The world is full of attractive young women," Cammie stated trying to reassure herself.

"Yes, Sweetie, but when the rumors are they are seen near the Holiday Inn almost every week…," Linda stated regretfully.

"What?" Cammie almost shouted with tears forming in her eyes.

"Sweetie, they are just rumors. As your friend, I'm telling you that you need to know those rumors are out there. I am so sorry to be the one to tell you. I just assumed…," Linda said able to finish the sentence.

"Assumed what?" asked Cammie.

"Assumed you knew," said Linda apologetically.

"Why would you assume I knew of something that's a rumor?" asked Cammie with her voice rising.

"Because Roger says it's pretty blatant, like they don't even care who sees them," finished Linda who now also had tears in her eyes.

Linda reached out to give Cammie a hug, but Cammie turned away with more tears building atop her lower eyelids. She wanted to make it to the locker room before the flood began.

That night when her husband returned from the hospital, Cammie told him of the rumors bouncing around the tennis courts to gauge his reaction. He without hesitation joyfully stated that he and Ava went to the Holiday Inn almost weekly, and sometimes twice a week. Cammie became pale and nauseated, her vision went grey and blurry as he walked toward her with a smile breaking out and said, "to get coffee. It's the closest place. That crap in the hospital cafeteria will kill me if that's the only coffee I drink. You are welcome to join us anytime, but we tend to go at the last minute whenever things quiet down. It gives us time to go over the upcoming schedule and discuss patients' problems. It's not exactly a social event." He then dug a receipt from his jacket breast pocket dated Wednesday of last week and said snidely while handing it to her, "See, two coffees at the café there. Not room service." He stood there waiting for her reaction.

Emotions flooded Cammie's consciousness. She felt relief in hearing an alibi with objective evidence to combat the rumors. She felt anger toward her husband, however, that their marriage had devolved to the point where she believed the rumors told her. She was overwhelmed with disappointment. Part of her wanted to confirm the rumors to explain her husband's growing indifference toward her and give her the license to strike out at him. Frustration boiled inside her. There were a thousand things she wanted to say to him, but she could not form a coherent sentence in her mind to express one of them. She looked at the receipt as though it would give her the inspiration to say what she was feeling, but the more she studied it the more foolish she felt. Eventually she crumpled the receipt in her hands and threw it at him before turning and walking away feeling powerless.

Her husband remained standing and as she walked away, he muttered, "crazy bitch," just loud enough for her to hear. Tears cascaded down her cheeks. She began to question her sanity and her marriage. How could these rumors seemingly be so widespread and so wrong? Why did she listen to Linda? Nothing was making sense to her right now. Was she a wronged wife by a cheating husband, or a woman duped by gossip on the tennis court? Either option left her wanting to run, scream, and escape to another life.

The next day Dr. Moss was operating most of the day. He had two cases. The first case was an aneurysm clipping and the second was a carotid endarterectomy. Between the two cases he made sure to speak with Ava privately about the night before and his wife's accusations. While in his office between cases he made it clear to her that any visits to the Holiday Inn could only be for coffee, at least for a while. Ava momentarily looked forlorn, but then straightened her posture, looked at Phillip, and said, "It was time for us to get an apartment anyways. That will be so much nicer than the hotel or this office." He displayed a look of doubt on his face at this comment, and before he could say anything she walked over to him and with her lips millimeters away from his lips she grabbed his crotch through his scrubs and said, "That wasn't just a suggestion Phillip. I need *this* when I want *this*. Make it happen my dear," and then released her grip and walked out of his office. He needed to sit back down for a while before he could leave the office and return to the operating room.

The relationship between Ava and Phillip seemed never to be one between equals. Given each personality, one or the other had to play the dominant role in *everything* they did or discussed. Phillip could not help but notice, however, that Ava was becoming more assertive. Whether this was an expression of her becoming more comfortable around Phillip and showing her true self, or an evolution in her personality remained unclear to him. Either way he was disturbed by this trend and felt a need to reestablish a stronger position in their relationship, but after he found them an apartment. While slim and sexy, she could be terrifyingly intimidating at times.

Like most urban academic medical centers, the surrounding area was replete with housing options for residents, medical and nursing students, undergraduate and graduate students, and the myriads of other professionals and support staff necessary for such an institution. Dr. Moss asked for a list of the residents' home addresses. If he was going to lease an apartment, he did not need one of his residents as a neighbor. He certainly needed a place within a short walk as his Jaguar would draw attention outside of the faculty parking area or country club. He started looking through the residential classifieds in the Post-Gazette and within a couple weeks had located a suitable option. He arranged the lease in Ava's name and ran the funding as an expense through his endowed professorship. The latter was another serious ethical lapse in addition to adultery. He was now stealing and cheating.

The apartment would be available on the first of the coming month. It was now the twentieth of the month. Ava had cooled toward him considerably. There had been no rendezvouses in the office since declaring the Holiday Inn off limits. He had quite expected an increase in such meetings while he searched for their den-of-iniquity. Ava was behaving increasingly distant. He had planned to surprise her the day the apartment became available, but now he felt he was losing her. He was also amazed that she could control her libido. If he ever would describe her sexuality to somebody, then there was only one word, insatiable. He found himself irritable, angry, and even betrayed. He feared Ava was holding his sexual satisfaction hostage until they had an apartment to share. Now he hoped that was the situation. To a degree this was the case. If he went through the process of leasing an apartment and all the associated moral hazard, he had brought on himself, then he did not want his mistress to abandon him. Ava remained quite happy during their little break from sex two to three times a week, as she had a standing invitation into Ella's bed. Ava took full advantage of this opportunity while she awaited word from Phillip. She was not irritable at all.

Phillip eventually corralled Ava in his office. As he closed the door he angrily asked, "What the hell is going on Ava?"

"Whatever do you mean, Phillip?" she coolly replied.

"You know exactly what I mean," he sternly answered.

"Oh, so Mrs. Cammie Moss has not been riding you to the rescue?" she sarcastically asked.

"Damn it, Ava. Why do you think we are…," he said failing to find the words he wanted to say.

"Are what, Phillip? So, you don't love me? Am I just some whore for you to pump your load into? If so, I think you owe me A LOT of money," she said with a smile and words dripping with sarcasm. She was enjoying watching him swing in the wind.

"Jesus Ava, I wanted to tell you I found us a place. I am trying to keep you satisfied and happy," Phillip pleaded without asking.

"Phillip, I can take care of satisfaction and happiness myself. I want fulfillment," she stated with the smile evaporating from her face.

"Fulfillment? What the hell do you mean? Do you want me to leave Cammie and marry you?" he responded loudly enough that if his secretary had been present at her desk, she would have heard.

"Maybe. I simply want to be more than your concubine. Now tell me about our place; because that is a start," she said with a business-like demeanor.

Phillip gave her the details regarding the modest yet convenient apartment he had leased for them. She was chagrined to hear it would be almost another two weeks before they could inhabit their new lair. Her mood though, did become more inviting toward Phillip. She walked up to him, embraced him, and kissed his cheek. She said, "I think we should *meet* here again tomorrow. You've been a good boy." She walked herself toward the office door and before leaving turned around and said, "wear scrubs for our meeting tomorrow," and left.

This woman had Dr. Phillip Moss wrapped around her little finger. He immediately dismissed, however, any thoughts of leaving his wife. That would be pure lunacy, and he considered the concept of marrying Ava as even crazier. He and Cammie had raised three wonderful and intelligent children. They had built a life and reputation together. While he recognized fully that their relationship was not the same as when they were younger, and never would be, he still valued her as his wife and lifelong companion. He also needed, however, the physical intimacy missing so long from his marriage, he told himself. If there was no intimacy at home, then damn it, he will gladly continue to take full advantage of Ava's attraction to him, or use of him. He did not care what Ava's motives were. He did not want her love or affection. He simply wanted her body. He had assumed her sentiments were similar until just now. She had clearly stated she wanted more. He was never going to give it to her. If Ava walked up to Cammie and told her about the whole sordid truth in an attempt to destroy their marriage so that she could marry Phillip, then her efforts would fail. While the Moss marriage would end, winning Phillip as the spoils of the divorce would not come to fruition for Ava. Phillip pondered whether to share these convictions with Ava to stave off any such maneuver by her. He concluded that his position would best be an arrow kept in its quiver. He did not want to say or do anything that would jeopardize their next and, unbeknownst to both, final office *meeting*. He needed her. He needed his fix. It had been too long already.

## Chapter Eleven: Terms of Endowment, 1995

Phillip kissed Ava tenderly goodbye as she left the apartment. For almost three years they neither arrived to nor departed from the apartment together. Neither one ever spent a night in the apartment, but together they spent hundreds of hours there over the recent years. Ava no longer spoke of divorce or wanting more. She had been a guest at the Moss home for some holiday meals and small department gatherings. She felt as though she were within the "inner circle" of the department and that seemed to satisfy her desire for more, or so Dr. Moss thought. She had received several pieces of fine jewelry from Dr. Moss as well that she always made a point to wear whenever in the company of Cammie Moss at functions. While rumors of their affair still swirled around the hospital, the gossip was so old that nobody really cared. Cammie had convinced herself such stale rumors were only running on the fumes of what she hoped were just the innocent coffee meetings at the Holiday Inn long ago. Home life at the Moss's was comfortable. The success of the department was nationally legendary by now. Dr. Phillip Moss felt on top of the world. His son was following in his footsteps. He would tell himself that he had it all. When he had waited the customary 15 minutes, he grabbed his jacket after brushing his teeth and returned to the office.

His secretary had gone for the day. Her routine was to always leave a handwritten note outlining the next day's appointments, cases, or meetings. Dr. Moss's routine was to always read this outline before leaving for the day. Tomorrow was an "urgent and mandatory" meeting called by the dean with all department chairs. Shit, he thought, there goes another hour of my life listening to that blubbering toad whine about recruiting more women and minorities. He did not give the meeting another thought beyond noting the time and place. At least it was at seven thirty a.m. and not later; otherwise, his clinic would be significantly delayed prompting another emergency meeting discussing patient satisfaction in the clinics.

The next morning after discussing the clinical service with the chief resident, Dr. Moss headed to the board room where the dean was holding the "urgent" meeting. Dean Detrick began the meeting by saying, "Lady and gentlemen, I want to let you know that all current chairs are in this room now."

No shit thought Dr. Moss. We are supposed to be here. Are they going to seal the doors shut or something and turn this into an escape room he half wanted to say out loud. Phil looked to see how Dr. Bryant, the orthopedic chair, was reacting, as Bryant always had the bravado to speak up and say what most were too scared or shy to say, even amongst a group of egocentric megalomaniacs. Bryant did not say anything, because he was not present. At that moment, Dr. Moss knew something was very serious, because Bryant was a giant in the world of orthopedics academically and clinically. He made the university tens of millions of dollars, and he was gone.

"We are in trouble," the dean continued without looking very troubled himself, "The Department of Justice working through the FBI has brought some very serious charges against the school of medicine. While I do not have all the information and cannot speak with authority on the legal aspects of the charges, let me tell you in the simplest of terms what allegedly happened, and what will happen. One of our departments has been accused of diverting funds into 'endowments' beginning more than five years ago. These endowments *appeared* to have been sanctioned by the university at the time of their creation. While seemingly altruistic to take money that could be used for salary support now and put it toward something long term for current and future faculty worthy of support would appear benign or even laudable, but in these cases it was not. These funds were diverted into shadow accounts bearing similar names as the true sanctioned endowments. What has now made this situation much worse, is that contributions from donors, and I'm talking about some big donors, were also shuttled into these shadow accounts. These now tax-sheltered and tax-free shadow funds under the umbrella of the school of medicine were allegedly used to fund every manner of nonclinical and nonacademic pursuit. Yes, think the worst. I am told the FBI has more than bank records. They have phone recordings, photos, and videos from around the world, as well as right here in Pittsburgh. The FBI is going to give this school of medicine a rectal exam with both hands once warrants come through that I am sure they will seek soon. I am charged by the University President and chief counsel to do that self-exam before the FBI does it for us. The more we can come clean, the better the chance we have for a leaner penalty. As is obvious to all of you, Bryant is gone. His faculty, or should I say his former faculty are aware. It is likely others from his former department will receive a similar fate. I encourage any of you with any knowledge of anything related to the inappropriate use of endowment funds by the orthopedic department or any department to come forward immediately. This may be the only way we can stop the bleeding. And while the seriousness and gravity of this situation will most certainly see the light of day in the media, I demand your discretion at this time. What was said stays in this room. All communication goes through me or the university counsel unless you are speaking with law enforcement. And if you find yourself being questioned by law enforcement, I insist you have our university legal team with you. That's all I am saying. You know how to reach me." Dean Detrick squeezed past the stunned department chiefs still sitting in their chairs and left to return to his office.

    The room was silent as an immediate and intense amount of introspection occurred. If anybody in the medical school was untouchable, it was Dr. Bryant. He was gone in a flash. And by the sound of it, he may very well be on his way to exchanging his Armani suits for an orange jumpsuit. Now the various chairs were probing their minds trying to remember if the magnum bottles of Dom Perignon, ocean view hotel suites, and first-class airline tickets for family members when attending conferences were reimbursed through their endowed chair accounts, and how the university or FBI would frown upon such luxuries. A few select chairs were much more worried about much more flagrant uses of the funds that they had come to consider their own. The gravity of the situation was not lost on Phillip Moss. He controlled the funds of his endowed chair, and self-reported withdrawals to the dean's office annually, as was university policy. While he wrote monthly checks from the endowment to Oakland Property Management, he reported this expense in his report to the dean's office under "microvascular lab expenses." The amount was not eye rolling in its amount, but if every stone was turned over by either the university or certainly the FBI, it would lead them straight to an apartment lease in the name of Ava Chelidon. He could already imagine her being questioned by the FBI. She would not panic or be anxious at all. She would simply tell them the truth in her brutally honest way, that she and Dr. Moss fuck each other's lights out in the apartment. She would not give a damn about any repercussions. All she ever did was show up at the address Dr. Moss told her and sign whatever she was told to sign. Dr. Moss considered having the lease switched into his name, and claiming the apartment was used as his "call room" for when he needed to be immediately available all night at the hospital. While that excuse could fly with the FBI, he knew that Detrick and any other upper-level person in the school of medicine would find it laughable and see right through it. He lived one mile away with a flat sidewalk connecting his home to the front of the building housing his office. The apartment was about one-half mile away and up a hill. If he marched to Detrick's office immediately and told him the truth, then he risked his job. At best it would place him and Detrick in somewhat of a stalemate. It could also result in mutual self-destruction. Detrick no longer was married, and the word was that he was estranged from his adult children. Detrick had "only" his reputation and job to lose. Phillip Moss had much more to lose. This fiasco with Bryant likely would take Detrick down anyways. If Detrick knew he was going down, he would most assuredly take Phillip Moss down with him. For the moment, Phillip Moss considered no action to be his best course of action. He chatted briefly with the chief of radiology about issues with the angiography suite in an attempt not to appear flustered and headed to clinic.

Two days later a sealed envelope labeled confidential and addressed to him was on his desk. It was from the university counsel's office with contents instructing him not to destroy any endowment account information or related receipts, and to bring all such documentation from the prior five years along with personal tax returns and personal bank account statements to a meeting next week with the dean and university counsel. Every chair had received the exact same letter. The dean was donning his gloves and applying the lubrication jelly for the exams he was about to perform.

    Phillip Moss surmised there was no way he would hand over the cashed checks that had been made out to Oakland Property Management. He would have to explain a monthly check written however for an almost unchanging amount over the past three years present on each monthly statement. He was at a loss as to how to explain this. Even with the actual checks returned to him and under his control, the bank kept mimeographed copies of each check in their records. The FBI could obtain that information in a heartbeat. The FBI would be unlikely to pursue the matter as the dollars amounted to peanuts in the grand scheme of things, but they very well could inform the dean of their findings. The dean also could pressure him to obtain the copies of the checks if he claimed to routinely destroy the cashed checks after receiving them. If he offered any resistance, then the only interpretation would be that he was hiding something or trying to, and they would dig deeper. He was more frustrated than ashamed with his predicament. While nothing he did would be deemed "criminal," he realized he certainly had skipped over a few ethical and moral lines. Others would say he did not simply skip over lines but traversed chasms on bridges of sin and deceit. Those indiscretions, he told himself, would be grounds enough to force him to surrender the endowment, lose the chairmanship, or even be ousted from the faculty. Any of those results would be a tough pill to swallow for Phillip Moss, and a very difficult scenario to explain at home. He felt the walls of his impropriety and adultery closing in around him. He was going to need aid from someone who he could trust implicitly. He began thinking of attorneys he knew, but he realized if he had to explain himself to anyone, he would have already lost the battle. He needed to close this down before needing an attorney. He picked up his office phone and called his favorite restaurant in Chicago.

Phillip Moss was quickly connected by the maitre d' to Jack Moretti's desk phone. Jack's gravelly voice was a comfort to Dr. Moss. Phillip gave Jack a quick overview of his dilemma. Jack could not promise him anything. To Dr. Moss's amazement though, Jack told him to do everything he could to have the FBI investigate the case. "I have no connections in the dean's office, but as for the Bureau, I do have friends," said Jack. Dr. Moss could almost hear Jack winking and smiling. Holy shit, Phillip Moss thought, this was going to be a roll of the dice.

The next two days were agonizing for Dr. Moss. He readied all the bank statements concerning the endowment, including records of donations made to the endowment, and destroyed every single cashed check returned to him over the past five years. He did not get his tax returns or personal account information prepared. Screw the dean, he thought, I am not going to simply bend over for his exam. He had nothing to hide in his tax returns or personal accounts anyway. His tactic was to give them numbers and honest statements but stall on the rest. He was going to make the dean either clear him at once or push the investigation to a higher level.

Dr. Moss entered the dean's office at precisely the appointed time carrying a stack of statements. He purposefully shuffled the statements to eliminate any chronology from the pile for the pure satisfaction of pissing the dean off. Marshall Henderson was the university attorney tasked with overseeing these "interviews." Having an attorney present made each of the meetings "privileged" so that nobody could be compelled to testify as to the specifics of the interviews. Henderson was a decent fellow with a long history in corporate law with US Steel. When he finally sickened of the board and executive teams at US Steel failing to make anything of what was once an iconic American company, he left to join the university. Pleasantries were exchanged and Dr. Moss handed Dean Detrick the sixty bank statements and a tabulated list of donations that matched to the penny the deposits listed on the statements. "Nice Phil, did you have one of your brain damaged patients arrange these," Detrick growled searching through the pile.

"Sorry about that, the department accountant has a drinking problem," replied Dr. Moss sarcastically.

Henderson asked impressed, "You have a departmental accountant?"

"God no. We could if we did not have to give so much money back to the dean though," Dr. Moss shot back directing the answer to the Dean more than Henderson.

Henderson sensed the tension between the two physicians and strapped in for a bumpy ride. "Dean, give me the papers please," Henderson politely interjected. The attorney began flipping through the statements and said, "Dr. Moss, thank you for bringing these statements. They do indeed date back five years, but I see no cashed checks, no receipts, no tax returns, and no personal account information."

"Well, I routinely destroy the cashed checks returned. You can cross reference the statements with my annual report to the dean concerning the endowment, and as for my personal financial information you both can suck my cock. But the dean second, I want him to swallow," concluded Dr. Moss as Henderson's eyes went from their perpetual half-awake status to popping out of his head, and the dean had a sudden coughing fit.

"Dr. Moss, I really do not think that is appropriate," stated Henderson trying to reinstate some decorum to the meeting.

"My apologies Marshall. You are correct and you are the guest here. You should be the one to swallow," Dr. Moss matter-of-factly replied.

"God damn it, Moss!" Detrick screamed slamming his fist onto the pile of papers, "Give me the damn information I asked for! The FBI is already crawling up my ass wanting me to give them anybody suspicious. I am trying to make this all go away for all our sakes. I promised them I would get this done!"

"Dean, I don't have the time to be your errand boy. I have nothing to hide. Go ahead and tell the feds I'm not cooperative. Let them do the work. They'll have it all with a snap of their fingers. My job is to run a neurosurgery department!" Dr. Moss exclaimed with the volume of his voice rising with each word.

"Phil, I lose all control if the FBI steps in. I, we will not be able to help you," Detrick said with false sincerity pointing at Henderson and himself.

"Now you are a comedian. You, help me? Ha!" said Dr. Moss as he stood to leave.

"Phil, so help me, if the FBI comes back with anything I will make you pray you were a resident again," said Dean Detrick turning red and plethoric. Moss was out the door and gone. The dean looked at Henderson and muttered, "Fucking brain surgeons think they can do anything they want. I need to fry his smart ass."

Dr. Moss returned directly to his office and immediately called Ava. He told her to meet him at the apartment in two hours and hung up as his secretary came in. He and Ava had not been to the apartment in five days, which was longer than usual. He needed to tell her what was transpiring as she would likely be questioned by an FBI agent. He knew he could not tell her what to say, because she would do what she wanted. He did feel an obligation regardless though, to warn her.

When she entered the apartment Phillip Moss was already there. He grabbed her and kissed her with a ferocity not expressed for a long time. She liked it and reciprocated. Not a word was spoken but many sounds were made. After thirty minutes they both lay exhausted and naked on the bed. She spoke first, "So Phillip, now that your tongue is no longer busy, what did you need to tell me?" He told her the entire story other than his discussion with Jack Moretti. She quietly listened and uncharacteristically chuckled when describing the morning's meeting with the dean and attorney.

"What are you laughing about?" he asked.

"It's just that when you were having your little pow wow with the dean this morning, I was talking to a very nice man named Vincent Maggio. Special Agent Vincent Maggio to be exact. Would you like his card? I have it in my jacket you ripped off my body by the door," she concluded without a care in the world.

Phillip's heart felt like it stopped. "Why didn't you tell me? Jesus Ava, this is serious!"

"Well, my stallion, it is a bit difficult to speak with you down my throat like you were. You gave me no time to say a word. Talking did not seem to be a priority of yours," Ava flatly stated without a hint of complaint.

"What did you tell him?" a frightened Phillip Moss asked.

"I simply answered some questions," she replied.

"Ava, what did he ask you?" Moss asked with impatience building in his voice.

"He asked about you, and us, and here," she said waving her hand around on the final word.

"Oh my God, Ava, how did he respond?" Moss pleaded.

"He did not say much. He did say he would be in touch if he needed to ask me anything more and that he would be speaking with you too, soon," she said.

"Sorry, but I need to get going," he said, and Phillip jumped out of bed, showered, dressed, and headed to his office.

As he kissed her goodbye she said coyly with a pout, "You must be worried, no repeat performance for me today? I'll remember this."

She can be so bizarre; he thought as he rushed out. Fifteen minutes later he was almost at his office.

Before Dr. Moss made it down the hall to his office, his secretary stopped him and said, "Dr. Moss, there is a man who insists on meeting with you. I told him I did not know when you would return, but he said not to page you. He is nobody I've met or seen before. His name is…"

"Maggio," Dr. Moss said completing his secretary's sentence.

"Yes, but…," she stammered as Dr. Moss tore around her and headed to his office.

Vince Maggio was not a large man. He was in his early thirties of average height with a wiry frame, shortly cropped dark hair and serious, almost sad brown eyes. His poorly fitting grey suit did little to conceal the leather harness securing his Springfield Armory .40 Smith & Wesson. He waited respectfully outside of Dr. Moss's office looking through an old Sports Illustrated with Mario Lemieux on the cover. When Dr. Moss rounded the corner, he almost ran into him. Special Agent Maggio looked up at the stunned surgeon and said, "Do you mind if we talk Dr. Moss?" and gestured toward the chairman's office.

Dr. Moss directed Maggio into the office and indicated a chair opposite him on which to sit. "Well, that was fast," said Dr. Moss trying to process the situation and deal with his fear.

"How do you mean sir?" asked Maggio.

"It's just that I told the attorney and dean this morning…," Dr. Moss said before being interrupted by Maggio.

"Sir, I do not want to be told privileged information," Maggio said holding up one hand, "I simply needed you to review some documents for me. I am quite tired of carrying them around." Agent Maggio pointed to a thick manilla folder on Dr. Moss's desk. He continued, "The first several pages are what I am most curious about. The remaining include your tax returns and personal bank accounts. Please open the folder, Doctor."

Phillip Moss felt like he was opening a door that led to hell. He immediately recognized reams of mimeographed cashed checks from the endowment account. He could not bring his eyes to focus quite yet and looked across at the nameplate on his open door that said, Dr. Phillip Moss-Chairman-Department of Neurological Surgery. He took a deep breath and looked down at the sheets with three checks copied on each sheet. The first sheet showed checks from the last three months with the exact same amounts and his signature made out to *Baxter Laboratories, Inc*. The next sheet showed the prior three months, the next sheet yet again, over and over. All made out to *Baxter Laboratories, Inc.* He looked up at the agent trying to look underwhelmed.

"Do you notice any discrepancies, Doctor?" asked Agent Maggio.

"No, everything appears in perfect order," said Dr. Moss.

Agent Maggio looked over his shoulder at the photos of Dr. Moss in Vietnam and at his son's college graduation from Northwestern and said, "My dad served in 'Nam. He didn't make it home. One of his buddies risked his own life to drag him out of the jungle before he died. My dad told him to send me his helmet and he did with a note describing my dad's last minutes and what he said. I cherish that helmet and am grateful for the man who tried to save my dad. I also love to eat Italian when I'm in Chicago. I'll be giving this portfolio of documents to the university attorney and dean's office if that's okay with you, sir." Agent Maggio stood up, closed the manilla folder, tucked it under his arm and headed toward the door. Before he left, Agent Maggio turned and said, "Doctor, just be careful what you say on the phone or type on the computer until the investigation is complete, as well as how you pay for certain things going forward."

Dr. Moss sat stunned at his desk for just a moment but then jumped up, left his office, and started to walk past his secretary who asked if everything was okay. The determination on his face concerned her. He told her nothing could be better and cracked a smile. Jack Moretti had saved his ass he thought. Given his recently obtained advice, he needed to give Ava the news in person. He covered the half mile walk to the apartment in less than ten minutes. When he arrived, she had already gone. Her scent still lingered. He imagined her winsome figure still collapsed among the tussled sheets and what he would do if she were there. He picked up the pillow where her head had been resting only an hour or two before and inhaled deeply. She was intoxicating to him with all five senses. He remembered being similarly affected by his wife, but in addition to having been intoxicated by Cammie with all five senses there was love. While there was affection toward Ava, there was no love. The physician part of his brain told him he was an addict. He was addicted to her. This addiction almost cost him his career and reputation, and in turn would have cost him his marriage. He realized all these things, and like an addict, started simply to think when he could get his next fix.

## Chapter Twelve: Ricki, 1996

Ricki Bouba spent the final six weeks of his sixth year of residency in the land of his birth, Cameroon. He still had several family members in the Douala area. The Pittsburgh neurosurgical residents were encouraged to spend one to three months in an underserved area of the world. It was by no means mandatory, but those residents without a spouse routinely left the country more for the sense of adventure than the pull of any missionary altruism. For Ricki the choice was easy. Almost the entire continent was severely underserved by specialized western medicine.
Neurosurgery was one of the most glaring deficiencies. Most Africans with the means, intellect, and drive to become fully trained neurosurgeons saw little future for themselves remaining in their respective country of birth. The lack of resources and overwhelming need crushed the will and resolve of most who tried to do "the right thing" by returning home. Help of any kind from the west was always welcomed by the communities in need, whether money, supplies, organized mission trips, or individuals. An erratic yet constant rotation of western neurosurgeons ranging from mid-level residents to senior faculty helped to ease the burden of delivering care in Cameroon, but it was never enough, not even close. Douala was one of two cities in the country that had the resources to support a fledgling and primitive neurosurgical practice.

Ricki arrived the third week in May at the Douala International Airport. His cousin, Pierre, was waiting for him and excitedly gathered Ricki's baggage and threw the luggage in the back of the dusty small Toyota pickup bed. Ricki had not been to Cameroon since his family visited when he was yet still in high school. It had been sixteen years, and the place looked exactly as he remembered. In fact, the Toyota pickup was strikingly familiar. The extended family was immensely proud of Ricki Bouba, a *brain surgeon* from *America*. They also collectively assumed he was wealthy beyond words; and while he was relatively much better off than most in Cameroon on his resident's salary in America, he was not wealthy by any metric. The excitement amongst many in the extended family and those claiming to be extended family died down quickly when they realized that he did not arrive to hand out hundred-dollar bills to everyone. Fortunately, there was a core of cousins, aunts, and uncles whose only selfish motives were to make him so comfortable and loved that he would want to return and practice in Cameroon.

Ricki was directed to a small room with a cot in his cousin's home. He could smell the manure from the animals on the other side of the wall wafting through the high open port above the cot. The scent was thick, sweet, and musty. He would need some time to adjust and was hoping the hospital had a call room for at least some of the forty nights he would be in Cameroon.

The next morning Pierre insisted on driving him to the hospital. It was a short walk by Cameroon standards, but Pierre cautioned Ricki that while everything may look the same, the streets had become more dangerous. Ricki learned the second and likely primary reason Pierre insisted on driving him was so Pierre could tell every single woman he knew that he was driving his brain surgeon cousin to the hospital. Ricki was unsure whether Pierre was trying to play matchmaker or was trying to impress women. After the third intersection at which hurried introductions occurred through the rolled down Toyota windows, Ricki begged Pierre to just drive him to the hospital.

The residents and faculty in Pittsburgh had recently received university email accounts. The office staff were clumsily trying to introduce this new means of communication into the workflow of the department. Ricki could not access that account from Cameroon, but he could send emails from his AOL account he had set up prior to leaving, utilizing one computer in the hospital. This solitary IBM computer was routinely occupied during the day but at night Ricki could often sign on to his AOL account for a few minutes. He exchanged messages with his father once or twice a week. He took advantage of any opportunity, however, to send Phil Moss an email at Phil's university account, as Phil had no other email account or World Wide Web access outside of the medical center. He and Phil bonded closely during their time at the children's hospital. They both developed an affection for each other and expressed that affection physically behind closed doors on more than one occasion. They missed each other. Had Ricki known that he would be in the incipient stages of a romantic relationship, he never would have jumped through all the hoops to spend six weeks in Cameroon. The pace of clinical work kept him busy though, and the time passed quickly. The other surgeons soon realized how talented Ricki was in the operating room. His time in Pittsburgh had served him well. Soon the other two neurosurgeons were asking him to either help with or flat-out perform what they considered the more complicated cases.

As the weeks went by the emails between Ricki and Phil transformed from simply sharing the neurosurgical experiences in which each was participating an ocean apart to a much more romantic tenor. For the month of June, they had become out of necessity, long-distance lovers. The cliche that distance makes the heart grow fonder proved true for Ricki and Phil. These seemingly innocent love letters, however, were being read by not only Ricki and Phil, Jr.

The endowment scandal investigation had continued for over a year. The dean actually requested that the FBI maintain surveillance for as long as practical in case any behavior muted by the sudden ousting of Dr. Bryant resurfaced at a later time. The FBI honored the request but did nothing more than skim emails every few weeks from what they thought were the department chairs. When the FBI provided lists of physicians for whom they wanted warrants to allow surveillance the name of Dr. Phillip Moss was on the list. Unbeknownst to the clerk assembling home and cellular phone numbers, home and vacation home addresses, and email addresses, the email addresses of both Dr. Phillip Moss, Sr. And Jr., were included in the approved warrant. Hence, the assigned agent for Dr. Phillip Moss was supplied with emails written or received by both father and son via their respective university accounts. The assigned agent, Vincent Maggio, quickly realized the "mistake" that had been made. He obtained copies of all transcripts and felt the contents may be something of which Jack Moretti would want to be aware. Nothing criminal was being unearthed, but personal secrets were. Agent Maggio knew very well that Jack Moretti valued secrets. Maggio contacted Jack Moretti with the information and for guidance. Jack Moretti told Maggio that the best thing to do would be to give Dr. Moss the transcripts of the emails between these two neurosurgical residents and thanked the agent for the information.

Dr. Phillip Moss, Sr., had somewhat suppressed his suspicions regarding his son's sexuality. The fiasco of Thanksgiving created enough confusion for him to simply dismiss his son's motives entirely for inviting Ava or Ricki. Agent Maggio had the transcripts anonymously delivered to the chairman's office. Maggio was going to keep his distance from what were personal matters unrelated to any investigation but needed to respect the recommendation by Jack Moretti to provide Dr. Moss with the information.

The day prior to the chief residents' graduation party in late June Dr. Phillip Moss returned to his office following a long day in the clinic to find a sealed large envelope with a Washington, D.C. postmark and no return address or identifiable markings. After grabbing a cup of bad coffee, he sat down with his voice recorder to dictate notes from his clinic that day but decided to open the envelope instead. Initially he thought there must have been some mistake as he was reading correspondence from the residency coordinator to the residents outlining conference schedules and teaching sessions. He then noticed however, that some emails were written by his son, responding to the residency director's questions or requests. He cussed as he had no idea why someone would waste his time sending him such garbage. He tossed the entire pile of papers into the trash bin and then noticed the corners of some pages with highlighter marks. He retrieved these pages and read every single one of them. In disbelief he read them again. As much as he did not want to admit it to himself, everything he was reading made sense. His son was in love with another man, a man who was about to become his chief resident next week. As a father he felt as though he had failed. He kept asking himself stupidly what did he do wrong in being a parent to cause this. As a chairman he felt a need to fix this "problem." He recalled how commanding officers dealt with this issue in Vietnam, reassignment or discharge.

As Dr. Moss was reading the email transcripts, Ricki Bouba was thirty-eight thousand feet above the Atlantic Ocean headed to Laguardia Airport on his way back from Cameroon to Pittsburgh. Ricki was looking forward to the end of the year party thrown in honor of the finishing chief residents. The event, while black tie, was always a great time for the residents to let loose with live music, dancing, and an open bar. The faculty made every effort possible to reduce the clinical workload in the days leading up to the celebration so as many residents and faculty as possible could be present. A skeleton crew had to be on call, as it was a neurosurgery program that covered a Level One trauma center. Typically, one of the finishing second year residents, and one of the rising chief residents would need to remain available at the hospital. Ricki was hopeful that Phil, Jr., would not be stuck taking call that evening. Ricki was looking forward to seeing Phil again. He reminisced to himself about his time in Cameroon. He loved reconnecting with family members. He worked very hard while there, but the stress of being a resident and being judged was not present in Cameroon. People relied upon him. They looked up to him. He took great satisfaction and pride in contributing to the welfare of the people in Cameroon. He also was impressed with the ingenuity of the neurosurgeons there, and how they did so much with so little. He learned many tricks from them that he would incorporate into his own skill set and looked forward to sharing these tricks with the other residents and even some faculty. His Cameroon family members begged him to return to work and live there before he left. He promised he would visit in the future, but his career plans would keep him in the United States. As he dosed off somewhere over the north Atlantic, he thought to himself there would be no way he could ever return to Cameroon to live and practice neurosurgery.

    Ricki's flight from Laguardia touched down at Greater Pittsburgh International Airport at five minutes past ten that Saturday morning. Phil, Jr., had rounded early and taken care of all necessary work before meeting with the chief resident and other fellow residents on the university team at seven a.m. After rounds the residents were excitedly talking about the upcoming party. Phil, being one of the two junior residents, politely waited for the story telling of the more senior residents to exhaust and then hurried to the parking garage. He had every intention of being at the airport by ten a.m. He was on call Thursday night, so he was due to be on call next Sunday, or tomorrow. The luck of the draw had left the other junior resident on the university service, Pranav, taking call, and hence in the hospital for the night of the party.

Before long, Phil was motoring across the bridges spanning the Allegheny and Monongahela Rivers in rapid succession as he looked down on their confluence forming the Ohio River at Point State Park on his way to the airport. He was able to park and be at the gate at ten fifteen a.m. as Ricki's flight was being guided into the gate. Ricki had anticipated taking the bus back into town. Both of their faces lit up at the sight of one another. As they embraced Ricki apologized for his need to take a shower. Phil could care less. He was thrilled to have Ricki back in Pittsburgh. On the drive back into the city they shared stories since their last exchange of emails. Phil asked if Ricki needed any help getting his things up to his apartment. Ricki laughed as he had only one suitcase. They shared a kiss and expressed how much each looked forward to seeing the other later at the party.

Phil took advantage of his rare window of free time. First, he went to the barber shop for a haircut. Next, he went by the grocery store to restock his meager provisions in his apartment. When he got home, he saw the phone message recorder light blinking. He rewound the cassette tape and then listened to his father's voice explaining how it would be best for the chairman's son to take call tonight at the hospital. Dr. Phillip Moss, Sr., did not want any perception of favoritism on the night of the chief resident celebration. Phil looked at his tuxedo hanging from the doorknob to his bedroom and put his head in his hands and screamed. He called the sixth-year resident, Bart Wozniak, who was covering as chief resident that night, to confirm the chairman's request. Bart concluded the short conversation and said, "Phil, If I could, I'd take call for you so you could attend the party. Your dad made it very clear to me that nobody takes junior resident call but you tonight. Fucking Pranav does not even have a tuxedo. I thought those guys from Duke wore tuxedoes for pajamas. Anyways, I'm sorry man. I told Pranav you would take over at five p.m. But this means next year, you'll definitely be at the party for me and Ricki." Bart's last comment raised Phil's spirits somewhat. He remained pissed that it would be another year before he could attend the storied chief resident celebration. He was learning that so many aspects of a neurosurgeon's life are measured in years, be they patient outcomes, training, or being able to do anything fun. He then called Ricki and explained. Similar thoughts coursed through their minds as they conversed. It is easy to call the chairman a prick, but more difficult to label a lover's father or your own father as one.

    The evening in the hospital had been slow, but that made it all the worse for the young Dr. Phil Moss. He brooded over being on call and not at the party and especially being robbed of more time with Ricki. After a year as a neurosurgery resident, the anxiety of being on call was largely gone. Whatever the emergency room threw at him, he knew what to do. It was the pace that could create problems. A good hitter in baseball can connect on fast balls, curve balls, sliders, and change ups, but not if all four pitches are thrown simultaneously by four pitchers. Many nights on call were spent trying to deal with the neurosurgical equivalent of this baseball metaphor that many of the residents used. They would joke that they did not mind knuckle balls, because nobody was ever expected to hit a knuckle ball. As luck would have it, just when Phil was about to head down to the cafeteria to get a late dinner, a patient who had a brain aneurysm rupture came to the emergency room. The next three hours were consumed with admitting the patient, placing a drain in the patient's head, and arranging for assorted studies, and scheduling for the operating room. By eleven p.m. he decided to try and sleep some rather than eat and returned to the call room. As he sat at the call room desk reviewing lab work on the recent admission, he heard what he thought were "cat calls" coming from the nursing station. There was whistling interspersed with a few *oh my lords* and *if I weren't married*. A knock came upon the call room door and there stood Dr. Bouba in a tuxedo holding a covered plate loaded with filet mignon, garlic mashed potatoes, thick crusty bread, and a slab of cheesecake. Ricki simply smiled and said, "Room service."

The next morning as Phil signed out the activity of the prior evening to Pranav and Bart before they went around to see all the patients, Pranav turned a strange color, made a few bizarre guttural sounds, spun 180 degrees, and while holding vomit in his mouth slid into the adjoining bathroom on his knees expertly right in front of the toilet, only to vomit directly atop the closed toilet lid. Bart just looked at Phil and said, "I don't think the P-Man gets out a lot. I heard he enjoyed the open bar last night a bit too much." After helping clean Pranav and the bathroom they retrieved a cup of coffee for Pranav and told him to stay in the call room.

Bart and Phil took care of rounding and all the note writing before Bart headed to the operating room to assist with the aneurysm clipping. Phil returned to the call room to check on Pranav. Pranav assured Phil that he would now be fine to take call and apologized profusely. Pranav blamed his condition on the cheesecake he ate last night. "Yea must have been the cheesecake," Phil said with a smirk as he left to go to his car. As he drove toward his apartment he realized when he returned to the hospital on Monday, he would be a third-year resident.

## Chapter Thirteen: Fulfillment, 1997

After a short but tense discussion with Ava, Dr. Phillip Moss, Sr., told her that it was too dangerous to keep their apartment unless she wanted to pay for it herself. She told him she was disappointed that he was so easily bullied by the FBI and the Dean. He could not find words to reply. What planet is this sexy creature from is all he could think. The annual lease would end in 6 weeks. He informed Oakland Property Management that the lease would not be renewed and went to their office to deliver cash covering the last two payments. A one-time cash withdrawal would not seem evil or suspect through the eyes of any entity. He could no longer rely on Jack Moretti's influence with the FBI to bail him out a second time. His greatest fear was, as when shortly before obtaining the apartment, Ava would withhold her affection from him. Much to his surprise, quite the opposite response occurred. Within a week he was wandering the aisles of a health and fitness store looking for any vitamins or supplements that could help him continue to perform at the pace being demanded of him. The young man working in the store that day asked if he was looking for something for his prostate, because those supplements were two aisles over. Dr. Moss simply replied, "kind of." Physically he was in better shape than ten years prior, but Ava left him feeling like he was running a marathon almost every day. If he considered her insatiable in the past, he could not even construe the appropriate word to describe her now. All he could think of was, *possessed*.

On the last day of the apartment lease as the couple lay in bed together, Phillip Moss asked with some hesitancy, "So where next? Your place?"

"That would be lovely, but you know I live all the way up in Butler, so not very practical. Plus, I think you deserve a break. You've performed admirably Phillip. Let's take some time off," Ava said with her head resting on his chest and her hand playing with his spent and deflated member.

"Time off? How long were you thinking?" he asked with concern in his voice.

"Oh, I suspect it will be about nine months," she said as the corners of her mouth turned up forming an impish grin.

## Chapter Fourteen: Chief Resident Bouba, 1996

"For God's sake Bouba, give me the damn drill!" an impatient Dr. Phillip Moss growled. "You'd think by the time you were in your seventh year you could open the skull efficiently," he continued as he grabbed the drill from Ricki Bouba and started drilling into the patient's skull.

"Yes sir, but I was being careful here because--" Ricki said and halted his speech as the drill plunged into the patient's brain and the field flooded with blood, "because the skull was deformed by the large vascular malformation underneath," he finished saying more under his breath than aloud.

"Goddamit!" Dr. Moss yelled. The two of them then worked feverishly to regain control of the operative field. Four hours later the patient was awake and doing well in the recovery room with no knowledge of the bullet he dodged, or more aptly, the bullet he took and survived.

Ricki Bouba was not enjoying his chief residency so far. All prior experiences with Dr. Moss had been tough but worthwhile and collegial. Ricki had always learned a lot from Dr. Moss and soaked in everything he could, whether it was discussing surgical indications or learning and observing operative techniques. Ricki had immense respect for him, but now his opinion was shifting. Ricki called two of the past chief residents who had just completed their training the prior year to ask how they were treated. Both recalled some tough and tense times, but the experience in its entirety was fulfilling and they never felt persecuted. Ricki felt as though he were on trial for high treason every day. The other residents on the service, including Phil, Jr., witnessed the abuse Ricki was taking from Dr. Moss. The chairman seemed to relish any opportunity to embarrass Ricki in front of others. The public attacks became so absurd that even some of the other faculty started to openly defend Ricki at conference and in the halls, wondering what the hell was wrong with the chairman. The other residents did their best to support Ricki emotionally as colleagues and friends, but none of them, except for maybe one, were going to confront Dr. Moss for another resident's sake.

Phil, Jr., also felt like he was being treated differently by his father. His dream of training in his father's program and working side-by-side with him now seemed to be a ludicrous fairy tale. His dad for lack of better words, was a real asshole. He watched his father treat Ricki like shit. In the short term, he could handle his dad treating him like he did not exist or matter, but to also witness the malevolence piled atop Ricki was almost too much to bear. In this weird two-way bifurcated relationship between father/chairman and son/resident Phil thought it better to approach him as the chairman, at least initially. Whatever was going on had to stop. Phil could not imagine another four years after this year's experience so far as being a manageable situation. For the first time Phil, Jr., realized that it may have been a mistake to return home for his neurosurgical training.

It was early October as Phil, Jr., began his fourth month as a third-year resident and Ricki Bouba was about to start his merciful last month as the chairman's chief resident, before rotating over to the adult spine service. Phil had been on call the night before so was relatively less burdened with tasks in the afternoon when he made an impromptu visit to his father's office. Phil knocked on the door and heard a grumbling string of syllables that he interpreted as a green light to enter. His father seated at his desk looked up over his half-moon reading glasses at his son with a forced half smile. Phil said, "Dad, can I bend your ear for a moment?"

"Of course, but be quick, I have a meeting in ten minutes in the OR conference room," replied his father while looking back down at the papers on his desk.

"Am I doing a good job?" Phil asked as he plopped down onto the same sofa he would curl up on as a young child when his mother would bring him and his sisters to surprise their father with cookies on their father's birthday.

"I've heard no complaints," his father curtly replied with his gaze remaining fixed on the papers he was reviewing on his desk.

"Every other attending gives me feedback on my performance, recognizes the work I do, and can look at me *when I am speaking*," Phil emotionally stated with special emphasis on the last four words and continued, "Jesus, Dad, I am working my balls off to make you proud and be the best I can be."

Dr. Phillip Moss finally looked over his reading glasses at his son and said, "Well Phil, interesting choice of words. I've been made aware of you making some bad decisions. Choices you are making can hinder you from becoming a neurosurgeon, at least in my program."

"You just told me there have been no complaints about me. I'm unaware of me screwing anything up. I don't get it, dad?" a frustrated young Dr. Moss concluded.

Dr. Phillip Moss finally fixed his gaze upon his son and said, "You need to be careful who you *befriend* in this residency. People could get the wrong idea about you. I cannot have my, I mean the reputation of this department weighed down and tarnished with such nonsense. Find yourself a girlfriend or I'll find one for you. Now, I need to get to this meeting." His father stood and cooly left his office leaving his son speechless, wide-eyed, and fighting the urge to scream or cry, or both.

"So that explains why you treat Ricki like you do!" Phil yelled as more of an epiphany than a question or statement at his father walking away.

Dr. Phillip Moss turned and charged back toward his son with hatred in his eyes. He halted just inches away from his son and in a measured voice unsuccessfully holding back anger he said, "Yes, Dr. Bouba does seem to be in a similar situation as you. For him it would be a shame if something happened that did not allow him to complete his residency since he is so close to finishing."

"What the hell, dad! You can't fire him because of who he is!" Phil, Jr. fired back.

"Who said anything about firing," his father retorted with a sly grin before turning and walking away.

Phil, Jr. was stunned by the emotional interchange that had just occurred. His own father threatened his career. His father also threatened Ricki Bouba with something potentially more sinister. Both he and Ricki's careers and maybe something more were at risk simply because of who they were. Phil, Jr. knew several gay physicians, both residents and faculty. None of these gay physicians were neurosurgeons, in fact, none he knew were in any field of surgery. They were all good doctors. Phil loved the field of neurosurgery. Despite his father's bigotry, he also loved his dad and desperately wanted his father's approval for all aspects of his life. He was not going to give up on becoming a neurosurgeon, and for the moment, was not going to give up on his dad.

If Phil, Jr., went to the dean or some administrator, he would risk destroying his father's career and hence, their relationship. He could also be the victim of a backlash from his father that could end his tenure as a neurosurgery resident in Pittsburgh, and depending on how spiteful his father could be, prevent him from transferring anywhere else too. He was not ready to go that far yet. Ricki's words of caution about the chairman when Phil invited him for Thanksgiving were now ringing loudly in Phil's head. Phil thought how Ricki knew his dad better than him in some regards. Phil also realized, however, that Ricki was unlikely to be aware that Phil's dad somehow knew about the two of them. He knew he needed to alert Ricki about all that had just transpired between his dad and him.

Phil headed down to the operating room charge desk. The large white board with assorted colors of erasable marker listed surgeon, room number, case type, and age of the patient. Phil surveyed if all three neurosurgery rooms were still occupied; and they were. He looked through the glass over each scrub sink outside into the operating rooms, and spotted Ricki helping a junior resident close the incision from a craniotomy. He donned his mask and entered. "Hey chief, could I catch up with you for a second when you are done here?" Phil politely asked.

While Phil's voice carried little concern, Ricki could read the worry in Phil's eyes and responded, "Give me about 15 minutes and I'll meet you in recovery."

Phil gave a half-hearted salute and headed to find some free coffee somewhere before parking himself near the entrance to the recovery room. Everyone who worked in that unit insisted it be referred to as the PACU (PACK YOU), short for the post anesthesia care unit. This request went largely ignored as everyone knew what *recovery room* meant and there were already too many places in the hospital ending in "CU"; why add to the confusion. Hence, as he was making his way toward the recovery room with hot coffee in hand, one of the nurses, who worked there and had a particular dislike for residents, asked where he was going looking like shit. He reflexively mumbled, "the recovery room," without even looking up to see who asked him, as he frankly did not care. His unbuttoned white coat must have somehow shielded the coffee he was carrying from the nurse, because as she yanked his arm get his attention and explain to him that it was not the recovery room but the P.A.C.U., she showered herself with Phil's hot coffee. Phil simply looked at her infuriated face and recognizing who it was, asked, "Do you guys have more coffee in the *recovery room*?" The only answer he received was a stream of curse words yelled so loudly that patients emerging from their narcotic slumber in the recovery room were suddenly made alert.

Phil found an empty stool next to the space where the patient Ricki had helped operate upon was being rolled into. Once the patient was safely situated Ricki and Phil left the recovery room and headed down the back hallway. Phil gave Ricki the details of the recent exchange with his father. "I appreciate you trying to help Phil, but I wish you had not mentioned my name," said Ricki and continued, "I think your dad has always known or suspected that I'm gay. But something has changed with how he treats me now. I thought it was maybe because I'm chief now, but I asked prior chiefs, and they did not have the problems I'm having with him. Then I thought maybe he's a racist, but other black residents have had no problems with him, and prior to this year he has always been tough but fair with me. Then I started getting real paranoid that he must selectively hate gay black men from Cameroon." It took

Phil a moment to realize Ricki was now joking and they both managed a brief chuckle.

"He never knew I was gay. At least I don't think so," Phil stated solemnly. "Somehow he knows now, and that you and I are….," Phil finished unable to find the right word. "I guess I was always too scared to tell him, knowing how he'd react. Ever since I was in grade school, I have wanted to be a brain surgeon and work with my dad. Maybe I should have come out a long time ago. I just never wanted to jeopardize my dream. I'm sorry, now I'm screwing up your life too. I'm the reason you are forced to endure my father's wrath," said Phil, "but damn it, Ricki, you have to finish this program. The crap he was saying scares me."

"Yea, maybe we should lie low for a while," said Ricki.

"Lie low? How much lower can we lie? We have been the definition of discreet! Unless he has bugged our apartments, I have no idea what to do differently," said a frustrated Phil.

"Well, you said your dad told you to get a girlfriend. Maybe, we should both get a girlfriend," Ricki said half-jokingly. "I just wouldn't ask Ava out again. That was cruel of me last year to suggest her at Thanksgiving," Ricki said contritely.

"She is *unique*. But why was it cruel? You helped me out of a jam by suggesting I invite her," asked Phil.

"I am so glad it worked out that way, but Phil you know the rumors about her and your dad, right?" said Ricki.

"So, they get along! Who cares! That doesn't mean anything," Phil responded defiantly.

"You are probably correct. I am sorry I brought that up," said Ricki to diffuse Phil's rising emotions, "but still a good idea not to have Ava be your fake girlfriend."

"Yea, agreed. She can be your fake girlfriend," said Phil with a smile and a shoulder bump into Ricki.

"No way. She's all yours then. She scares me white," replied Ricki smiling as they both broke into laughter. "Let's get together this weekend sometime and talk about this more. We are both too tired now. Go home and get some sleep," said Ricki.

Two days later on a Friday morning at nine-thirty both Ricki and Phil were told to be at the chairman's office at ten a.m. to meet with the chair and the program director, Dr. Kleinwurst, for their quarterly review. Since traditionally the program director met with each resident for only yearly reviews, in January, this did seem to be an unusual impromptu meeting.

Dr. Kleinwurst did most of the talking. He serially went through each of their files. Multiple instances were now recorded in each of their files beginning in February of this year of complaints by nursing staff, patients, clerks, and other physicians, all anonymous. Each documented complaint was either a flat out lie, or an extreme embellishment of some interaction. The most recent complaint about Phil from a nurse described him as having thrown hot coffee on her and cussing her out in the hallway. At the conclusion of this charade the chairman informed them that there was enough in their files to justify termination from the program, but that as a first step they would both be placed on a six-month probationary period. Dr. Moss, Sr., then described possible interventions if these two residents' "behavioral problems" did not improve during the probationary period. He hinted that Dr. Bouba may benefit from a much more prolonged return to

Cameroon, and that Dr. Moss, Jr., could benefit from a year at Queen Square in London studying neurology. The chairman made it very clear to the two residents sitting in his office that they will be watched very closely. Dr. Kleinwurst concluded by telling Ricki and Phil that he would meet with them again in January, or sooner if needed. "Though if I meet with you sooner, it's probably to tell you that you are fired," he said with a smirk before telling them both to leave.

"Did you see the folder on your dad's desk?" Ricki asked Phil.

"No, I was too busy trying not to scream or strangle Kleinwurst," responded Phil.

"Well, he had a folder full of printed emails. I saw my AOL email address and June dates on the two top sheets," said Ricki.

"Why would he have...Oh fuck," Phil said as he swallowed hard.

"Yea, I don't know how he got them, but that's how he knows," said Ricki.

"They've got us by the balls. Shit, Kleinwurst makes my dad look like Mr. Rogers," said Phil.

"Mr. Who?" asked Ricki.

"Never mind. Ricki, I really like you. I'm pretty sure you feel the same about me. But I have got to finish this residency," said Phil.

"Of course! And I need to finish too. I haven't told anybody yet, but I've been talking to the Cleveland Clinic about their fellowship. Cleveland is a lot closer than Cameroon," said Ricki forcing a smile.

"I don't want to think about you being gone yet, and we have to get down to the OR. We are already late," exclaimed Phil.

"Don't worry, we have a great excuse," said Ricki.

"I'm not so sure after this morning. I half expect another complaint in my file for being late to the OR today," said Phil seriously.

"Good point," said Ricki with an affirmative nod.

"Six months' probation. We have to be perfect until early April. Actually, worse than that, we have to be robots," said Phil.

"No man, worse than that, we have to be straight, or at least act it," said Ricki.

"What are you talking about?" Phil asked.

"How do you think I stay alive and out of prison when I am in Cameroon?" posed Ricki, "We have to pick our fights. Too many times people like us are guaranteed to lose. If I were 'out' in Cameroon I'd likely be dead or in jail, and then probably killed in jail. If we told your dad and Kleinwurst to go to hell, they'd have us fired and blackballed with their concocted files to back them up. Righteousness will not keep you alive or keep you in this residency. Would the noble act be to quit? Quit this program? Quit neurosurgery? I say no. How does that make it more fair for the next gay person to come along wanting to become a neurosurgeon. The noble act is to finish training, become an excellent neurosurgeon, and show your father and everyone like him that being gay does not matter. I am going to be a great neurosurgeon. You can also be a great neurosurgeon. You are smart and talented Phil. Let's keep our eyes on that prize. Like you said, they have us by the balls now, but in the end we will win. We will be the heroes. Unfortunately, we have to sacrifice some things temporarily, and those things are our identity, our happiness, and our time together. My love for you will not be sacrificed though, that endures. But like I said, we will win, and we win by reclaiming our identity, our happiness, and our relationship. We win by clearing the path for the next person."

"I don't know if I can do that Ricki. I have years to go, and you only have months," responded Phil with tears forming.

"Phil, you have to, for both our sakes," said Ricki as he donned surgical cap and mask and headed into the OR with tears pooling in his eyes too.

## Chapter Fifteen: Pulizie, 1997

Dr. Moss, Sr. could not fall asleep. Since Ava told him she was pregnant earlier that day, his mind was a constantly spinning hamster wheel, never stopping yet never moving forward. He considered every plausible scenario and option as to how to remedy this situation for himself. He would beg her to get an abortion, even though the odds were slim of convincing her. He could sense the pure joy she felt being 'with child', their child. He could sense the changes in her body too. She was not lying. Soon the department and medical center would be witness to this unmarried woman's pregnancy and rightly assume he was the father. His reputation and career would be devastated. He considered firing her to avoid this, but if Ava were to be left marooned by him, she would have all the impetus necessary to be very public and brutally honest with whomever she liked. She would not go quietly. She would not be ashamed. He considered bribing her, but the sums of money to induce her to leave her job, vanish from Pittsburgh, and support *his* child for decades would be astronomical and impossible to hide. It was also extremely unlikely that money alone would satisfy her anyways. She had never asked for anything material in the entirety of their several-year affair. For a moment he thought maybe he was not the father but given the ferocity with which they had been having sex the past several weeks, that seemed very unlikely. Ava Chelidon was going to have a baby, and that baby was going to look like him. Even if the baby did not look like him, it would have to be a different race altogether to have anyone think he was not the father. No remedy he pondered considered the welfare of Ava or the baby. He needed this *problem* to go away for his sake. Tomorrow, he thought to himself, I will call my favorite Italian restaurant.

After hearing Dr. Moss begin to describe his predicament Jack Moretti complained that he could not hear what the doctor was saying that they must have a bad connection and then hung up. Dr. Moss repeatedly called back, only to have nobody answer in Chicago. He took that as Jack's way of saying I've done enough already for you. Dr. Phillip Moss was saddened by Jack's apparent unwillingness to hear him out. He sat at his desk cradling his head in his hands for a minute or two. His phone rang. He readily picked up the receiver expecting to hear the scratchy voice of Jack Moretti, instead it was the OR circulator letting him know that his second patient for the day was being put to sleep and would be ready for positioning in about ten minutes. Dr. Moss tried to extinguish thoughts of a pregnant Ava and Jack's betrayal from his mind and headed to the OR.

Three hours later Dr. Moss was returning to his office when his often overly nervous secretary stopped him saying, "Dr. Moss, there is a man here to see you. I told him you were busy. He's no doctor, but I think he brought you a case of wine." Jack entered the office and there stood the same man Jack met on his doorstep two Thanksgivings ago.

"Doc, sorry to arrive without an invitation," Joey Scarlucci said, "but Mr. Moretti wanted me to drop this gift off for you along with a note. I'm to stay until you have read the note in case you have any questions."

Dr. Moss tore the envelope open and read it, *The FBI still has ears and eyes on your phones and emails. Call me from a phone outside of the medical center and your house- JM.*

"Please tell Mr. Moretti thank you for the note and the Sangiovese. I have no questions," said Dr. Moss.

"I will tell him doc. Could I trouble you to return the note to me? I need to destroy it. Mr. M's orders," said Joey Scarlucci.

"Oh, of course," said Dr. Moss as he handed the paper to Joey Scarlucci, who then promptly chewed and hastily swallowed the note.

Dr. Moss headed back to the hospital to round on the patients that he had operated upon that day. As a routine he would always have Ava round with him. Today he would go solo. He twinged with some remorse and guilt that his long-time accomplice was now suddenly an adversary, or so he thought. As he walked over to the hospital, he wondered from what phone would it be safe to call Jack. He had not looked for a payphone in years, and was not certain any were still around, at least in places he would feel safe being overheard or seen. He decided he would drop by the country club on the way home. The club had several private nooks and crannies with old rotary phones still functional.

Jack picked up on the second ring and began the conversation, "Phillip, did I hear you say that this Ava woman is pregnant? And I'm assuming by you?"

Dr. Moss replied, "Yes. And she will be hell bent on having the child. Ending her pregnancy is not going to happen. And she is somebody who cannot be bought with money. I was wondering if you would be able to help me."

"Phillip, that is a big ask. My guys can influence, but nothing more than that. If you like, I can connect you with someone's team who can do more than influence, but it would not be gratis with him. This would be purely business. You will never see or speak with him. He is untouchable. You, my friend, are not untouchable if you head down this path. I'd encourage you to think long and hard before pushing this button. You'll hear from his team if you truly want this, but I encourage you to give this serious thought and think of another way to achieve your ends," Jack replied earnestly.

"Have them contact me," Dr. Moss replied without hesitation.

"Phil, are you sure?" Jack asked.

"Damn it, Jack. I need this to go away. Yes," Dr. Moss curtly responded.

"Okay. We never had this conversation," Jack said and hung up.

The next day Dr. Moss walked alone to clinic. For years it had been routine for Ava to meet him in his office and they would walk to clinic together. As he passed the receptionist, she bid him good morning and told him Ava was already here. As he went toward his clinic desk, he heard someone throwing up in the staff bathroom across the hall. After a few minutes, Ava emerged from the bathroom looking gaunt but with a fresh application of lipstick. She nonchalantly wished him good morning as she walked past him standing near his desk and grabbed his rear when nobody else was watching.

The day's clinic went well enough from the patients' perspectives, but there was a new tension that grew throughout the day between Ava and Moss. Their usual banter and flirting were absent. As they sat in the workroom with other physicians and nurses present, she made several oblique comments referencing her morning emesis in an attempt to stir a response from Dr. Moss. When she said, "I am glad you didn't eat what I ate yesterday. I can only imagine you eating what I did and getting what I have," and then smiled and winked at him, he could no longer remain silently stoic.

The pencil with which he was sketching a surgical approach for a patient snapped in his fingers. He abruptly stood with his chair toppling with a clatter behind him. Everyone in the room turned to observe the commotion. His impulse to walk the three steps and throttle Ava was tempered by the several witnesses in the room. He grabbed the paper upon which he was sketching almost crumpling it into a ball, walked over to Ava and slammed the wrinkled sketch onto her desk and said through gritted teeth inches from her face, "would you kindly give this sketch to the Dicksons in room 7."

She calmly replied with a whispered last word, "not a problem, daddy." Dr. Moss's eyes widened and bulged before he stormed out of the work room. Ava simply smiled and looked directly at all the onlookers who hurriedly tried to appear as though they had seen nothing happen.

Dr. Moss was still fuming and muttering to himself as he passed his secretary without saying a word. On his desk was a simple sealed unmarked white envelope. He yelled out to his secretary, "Who left this envelope here?"

She arose and walked to his doorway and answered, "What envelope?"

"This envelope," he barked holding and waving the envelope in front of himself.

"I've been here all day. I even ate my lunch at my desk. The only other person to be back here was the woman who empties the office trash bins," stated his secretary. He finally stopped waving the envelope around and set it on his desk in front of him and just stared at it. "Is everything okay Dr. Moss? Can I get you anything?" she asked with sincere concern.

"No. No thank you, Lucy. Sorry, I've had a tough couple of days," he said. Lucy simply nodded and backed away and returned to her desk.

Dr. Moss then opened the envelope. On a memo pad sized piece of paper was typed, "Cathedral of Learning. 29th floor. Noon. Friday."

Friday was typically a day spent in the operating room, and this Friday he had multiple cases scheduled. He knew he could be finished with the first case by eleven o'clock in the morning. He would just have to delay starting the second case until after this "meeting."

That Friday morning went smoothly, and he changed out of scrubs into his regular clothes. He told Ricki Bouba that he had a meeting outside the hospital and would call the OR desk from his cellular phone when his noon meeting was over. He grabbed his heavy jacket and cellular phone and began the short walk to the Cathedral of Learning. It was just cold enough to not be comfortable, and the cloudy skies were threatening rain. Just as he was about to enter the building his cellular phone rang. He pushed the answer button on his Nokia. Before he could say a word, he heard a muffled voice instruct him to go to the twenty-seventh floor instead and to sit in one of the benches paired back-to-back with another bench and face the windows. The caller hung up immediately.

Dr. Moss entered the main level wondering if the mystery caller was watching him at this very moment. He walked over to the elevators and pushed the up button. The doors opened revealing an empty compartment. He entered, but before the doors closed several ROTC students in uniform clambered inside. He pushed the button for the twenty-seventh floor, and one of the ROTC students bumped into him as she pushed the button for the twenty-ninth floor. He had not been that close to a military uniform since he wore one himself, he thought. He exited on the twenty-seventh floor and eyed one of the pairs of benches described in what was a lobby despite being on the twenty-seventh floor. He seated himself facing the windows. Shortly thereafter a young lady with a book bag sat on the bench behind him. He heard the unzipping of the bag and rustling of paper. Suddenly she spoke, startling him, "Do not turn around Dr. Moss. Keep your gaze transfixed upon the window in front of you. Bad things happen to people who turn around. Someone will be here to speak with you shortly." He heard the paper rustling again, and the book bag zipper. He sensed her motion and standing that released a waft of delightfully erotic perfume in his direction. He inhaled deeply, fighting the urge to turn and see the body that carried the delightful scent.

He kept his gaze forward, looking at his wristwatch every minute or two. After several minutes he felt a much larger body land on the bench behind him. The same voice from the phone call said, "Eyes forward doctor. These are the rules: You do not watch me leave. You wait ten minutes after I've left before you leave. When we next speak, you give me a name or names and addresses. You give me ten thousand cash per name up front and fifteen thousand cash per name after all the work is completed. If you are in agreement with these nonnegotiable terms, then I will meet you on Monday at noon. I will call you at eleven o'clock on Monday morning with the meeting place. You give me targets and dollars, and in turn, I will give you results. Nobody else knows about this. You have lovely daughters doc. Capiche?"

"I understand. Monday it is," said Dr. Moss with a tremulous voice.

"Ten minutes doc," said the voice.

Special Agent Vincent Maggio and his partner were parked one hundred yards away near the Carnegie Museum of Natural History. They had received a tip a few days ago that if they shadow Dr. Phillip Moss outside of the hospital, then they may encounter people connected to organized crime, and in particular various henchmen who worked for a mob boss known as Pulizie. Pulizie was known to be an orchestrator of contract killings, or more correctly, disappearances because bodies were never discovered. If the last known location of the victim was their home it was always spotless, even immaculate. There were never broken objects, signs of a forced entry or physical struggle. Neighbors would never report seeing or hearing anything unusual. If a dishwasher was present at these "crime scenes", then it was routinely full of clean dishes. If a washer and dryer were present, the laundry was always done and folded.

The pair took turns watching the main level entrance with binoculars and taking control of a camera. On the other side of the building another pair of agents that included Vietnam veteran, Luther Robinson, similarly kept watch. Special Agent Robinson had been brought up from the Atlanta office. He was lead on a task force that had hunted Pulizie for three years and knew by either appearance or name several of the thugs in various cities allegedly associated with Pulizie.

Both pairs of agents had seen Dr. Moss round and enter the building earlier. Agent Robinson could not hold back a big grin and laugh when he saw the doctor. He muttered, "He's walking like he has a corncob up his ass. This must be some serious shit for him." The other agent rolled his eyes in bewilderment thinking of course it is serious; he is meeting with a hit man.

It was easier to screen people leaving the building versus those entering, as these people were face forward exiting. There was an agent inside as well, but her role was to follow Dr. Moss and report where in the building he went. She was to perform no further surveillance as the bureau did not want to spook anyone meeting with the doctor or anyone serving as a lookout for the encounter. Dressed in fatigues bearing the emblems and markings of an Air Force ROTC student, she rode the elevator with him and the other ROTC students and noted that he pushed the button for the twenty-seventh floor. She leaned forward and pushed the button for the twenty-ninth floor as that was the floor where ROTC classes were held. As she leaned past Dr. Moss, she deftly dropped something into his open coat pocket. After the elevator reached the twenty-ninth floor, she exited the elevator and found a private place to call Luther Robinson with Dr. Moss's location. She told Robinson he was on the twenty-seventh floor and that the bug was successfully placed. The listening device, or bug, had a very short range of transmission. Agent Robinson quickly alerted another agent dressed as a university janitor and wearing a headset attached to what appeared to be a Sony Walkman to get to the twenty-seventh floor with his broom, mop, and cart and to begin recording. With few walls in the open twenty-seventh floor lobby the agent was able to keep a good distance from Dr. Moss and obtain adequate reception. He moved his body to the imaginary beats of the Spice Girls, "Say You'll Be There", as he swept imaginary trash and looked for trash bins to empty. He had forty-five minutes of cassette tape to record with. Within a minute of hitting the record button he heard the young woman's voice speaking to Dr. Moss, followed by prolonged background noise and mumbling by Dr. Moss, and eventually the conversation they were hoping to record.

The agents outside knew to look for anybody wearing sunglasses. Sunglasses were a rare item to see adorning faces almost any time of year in Pittsburgh, but particularly rare on a dark cloudy early spring day. In each lookout vehicle one agent kept watch with binoculars while the other worked a camera outfitted with a telephoto lens. Random photos were taken of anyone presenting an adequate face shot. Everything could be magnified for analysis later, but two men were wearing sunglasses as they exited the Cathedral of Learning and received extra photographic attention from the FBI. Luther Robinson recognized one of the two immediately. This was going to be a productive day for the bureau.

All the agents held their positions. A dark sedan rolled to a stop along Forbes Avenue and the man that Luther Robinson recognized entered the front passenger seat. The vehicle and license plate were photographed. Several minutes later Dr. Moss emerged from the building. He retrieved his cellular phone from his jacket and called the OR desk to let them know he was returning and would be in the OR in twenty minutes. Luther watched all this with the binoculars and remarked, "Damn fool. Mother fucker is an amazing surgeon, but he is going to get an ass whooping if he has Pulizie do anything for him. I need to talk to Maggio about this."

A half an hour later all four agents were crammed into a booth at a Wendy's in a suburban town just outside of Pittsburgh. After lunch, Luther said he would drive back to the district office with Vince Maggio, and the other two agents could drive his vehicle back. "We need to loop Jack in," said Agent Robinson to Agent Maggio as soon as they were inside the vehicle.

"Who the fuck do you think gave us the tip!" replied Maggio.

"Then we need to update him," Robinson said firmly, "we can't let Moss go any further."

"Are you nuts sir? You've been the lead agent of this task force for years. We follow this through, and you could bag your man. You'd be a frickin' hero in the bureau," Maggio excitedly exclaimed.

"Jack gave us this tip for a reason. I don't think it was so we could catch Pulizie. He wants us to protect Moss or at least keep him from doing something stupid. If we get Pulizie, great, but we have to protect Moss. Why don't we find a pay phone before getting back to district and chat with Jack," Robinson said with an air of paternal authority toward agent Maggio.

The short conversation with Jack Moretti confirmed Luther Robinson's suspicions. Jack was such a man of principle having pledged that he would do anything Phillip Moss, Sr., wanted for the rest of his life, that he honored Moss's request for "assistance." Moretti could not bring himself to break that code, but he hoped others would step in and foil Moss's misguided intentions, or in other words, foil Moss's funding of the murder of an innocent pregnant woman.

"We need to let Moss know that the FBI is aware of Pulizie and it's out of our control. We can't protect him from law enforcement or even Pulizie. He needs to find another way to achieve his goal, whatever that may be," Luther Robinson said as he looked out the car window upon their return downtown. "We can offer our assistance, but we are not killing anybody. I don't care what he did for Jack or what Jack did for your dad, or what Jack did for me. I've not spoken with him since 'nam. He has no idea I'm in the bureau. It would be nice to see him again. I'll visit him tomorrow. I just wish it were under different circumstances," concluded Robinson.

On weekends, Phillip Moss, Sr., had established a routine when not on call to walk his family's aging Golden Retriever, Charlie, around the block in the morning, weather permitting. Moss was a little later with the dog walk this morning as he had made a trip to the PNC bank branch nearby to make a large withdrawal. Luther Robinson donned in sweatpants, hooded sweatshirt, and running shoes, began surveillance of the Moss home from his vehicle early that Saturday. He saw the front door open, and the white-faced Charlie stumbled out across the threshold still having enough vigor to pull Dr. Moss with the short leash connecting them. Robinson maneuvered his car to a discreet parking spot, exited his vehicle, and began running counterclockwise around the block where Dr. Moss and Charlie were now charting a clockwise path. He chuckled how a large black man running with a hooded sweatshirt in this neighborhood would be perceived. He half hoped someone would confront him, so he could flash his FBI badge and enjoy the look on his or her face. After roughly three decades he did not count on Dr. Moss recognizing him. If Moss remained incredulous as to whom Luther was, Luther knew he had an indisputable identifying trait. The two men had only crossed paths intermittently over a course of a few days almost thirty years ago. The day they did meet though was a defining day in each man's life. For Luther he had taken a bullet across his back and was expecting to receive a killing shot when Jack Moretti not only shot the man taking aim and firing at Luther, but took the bullet meant for Luther. For Dr. Moss it may have been just another day in Vietnam trying to save the mangled young men extracted from the warring jungle, but it was the time he saved Jack Moretti's life. Jack then became the closest thing to a best friend that Phillip Moss ever had. Luther thought whatever had become of Dr. Moss or whatever demons now possessed him, he was not going to let Moss flush his soul down the toilet by being party to a murder and being involved with Pulizie.

   Though in his early fifties, Agent Robinson had remained in excellent shape. After the war he found himself in Tuscaloosa as a college student where he ran track for the Crimson Tide. Running was like breathing for him still. He glided around the sleepy Shadyside block effortlessly and began approaching Dr. Moss without knowing what he would exactly say. As the distance closed from three driveways to two driveways, he decided to sprint another lap and think more. Dr. Moss looked up from having just picked up Charlie's fresh poop in a bag to see a large black man running toward him. He reflexively put the bag in his coat pocket and hurriedly retrieved his phone. As Luther blasted past him, they made eye contact and Luther said, "Morning, Doc." Dr. Moss was relieved that there was no confrontation but disturbed as to why this person knew who he was. The events of yesterday had instilled a degree of paranoia in him, and rightfully so. As he thought about it, the guy did look familiar. He must have been a patient of his, or more likely a family member of one of his patients. He comforted himself with those conclusions, as he slid his cellular phone back into his coat pocket, and unknowingly directly into the open bag of dog shit.

The block was only half a kilometer in distance, so Luther was fast approaching Dr. Moss again in only a few minutes. Though he could have kept running at a full sprint, Luther slowed to a trot and then a walk fifty feet away from Dr. Moss. As he did, he pulled his hood off his head and took a drink from his water bottle.

"Good to see you again, sir," said Luther as his signature smile spread wide and he extended his hand to Dr. Moss.

"Yes, I'm sure, but do I know you?" a worried Dr. Moss asked as he reluctantly extended his hand.

"Yes sir. Hue in 'Nam. May eighteenth, nineteen-sixty-eight. I was Private Robinson then," replied Luther.

Dr. Moss's mind reeled. He remembered a similar smile on a brave young man who did all he could to keep Jack Moretti alive despite suffering a painful injury himself. Whether it was Jack or the mob behind this accidental meeting, Dr. Moss found the likelihood of this man jogging on his block to be the same man from Vietnam as impossible; somebody was trying to mess with him. "Who the hell are you really?" spatted Moss.

"I'm Luther Robinson, sir. Jack Moretti saved my life, and I like to think you and I saved his," replied Luther Robinson.

"Well, I know *I* saved Jack's life," said Dr. Moss indignantly, "I suggest you just keep running, because I don't know who you are!"

Luther Robinson in one graceful fluid move spun 180 degrees, gripped the bottom of his sweatshirt and lifted it above his shoulder blades. A large and unsightly keloid scar stretched from left to right coursing upward dominating his upper back. He paused for a moment and then with equal fluidity returned to face Dr. Moss and lowered his sweatshirt. He looked into the eyes of a stunned Philip Moss and said, "Like I said sir, I was Private Luther Robinson, but now I'm Special Agent Luther Robinson with the FBI, and we need to talk." Agent Robinson produced his badge, though it went practically unnoticed, the keloid was all that Dr. Moss needed to see. "Sir, we should keep walking while we talk," Luther calmly instructed the still stunned Dr. Moss.

"What are you doing in Pittsburgh?" Moss asked as he reoriented himself to the situation.

"As I said, doc, I'm with the FBI. I work out of Atlanta now. You have crossed paths with a man I've been hunting for over three years," said Robinson as the two men walked and Charlie approvingly sniffed the legs of the FBI agent.

"And who might that be?" asked Moss, feigning any such involvement with a criminal wanted by the FBI.

"His name doesn't concern you, and it is safer for you to not know it," replied Robinson.

"Well, I still don't know what you are talking about," an indignant Dr. Moss retorted.

Luther Robinson then recounted the entire meeting at the Cathedral of Learning that the FBI observed and recorded between Dr. Moss and operatives of Pulizie. Dr. Moss suddenly felt weak, stopped walking, and extended his arm to brace himself against a tree, while his other hand grasped Charlie's leash. Charlie took this as an opportune moment to relieve himself against the base of the tree. Dr. Moss appeared as though he was going to be sick, and muttered, "Are you here to arrest me?"

"No sir, though you know I could. I am here to warn you and to help you. After you saved Jack's life along with his Sicilian code of honor, he will always help somehow with any request you make of him. But doc, his honoring your request is not in your best interest. If you get into bed with organized crime to have somebody killed, law enforcement will be the least of your worries. You will be a tortured soul for the rest of your life, and of course, I will still arrest you," Robinson said with a smile escaping at the end.

"So, you know everything? The reason why I was in the cathedral? What I was asking for?" Moss asked almost whimpering.

"Yes sir," replied Robinson.

"What should I do next?" Pleaded Moss.

"When you are contacted Monday morning simply state you can't go through with it. Do not say it's because you can't get the money. They'll offer you 'financing'. Do not say it's because the FBI knows. That would put Jack and you and your family at risk," Robinson firmly stated. "Doc, however troubling your situation is, it ain't worth killing over. Find another way. You were a good man when I met you. Don't fill your life with more regret and pain by doing something stupid. Call Jack if all you want to do is scare or blackmail somebody. That's my advice."

"I'll call Jack," Moss said resolutely.

Agent Robinson started sniffing the air, checking the bottom of his running shoes, and finally sniffing Dr. Moss and said, "No disrespect doc, but take a shower when you get home." Luther Robinson pulled his hood up and resumed a brisk run back to his car a block away.

Dr. Moss was left speechless but then was overpowered with a rancid odor as he put his hands in his coat pockets to warm them. He extracted his phone thickly coated with Charlie's morning feces. He doubled over and vomited as a neighbor retrieving her morning newspaper observed his misery from her front porch before rushing inside.

Later that day, Dr. Moss called Jack Moretti from a safe phone. Jack told him that he could not contact the man known as Pulizie on such short notice. He was careful not to share Pulizie's name with Dr. Moss. They discussed what Luther Robinson had said. They both agreed that Luther's plan was best, and they would talk again Monday evening about what next steps could be taken.

Most weekends went too quickly for Dr. Moss. This particular weekend lapsed at a glacial pace. On Monday morning he was just leaving a committee meeting that had run late when his cellular phone rang. Despite cleaning it as best he could with cotton swabs and soap, the phone still smelled like dog shit when he brought it to his face.

A woman's voice calmly said, "Good morning, Dr. Moss. Is there any information you would like to share before giving you a location?"

"I can't do it," stammered Dr. Moss.

"Dr. Moss, we know *you* can't do it. That's why you hire us," responded the calm voice.

"I don't want anyone to do it," Dr. Moss said with slightly more control.

"Well, today is Ava's lucky day I guess," said the calm voice.

"I never told you her name!" Dr. Moss somehow shouted in a hushed voice.

"We do our homework Dr. Moss. Maybe we will help you anyways. Just so the boys can have some fun. They are getting a bit stir crazy in your city. Good day Dr. Moss," said the woman before abruptly hanging up.

His mouth was dry. He felt helpless. The only other time he felt like this was when clipping a basilar tip aneurysm within the brain a few years ago. He watched the clip shear the aneurysm off the artery as he closed the clip around the aneurysm. He never knew why it happened. He only knew that he had just killed somebody. There is no "plan B" for an event like that. The bleeding cannot be controlled unless the artery is compressed against the brain stem. And the brain stem does not tolerate being a backboard. Compressing the brain stem kills the patient as readily as the bleeding. The only things left for the surgeon to do are to close the head and to go tell the patient's family the grim news. There is no more difficult task than telling a family your hands killed their loved one in an attempt to help him or her. Does he tell Ava, Luther, Jack, nobody? Ava would do something dramatic, and then he would be arrested. Luther said he would arrest him if Ava were murdered. Jack might be able to help. Maybe he could stop the bleeding without compressing the brain stem.

Dr. Moss immediately called the restaurant in Chicago. His call went to a recording informing all willing to listen that the restaurant was closed on Mondays, open five p.m. Tuesdays through Thursdays, and at noon Friday through Sunday. He hurled his Nokia at the painted cinderblock wall of the hallway outside the conference room as he cursed aloud. He was amazed the phone stayed in one piece. A few medical students witnessing the outburst sheepishly strode by the hyperventilating chairman of neurosurgery. After they had turned the corner, he picked up his phone and threw it with all his strength into the wall, successfully shattering it. Now he could purchase a new phone that did not smell like dog shit. He wanted one of the new Motorola StarTac phones anyway.

Since this was the first Monday of the month, it was the day of the monthly team meeting where office and clinic personnel met over lunch to discuss problems, solutions, projects, etc. He and Ava for years always sat next to each other for these round table discussions in the department conference room. He was late to the meeting, which was not unusual. The only remaining seat respectively had been saved for him next to Ava. He apologized to the group for being late and took his reserved seat, forcing a smile and a nod toward Ava, who reciprocated. After the mundane discussions of reducing wait times, patient flow, satisfaction scores, and whether ESPN or CNN should be on the waiting room TV, the meeting concluded. He remained seated, as did Ava, allowing everyone else to leave. "So how are you feeling?" Dr. Moss asked with an insincere smile.

"Well, it's not morning anymore. So, I am doing just fine," she replied with a wry smile, "And thank you for asking, even if you don't really care."

"Jesus Ava! I am trying here," he replied frustratingly.

"Well, try harder," she said matter-of-factly.

"Ava, I'm worried about you. Is there anywhere you could stay other than at your place?" Dr. Moss queried.

"Oh yes, our apartment! No wait, you took that away from us!" Ava sarcastically replied.

"What about Ella?" Moss asked.

"Oh, she is 'co-habitating' with someone now. There wouldn't be enough room for all three of us in her bed," Ava replied.

"But you told me you slept there often. Can't you just sleep wherever you slept then?" responded Dr. Moss.

"Phillip, I slept in her bed, naked, after she and I would love. Do I have to explain further?" Ava retorted.

A wide-eyed Dr. Moss rocked back and could only say, "Oh."

"Phillip, you should be fine with any of that. Look at young Phillip," Ava interjected as Moss's eyelids fell back into position.

"Stay with him," Moss quickly said.

"Stay with who?" a confused Ava asked.

"My son. At least for a few days," said Moss.

"Phillip, your son *is* more handsome and kinder than you, but I believe he plays for the other team. And why the hell do I need to stay with someone?" Ava asked with her voice rising.

"Because you might be in danger!" blurted Dr. Moss.

"Phillip why would anyone want to hurt little old me," she said with a chuckle.

"Ava, please. You need to be careful," Moss pleaded.

"I get it; this is you trying harder. Thank you. I can take care of myself. Remember, I grew up in a not very nice part of Philly. I can protect myself from all types of scum," she said confidently.

"Ava, you are a small woman, and pregnant," he said with a trailing hush.

"I am those things. I am also a small pregnant woman who sleeps with a nine-millimeter under her pillow. So, whatever has you worried, don't be," said Ava. She stood from the table and left. Dr. Moss simply looked up at the ceiling, spread his arms, and sighed. Then he stood and departed. He needed to buy his new Motorola.

That evening as Ava headed north toward Butler on highway 8 the traffic thinned rapidly as it almost always did. A large black SUV passed her at one point, but not before slowing down directly alongside her. She could see nothing through the SUV's tinted passenger window, so she simply rolled her window down and raised her middle finger toward the SUV. She smiled to herself as the SUV accelerated away. A mile later she saw it exit the highway. She was glad the SUV was gone, but half hoped to be able to flip off the occupants of the SUV again.

She lived much further away from Pittsburgh than most who worked at the medical center. She enjoyed the space that surrounded her little two-bedroom bungalow. It was quiet, and at night there were few lights allowing her to see stars like she never saw in Philly. She always wanted a dog, but now with a child on the way, a canine companion would have to wait. Once she arrived home, she took her vitamins and reheated the spaghetti she had taken for lunch and not eaten for a quick dinner and opened a can of Seven-Up. She briefly pondered Dr. Moss's bizarre behavior earlier in the day. He is not handling this baby thing very well she thought to herself as she rubbed her abdomen. She turned on the TV and flipped channels passing on *Diagnosis:Murder* and *Just Shoot Me!* before settling on *Home Improvement.*

Shortly after becoming pregnant, she developed a craving for Seven-Up soft drinks. During a commercial break she decided to retrieve a second can from the refrigerator. She looked at a pitcher of water she kept in the refrigerator thinking that it is probably healthier than another Seven-Up. Screw it, she said to herself, I want the pop. As she stood in the kitchen finishing her first and opening her second Seven-Up, she could have sworn she heard a vehicle driving past her home, but when she looked out the window over the kitchen sink, she saw no lights.

She chuckled when she threw her empty can into her kitchen garbage bin and realized it contained only empty Seven-Up cans. The clink of the empty can landing upon the others in the trash bin made for quite the noise. But the clink of the cans colliding was quickly followed by what she swore was the sound of a car door softly shutting. Once again, she looked out the window toward the road. She turned on the light that illuminated her car parked out front and saw nothing suspicious. She thought for a moment that maybe Phillip was serious about her being in danger but why be so vague and weird about it. And why would she be in danger? She returned to her small living room and watched the remainder of *Home Improvements*. Despite not being late, she needed to always be up early, and her energy had already been greatly curtailed by the pregnancy. It was time for bed. As she brushed her teeth she thought about Phillip's warning, the strange SUV on the highway, and the sounds she thought she heard. Before turning in she built a small pyramid of empty soda cans next to each of her two exterior doors. She confirmed the doors were locked as well as the windows. The windows were quite small though, so unless a small child was stalking her, nobody would come through the windows. She thought about calling Phillip or Ella, as she had no acquaintances nearby. She even considered calling the police, but what would she tell them, that she heard a car driving down a road? Better safe than sorry, she told herself. She picked up the phone and cradled it between her shoulder and ear and took a moment to decide who to call. It took only seconds for her to realize though; there was no dial tone.

    Pulizie's thugs had been out earlier in the day dressed as utility workers. On the rarely traveled rural road they could have been dressed as the Easter Bunny and Santa Claus because nobody drove by. They quickly snipped the phone line to Ava's house and assured there were no chain locks or bolts that would need to be cut to enter her home. After picking the door lock, they surveyed her refrigerator for anything open she may eat or drink that evening. There was a pitcher of water with a sliced lemon and slices of pizza in a takeout box. They liberally dosed both the pitcher and pizza with midazolam, a powerful sedative. They then returned to Pittsburgh and kept surveillance on Ava's Acura in the hospital parking garage and with the plan to follow her back to her house when she left the hospital.

For all her bluster and confidence Ava was now genuinely frightened. She wished she really had a handgun to keep under her pillow. Maybe Phillip would have been more forthcoming or concerned if he knew she was truly helpless. She was cursing herself for lying to him about having a nine-millimeter under her pillow. She kept all the lights off and went back to the kitchen and retrieved the largest knife she could find. She had not sharpened it in over a decade, but it was all she had. She made sure all blinds were closed and stuffed her two pillows under the sheets along with some clothing. At least in the dark it somewhat looked as though someone were asleep under the sheets. She took the comforter off the bed and went and curled up on the couch in the living room with her knife. Five minutes later she had to pee. She went to the water closet and relieved her bladder. Her mouth and throat were dry from the fear she was experiencing. She was not going to have a third Seven-Up so she poured herself a glass of water. She thought to herself she should filter fresh water tomorrow because of the taste. Everything tasted different with pregnancy. She returned to the couch with her knife, determined to stay awake all night, if necessary, with her eyes on the front door, and promptly fell asleep. The knife she was clutching fell to the floor as she began to snore. The midazolam was doing its job. She dreamed of trying to climb a mountain of Seven-Up cans that made a clanging sound with each step. She heard a man's voice yelling and cussing as the cans ricocheted down the mountain toward him punctuated by loud bangs. She remembers seeing a strange man's sleeping face being dragged down the mountain of Seven-Up cans away from her by some invisible force. Finally, there was peace, and she felt like she would sleep forever.

    She awoke at dawn's first light. She was startled that she no longer held the knife, and then realizing she was okay, startled that she had slept late. She picked up the knife and gasped as she looked toward the front door. The pyramid of cans was strewn across the small foyer. The front door was unlocked. She rushed to her bedroom with knife in hand. The pillows and clothing stuffed under the sheets were all as she left them, but there were three small holes perforating the sheets. She looked under the bed and saw where the hardwood floor had been splintered and pierced. She ran wildly around the small house opening every closet door and stabbing wildly before looking. She searched every corner and under all the furniture for anybody hiding in her small home and found nobody. She collapsed on her bed and began crying. She had never been late to work in her life. Today was going to have to be an exception. Somebody tried to kill her.

## Chapter Sixteen: Guardian Angels, 1997

In the basement of a safe house in Wilkinsburg, just outside of Pittsburgh, agents Robinson and Maggio drank coffee after a long night. They had tailed Pulizie's thugs while the thugs were occupied with following and tormenting Ava. Now one of them was in a body bag along the wall next to the agents and the other was shackled to a chair on the other side of the table gagged and moaning in pain. Maggio was almost too late intercepting the intruder at Ava's house. He fully intended to let the thug pick the lock and enter but was caught off guard with how quickly and silently the thug gained entry. That was until the clattering of the cans. The thug turned to leave with his gun drawn believing his target was alerted by the clamor, only to find him facing another figure in the dark. As the thug brought his weapon up, Agent Maggio put a .40 Smith & Wesson hollow point in the thug's chest and another between his eyes. Tap, tap he was taught at Quantico. His instructors would have been proud. The thug's lifeless body fell backward into the home landing on the empty cans. The other thug leapt from the SUV and drew his weapon as he passed the front of his vehicle. Thug number two could only see stars as Luther Robinson brought the butt of his .45 down on the back of his head. Agent Robinson handcuffed him, secured his weapon, and searched him. Thug two was foolish enough to be carrying his wallet with what appeared to be legitimate identification.

Agent Maggio entered the home and found Ava deep asleep on the couch and seemingly in good condition, but clearly sedated after not awakening to the crash of the cans and two gunshots. He saw the knife on the floor and chuckled, she knew they were coming. He then took the dead assailant's weapon in his gloved hand and fired three rounds through the decoy in the bed Ava had constructed. He collected the shell casings and dragged the body over the threshold outside. He thought he heard Ava let out a sigh as he dragged the body, but she had not awakened. The thug's leather jacket did a good job of containing the hemorrhage. He closed the front door and messaged Luther that all was secure. Luther arrived moments later with a body bag and zipped up the deceased Pulizie henchman. Luther threw the bagged body over his shoulder, and they walked back to their vehicle. After securing their prisoner in the agency vehicle Agent Maggio left for the safe house, while Agent Robinson followed in the thugs' vehicle with the bagged body. From the front door lock being picked to leaving the scene it was all over in under five minutes.

## Chapter Seventeen: IKEA, 1997

A distraught Ava stopped at the first pay phone she could find and called Phillip on his cellular phone. Unfortunately, Dr. Moss was picking up his new Motorola later that day and could not be reached. In a panic she called the Moss home, and Mrs. Moss answered. Despite the disdain Mrs. Moss held toward Ava, she was moved to the point of sympathy by the panic and fear in Ava's voice. Ava rambled about being followed, a black SUV, bullet holes, and a baby. None of this made sense to Cammie Moss, and she considered that maybe the poor girl was schizophrenic. Whatever the circumstances, it was clear to Cammie that Ava needed some type of assistance. A fellow human being was suffering, and so Cammie Moss swallowed her pride and told Ava to drive directly to the Moss home. Cammie told her she would call the hospital and let Dr. Moss know that she would not be in for work. She similarly called his cellular phone without an answer and made a mental note to call after Ava was situated.

While Ava continued her drive south toward Pittsburgh, Luther Robinson was already in Dr. Moss's office updating him on *some* of the events from the prior evening. He assured him that Ava was not harmed and did not witness the break in or the *neutralization* of the intruder. He explained that Ava appeared to have been drugged somehow. This was a suspected *modus operandi* of the Pulizie group, though it could never be proven because neither drugs nor bodies were ever discovered. It remained a viable theory because of the lack of any struggle or violence within the homes of the missing victims. Ava's home would tell a different story. A forensics team would be onsite that morning, followed by the cleanup crew that would restore everything exactly as it was before, minus any drugs. When Agent Robinson told Dr. Moss of Agent Maggio firing three rounds into the pillow stuffed decoy, Dr. Moss developed a confused look and asked, "Why the hell did he do that?"

"This conversation never gets repeated. Two reasons sir, one to help Maggio, and one to help you," replied Agent Robinson.

"Okay, now I'm more confused!" exclaimed Dr. Moss.

"While Maggio killed the thug in self-defense, it seems like anytime a bad guy goes down without firing a shot, it's somehow construed that we are trigger happy killers hiding behind our badges. Fuck those bastards that think that. Let them see what a bullet does to a man that is slow to defend himself. We leave a few rounds fired from the bad guy's gun and we are in a better place. But for this guy, we will keep his death under wraps. Pulizie can't know we have captured or killed either of his thugs. So, to answer your questions, that's how it helps Maggio. As for you and your problem, Ava knows somebody very likely thought they killed her in her sleep. She has no idea who, why, or where her failed assassins are. She will be frightened, scared for her life, for her baby's life. She will be vulnerable, able to be manipulated and coerced. Let her think what she wants or fill her head with threats. You will have leverage over her for a short while. Use the opportunity to gain control and steer the situation to your benefit. But absolutely no physical harm to her. I've got to draw the line somewhere," Luther Robinson concluded with a stare that shot right through the soul of Dr. Moss. "Not a word to anybody about this doc," said Agent Robinson coldly as he rose from the chair and departed the office.

    As Ava pulled up alongside the curb in front of the Moss home, she felt some relief. It was daylight, and as best as she could tell, nobody followed her. The Moss's neighbors with the pool had a for sale sign out front. She closed her eyes and tried to calm her nerves by imagining floating in that pool on a summer day but only started shaking and crying as she imagined bullets peppering the water around her. She remained paralyzed by emotion and unable to leave her Acura after turning off the ignition. Why would anyone want to kill her she thought? The only person that would want her dead would be…. "Oh my God!" she screamed out loud to herself. She looked up toward the Moss home to see Mrs. Moss peering through the window and beckoning her to come inside. She thought how stupid could she be. She practically stepped right into the spider's web to be insnared is all she could think. She turned the key and fired up the four cylinders. Her tires screeched as she rocketed down the quiet suburban street. Ava kept muttering out loud, "she knows, she knows, she knows," all the way to the hospital parking garage. Cammie Moss simply watched in bewilderment as Ava sped away thinking that girl is truly crazy.

    Every day that Ava worked she always arrived impeccably dressed in makeup perfectly applied. Neither were necessary to make her attractive as she was born with natural beauty. Both of these routines, however, did make her even more attractive. As she strode down the hallways toward the neurosurgical offices those that saw her would describe her as looking disheveled and distraught. Her face was streaked with dried tears and mascara. Her skirt and blouse were uncharacteristically mismatched with the blouse buttoned asymmetrically. She blasted past Ruth directly into Phillip Moss's office and slammed the door.

Dr. Moss was caught off guard by her blustery entrance as he looked up from his desk with surprise. Ava started sobbing and screaming, "she knows, she wants me dead, she knows Phillip, she knows! Why didn't you answer? Why didn't you answer? I almost died! The baby almost died! Our baby almost died!"

With the last pronouncement Dr. Moss sprung from his chair encouraging her to keep her voice down. He embraced her as she continued to sob saying, "calm down, calm down. You are safe here. What happened?"

"You tried to warn me. Why didn't you tell me she was going to kill me? How does she know? Did you tell her? Is that why your wife hates me so much to kill me?" Ava said between sobs. Ava then recounted the events of the night before, what she found this morning, and how she almost walked into a trap at his house this morning.

Dr. Moss now realized Ava's perceptions and recalled Luther Robinson's words from earlier in the morning as he embraced Ava, "use the opportunity to gain control and steer...."

Dr. Moss held her closely and said lying through his teeth, "I never thought she was serious. I can't believe she would be behind anything like this. That would explain why she took all that money out of our account recently though. If it was Cammie, then I'm sure she was just trying to scare you."

"Phillip! They shot me in my bed! Well, not me, but they thought it was me!" she cried out.

"Let me call the authorities. They need to take a statement from you and inspect your house for evidence," said Dr. Moss authoritatively as he picked up the phone and called Luther Robinson. Luther said he already had the house secured as a crime scene and that Ava was not to return there. He also said, he or someone else would contact her soon for her statement.

"Thank you, Phillip," she said with sincerity as the sobs finally ebbed, "But where am I going to live?"

"Well, if it were my wife behind this, there is only one place you'd be safe at night," said Dr. Moss.

"Where Phillip? asked Ava.

"With my son," responded Dr. Moss, "she would never let anything like you described happen where he lives. Go clean up and get a coffee. I'll meet you in the clinic at one p.m."

Soon thereafter, Dr. Moss called out to Lucy to have his son paged and to tell him to come up to the office as soon as possible, if not before.

Within the hour, Phillip, Jr., had cut himself free from the clinical grind in the ICU and made it to his father's office. "Is this a hi Dad, or a a hi Professor visit today?" asked Phil, Jr., as he knocked on the open door with a smile.

"This is a little bit of both," replied Phillip, Sr.

"How so?" asked Phil, Jr.

"Well, your probationary period seems to be nearing its completion," stated Phillip, Sr.

"Uh-huh," replied his son with his head nodding.

"You need to do your mother and me a favor," said Phillip, Sr. looking directly at his son.

"Sure, dad, anything," replied Phil, Jr.

"Ava needs a safe place to stay for a while, and that safe place is with you," Phillip, Sr., commanded more than asked.

"What? That's nuts, Dad. I don't even...," Phil, Jr., said struggling for words.

"You don't even what? Have the space? You do. Have the time? You are always here. What is it that you don't even?" his father responded with a prosecutorial tone. "Let me remind you that you are still on probation and your remaining in this program remains...uncertain. I could have the same discussion about Dr. Bouba, as well as about his *potential* fellowship at the Cleveland Clinic that he is excited about. I do sometimes think he may benefit from a full year in Cameroon before allowing him to graduate as well. I do need to give that more consideration. Ava will be staying at your apartment beginning tonight."

"What about my old place in the carriage house?" pleaded Phil, Jr.

"Your mother prefers she not be there," responded Phil, Sr.

"I'm on call tonight!" exclaimed Phil, Jr., rolling his eyes.

"Not a problem. I am not asking you to be her chauffeur. She can go there herself. Give me your key and I'll have Lucy make a copy for Ava. Lucy will page you when you can have your key back," his father concluded matter-of-factly. Phil, Jr., pulled his key ring from the pocket in his scrubs, removed his apartment key, and slammed it on his father's desk and left.

During the clinic Ava remained visibly shaken. Dr. Moss felt a pang of guilt but only for a moment. After clinic he told Ava he would meet her outside his son's apartment and make sure she got safely inside. But first she needed to meet with Special Agent Maggio so he could take her statement. The meeting with Maggio was brief. She noticed he seemed to almost finish her sentences for her, as though he knew the answers to the questions he asked. After the surprisingly short interview Dr. Moss walked her to her car and provided assurance that she would be safe at his son's place, "for as long as necessary." She kept muttering to herself unintelligible words and whimpering. He steadied her by holding her arm as he feared she would collapse to her knees at any moment.

When they arrived at her vehicle, she grabbed the lapels of Dr. Moss's heavy tweed jacket and looking him in the eyes cried, "Did you tell her? Did you tell her I'm pregnant? With your child? Did you tell her I want to have your baby? Did you tell her I want to make a family with you?"

"Ava, no. You need to get these silly thoughts out of your pretty little head," Dr. Moss said with a paternalistic tone.

"Why don't you tell her? Tell her you want me! Tell her you want to start a new family with--," Ava screamed. Her final words were cut short by a sharp blow to the side of her face.

Phillip Moss had heard enough. After his open right hand collided with the left side of her head and face, she fell sideways against her car but caught her fall on the driver's side door handle. "Get in your car you crazy bitch. I'm trying to keep you alive," he growled, "keep talking like this and you *will* end up dead. Now get yourself together and meet me at Phil, Jr.'s apartment like we discussed." He opened her driver's side door, pushed her in, slammed the door shut, and yelled, "Understand?" through the closed window.

Ava could feel her soul cracking. She was pregnant, frightened, threatened, and losing control of her life. The one man she adored and worshipped had not only brutally just slapped her but threatened and instilled more fear into her as well. Her dreams and plans of love and family were rapidly replaced with the singular desire to simply survive. She found a tissue and wiped the tears from her eyes. She took several deep breaths before retrieving the car keys from her purse. She cautiously backed the Acura out and found herself driving at half the speed limit when out on the road. She was scared to drive any faster and was trembling. She turned the heat up all the way. When she pulled along the curb and parked, Dr. Moss was already sitting on the steps waiting for her. As she approached him, he arose and walked toward her. She cowered as he raised his hand again. He gently caressed her reddening left cheek with the back of his hand and said, "Let's go in and get some ice on that. It's a shame you slipped and fell in the parking lot. You'll be okay though." She mustered a weak smile and thanked him.

Once inside they were both surprised by the sheer austerity of the apartment. It had all the warmth of an economy motel room. This was no home for Phil, Jr. This was simply a place where he ate, slept, and showered. The size of the apartment enhanced the austerity. There was room for much more furniture and furnishings. For now, a solitary love seat was against one wall with an old 32-inch Westinghouse TV on a stand all the way against the opposite wall. The bedroom was equally sparse with a queen-sized mattress and box springs on the floor and a large suitcase serving as a bedside table with a small lamp and alarm clock perched upon it. They began opening doors and discovered a water heater and furnace behind one. Another door revealed a stacked small washer and dryer. Two more doors were glorified coat closets and a third served as a small pantry that contained a single open box of Rice Chex.

Dr. Moss opened the freezer compartment and extracted a tray of ice cubes that looked to have been present since the previous tenants occupied the apartment. He ran water over the bottom of the tray to loosen the cubes' grip on the plastic, popped several out, and wrapped them in a clean dish towel. He handed the self-made ice pack to Ava. "You need to rest and let your injury heal before returning to work. That's an order," he said. He reached into his jacket pocket, pulled out his wallet, and extracted a credit card. "Here, take this. Go to IKEA and anywhere else tomorrow morning and get what you need to make this place a home. Just don't buy anything gilded in gold," he said with an apologetic look on his face, "Oh, and here is the key to the place." She held the key in her open palm looking down at it. He kissed her forehead and with no further words spoken left the apartment.

As soon as he left, Ava sat down on the couch and started envisioning what the apartment needed. She went into the bedroom, stripped the bed, and loaded the washing machine. Thank God she thought that Phil, Jr., at least had some laundry detergent. She washed the few dirty dishes in the sink. She realized she was famished. The refrigerator revealed a half a loaf of sandwich bread, a carton of milk two days past expiration, and a jar of grape jelly. Damn it, she thought, why does he not have peanut butter. Now that it was dark, she was going nowhere. She made herself a jelly and Rice Chex sandwich and inhaled it. She gave herself a pleasing smile at this surprisingly tasty creation. She poured a glass of milk, sniffed the carton, and detected no spoilage. This would suffice for tonight, she thought. She turned the TV on and watched a Penguins game despite having no interest in hockey, while the washer and dryer ran. By the end of the first period, she had clean, dry, warm bedding. She made the bed, stripped off her clothes, and collapsed asleep not knowing who she could trust or believe, but for some reason, she now felt safe.

Phil, Jr., had an uncharacteristically easy night of call. He was able to get four hours of sleep, which to his recollection was a personal record. On morning rounds he bragged to the other residents about his Van Winkle-like night of call. The more senior residents simply responded by saying he would be good to stay later than today until all the work is complete. He realized he should not have shared his good fortune with the team. While Phil, Jr., was washing his hands scrubbing into a morning case, Ava was showering and discovering the only soap present was a single well used bar of Irish Spring soap. There was no shampoo. She made a mental note to add toiletries to her shopping list and washed her hair and body with Irish Spring. She needed toiletries more than furniture.

As she functioned at work, Ava also was an efficient shopper. She no longer trembled and was comforted by daylight and sunny skies. She first went to a Wal-Mart and obtained toiletries and cleaning supplies. Next stop was the Kaufmann's department store for kitchenware, clothing, makeup, sheets, towels, and blankets. Then onward to IKEA where she quickly selected furniture for the kitchen, living room, and bedroom. She made sure to get a new sofa upon which she would be comfortable sleeping. She did not look forward to the assembly process for many of the items, but she was fortunate that IKEA could deliver everything by the end of business that day. Her final stop was the Giant Eagle grocery store nearby. She loaded up on essential provisions, including peanut butter and the ingredients for a spaghetti dinner.

She was back at Phil, Jr.'s place by one p.m. With some trepidation she made the multiple trips between her car and the apartment to empty the Acura of her purchases. There were enough people on the sidewalks, however, to give her peace of mind. Once ensconced inside she stocked the closet pantry and hung some of her clothes in a coat closet. Within minutes the entrance way buzzer rang, and she could see the IKEA truck parked in the street. Shit, that was fast, she said to herself. A sense of unease swept over her. Was she really going to just open the door for two men who happened to *look* like delivery men. She quickly unwrapped a paring knife she just purchased and held it tightly behind her at the small of her back. She proceeded down the stairs and opened the door. Both men were busy dropping the rear gate of the truck and beginning to unload. The first looked up and made eye contact with her and said, "You don't look like a Phillip Moss!"

"No, but he is coming by any minute," she replied forcing a smile and tightening the grip on the paring knife.

"Not a problem. You can sign for the shipment, as long as we deliver to the third-floor unit," he said as he looked at a clipboard lying on a box next to him that had already been unloaded. Give us about ninety minutes please, and we'll be out of your hair, ma'am."

"Ninety minutes! I didn't buy that much!" exclaimed Ava.

"No ma'am, but a, uh, Phillip, uh, Moss called and paid extra to have us assemble everything," he replied, again looking at the clipboard to remind himself of the name.

"Well, then please hurry. I have so much work to do today," Ava said.

"Yes, ma'am. Rupert and I are fast with our Allen wrenches. I just need you to sign the delivery invoice to confirm we delivered all you bought, and we will get it inside and assembled. And my name is Bart," said Bart cheerfully.

Ava walked down the stairs realizing she still was holding the paring knife behind her back. She just let her hand fall to her side and continued holding the knife in plain sight.

"We will open the boxes inside ma'am. But thank you for bringing a knife down," said Bart with his eyes glued to the brand-new knife.

"Oh, no, I, uh, was just starting to make something when you guys rang. This is for cutting onions, not you, I mean not the boxes," responded Ava, now feeling slightly embarrassed as she could not begin to imagine either of these two hurting anybody.

"Yes, ma'am. You just do what you need to do inside, but you will need to tell us where you want each piece of furniture," said Bart.

When she walked down to the street level, she noticed the silent Rupert likely had Down syndrome. He was also working like a machine getting the truck unloaded. The guy had an admirable work ethic and was strong as an ox. If he kept the same pace with assembly, they will be finished in well under ninety minutes she thought. Suddenly she realized she would rather have these two men hanging around for as long as they needed. They were not a danger to her; quite the opposite, in minutes her perception of them changed from being a potential threat to being a protector. Ava commented to Bart, "Rupert doesn't say much, does he?"

"No ma'am. He's the best partner I've ever had. He was a weightlifting champion in the Special Olympics. He was bummed they didn't offer boxing though. He works out in the ring every week with regular folk. Most guys are scared to mess with him once they see him in the ring. He lays most of them straight out with the upper cut he has. They never see it coming. Right Rupe?" explained Bart with a big smile. Rupert just nodded, grunted, and kept working.

As they worked inside, she made them sandwiches that they readily devoured. When they were done with the job, she gave them a cash tip for which they were very grateful. Finally, Rupert spoke and said, "Thank you, Miss Ava," and then he began to snigger and whisper into Bart's ear.

"What's so funny?" asked Ava.

"He says you are pretty, ma'am," replied Bart; and with those words Rupert turned a bright red.

Ava gave Rupert a kiss on the cheek and walked them to the door. Rupert smiled the entire rest of the day, and reminded Bart for the rest of the week, "Miss Ava kissed me!"

"Well, I know who to call if I need any heavy lifting done. Thank you, fellas," Ava said with an appreciative smile as the two men departed.

The apartment was unrecognizable compared to this morning. Ava had a Marinara sauce simmering, the furniture perfectly arranged, a few new rugs covering the hard tile floor, and some clean clothes on herself. All the work and activity partially helped keep her mind off the fact that less then forty-eight hours ago somebody tried to kill her.

Back at the hospital Dr. Moss informed Lucy to let the clinic know that Ava would not be in for a few days as she was not feeling well. Lucy picked up the phone and said, "I'll give her a call right now to check on her and see if she needs anything."

Quickly Dr. Moss interrupted her and said, "She is not staying at her house. She is at my son's apartment."

Lucy's face contorted into a shape expressing bewilderment and said, "Excuse me Dr. Moss, did you say she is at your son's place? Are they dating?"

"Oh, I think they are beyond dating Lucy," replied Dr. Moss with a coy smile, "they have tried to keep it quiet, but ever since he had her over for Thanksgiving the year before last, the relationship has been progressing." Knowing that Lucy was the largest gossip in the department office he then said, "Don't spread this around Lucy, I feel confident they will make their relationship known to everyone soon enough on their own terms."

"I thought…," Lucy said before pausing, and then finished, "oh, never mind," as Dr. Moss stared quizzically at her. By the end of the lunch hour the entire department's office staff was aware of the "Jr. and Ava" relationship. By the end of the workday, the operating room and clinic staff, and many residents had heard the same news, but not Phil, Jr., himself. Ricki Bouba on the other hand received an earful regarding the "romance" from a chatty operating room circulator while he assisted with a spine operation. He shook his head thinking that he told Phil, Jr., they would need to act "straight" to get through this bogus chairman manufactured probation period. He had no idea Phil, Jr., would take acting straight to this level though. Bravo, Phil, bravo, he thought to himself with a twinge of jealousy.

In the maelstrom of the neurosurgical service, he had almost forgotten about his father's bizarre directive concerning Ava. He recognized her car out front so was prepared to see the peculiar and beautiful Ava Chelidon upon entering his apartment. He was hoping she would keep to herself and just leave him alone. Phil, Jr., was able to leave early that day and was heading up the stairs to his apartment shortly after seven p.m. As he opened the door the scents of oregano, garlic, and tomato wafting through the air seemed other worldly compared to the expected stale air that greeted him hundreds of times before upon entering his apartment. His stomach immediately churned with hunger. He hung his jacket on the wall mounted coat hook, dropped his book bag, and kicked off his shoes at the door. When he turned the corner out of the small foyer, he was dumbstruck. For a brief moment he thought he had entered the wrong apartment, until he saw his old TV still perched on its old stand. There was now a small dining table set with plates and silverware in addition to piece after piece of new furniture as he continued to scan his rehabilitated abode. All he could muster was a weak, "Hello," with his voice almost cracking.

Ava emerged from the bedroom, *his* bedroom, as she had been in the adjoining bathroom. "Hello, Phillip, Jr., I hope you like everything. I know this is weird. No offense meant, but this place was so depressing. Something serious had to be done. Consider it emergency surgery. And don't worry, your father paid for everything," said Ava nonchalantly.

"Wow! This place looks amazing. Do I get to keep all this stuff?" Phil, Jr., asked himself as he had the eyes of a young child seeing a Christmas tree surrounded by presents just for him.

"Well, the furniture is from IKEA, so I won't be taking it with me," replied Ava.

The glow left Phil, Jr.'s face as reality sunk in and he seriously asked, "Ava, why are you here? And what happened to your face?"

"What has your father told you?" asked Ava as she took a seat on the new sofa and patted the spot next to her, encouraging him to join her.

"He pretty much told me that you were going to stay with me," replied Phil, Jr. shrugging his shoulders.

"And you agreed?" asked Ava in a critical tone.

"No, not at first. He can be a little threatening. I let myself be coerced by him," replied Phil, Jr.

"Well, at least he didn't hit you," said Ava gesturing toward her own face.

"Holy shit, Ava! No way! Dad did that?" exclaimed Phil, Jr. who suddenly found himself standing.

Ava simply nodded in the affirmative and said, "but he says I slipped in the parking lot," as tears began to form in her eyes.

"Oh God, Ava, I am so sorry. But why are you here? Or why do you need to be here?" asked Phil, Jr., with sincere concern in his voice.

"Let me tell you over dinner. The pasta is ready to be strained now," and she rose from the sofa, stifled her emotions, and headed toward the kitchen.

Ava told Phil, Jr., everything, beginning with the affair with his father, the pregnancy, his father's warning for her to be careful, the strange SUV and sounds at her house, the pyramid of cans knocked over, bullet holes in her bed and floor, and her sleeping through it all. When she tried to describe the circumstances when struck by Phil, Jr.'s father she melted in a pool of tears. She finished by telling him her house was now a crime scene that the police had locked down while the investigation was completed.

"Ava, I've only got one bedroom and one bathroom here. If my dad paid for all this furniture he could have paid for a hotel room for two weeks for you. I understand why you cannot stay at your place, but why with me?" Phil, Jr., concluded.

"Phillip said this is the only place I would be safe," replied Ava.

"That makes no sense at all! How am I going to protect you from guys with guns!" exclaimed Phil, Jr.

"Because your father said your mother would not send anybody after me here," Ava said with her voice shaking slightly.

"My mother! What the fuck! That's nuts!" an irritated Phil, Jr., exclaimed.

"Think about it, who would want me gone more than anybody else in the world?" retorted Ava.

Phil, Jr., sat in stunned silence. He could barely wrap his head around the alleged pregnancy involving his father. Was he in the room right now with a future stepbrother or stepsister in Ava's belly who would be twenty-nine years his junior? Was Ava pregnant, but now just psycho, and all the stories of strange SUVs and bullet holes and sleeping through a break-in and gunfire was just pure psycho bullshit? Ava had always been *different*. If everything she said was true though, then deductive reasoning would indeed point toward his mother. But he *knew* his mom. He could sense she was suffering in silence, but to say she would somehow order a hit on Ava? That seemed like pure lunacy to Phil, Jr. Some of his mom's tennis partners were grade A ultra-entitled bitches, but none struck him as having connections to assassins. Nothing made sense to Phil, Jr. He refused to believe his mother had anything to do with this current mess. He would go ask her at his next opportunity, but without his father around. With Phil, Jr.'s work schedule however, meeting his mother alone was going to be tricky. "I need to go to sleep," Phil, Jr., finally said, "I get up at three-forty-five, so I'll be gone by four-thirty. The place is all yours after that."

Ava walked over to the new sofa and said, "I'll sleep here, but can I pee and brush my teeth first?"

"Of course. And you can have the bed when I'm on call. It's every third night. And can I ask a favor?" concluded Phil, Jr.

"Certainly," Ava quickly responded.

"Please just call me Phil," Phil, Jr., requested.

"I will, Phil," responded Ava.

"Thanks for the spaghetti. I don't cook much, or at all really," said Phil, Jr., with a sheepish grin.

"You are very welcome, Phil. Now let's get to sleep," said Ava authoritatively.

**Chapter Eighteen: Who's Your Daddy?**

The next day at the hospital after morning rounds Ricki caught up with Phil on their way to the operating room. "So, I hear you are taking my advice seriously regarding a straight charade," said Ricki.

"Oh geez, did my dad tell you yesterday when you guys were operating?" responded Phil, Jr.

"Nope, but just about everybody else did," answered Ricki with a twinge of sarcasm.

"What the fu…fu…feathers!" Phil, Jr., caught himself reflexively responding as the hospital chaplain passed them in the hallway.

"Ricki, I wish I could tell you the full story now. Let's just say there is some crazy shit happening and I cannot even begin to explain it all. But we do need to talk about this mess, and soon," Phil, Jr., said as both of their pagers went off calling them to their respective operating rooms.

"Can't wait to hear," Ricki said, again with a dose of sarcasm.

"Jealous?" Phil, Jr., said with a smirk and turned to enter the room he was assigned to that day.

Other than a case Dr. Kleinwurst was completing with one of the other chief residents, about twelve hours later the neurosurgery operating rooms were now empty, and rounds in the ICU were wrapping up. Ricki suggested they head to the cafeteria and grab a coffee and talk. They found an out of the way table and sat down with their coffees across from one another. Phil gave Ricki the details of the discussion he had with his father. He made it clear that his dad used their current probation to coerce him to take Ava in, as well as threaten to upend Ricki's plans as well. Phil told Ricki he was not going to do anything to jeopardize Ricki finishing the program and moving on to his fellowship. Phil also knew his dad probably realized that too. Hence, it was yet another leverage point held by the chairman to strengthen the coercion. After concluding the debrief on Phil's discussion with his father, Ricki simply said, "This is crazy and makes no sense at all."

Phil, Jr., quickly replied, "Sweetheart, wait until you hear what Ava told me, then tell me what is crazy." Phil then spent the next half hour not only recounting what Ava told him, but also described Ava's injury to her face, and the miracle home makeover that occurred when he was on call. At the end of it all Ricki could only say, "Your mom, no way."

"Exactly! That was my reaction too. But if I did not know my mom, it would make sense. But, like you said, no way," exclaimed Phil.

"Yeah, but then who? Ava is a weird chick, but not exactly the *kill me* type," said Ricki looking up at the ceiling and stretching his arms.

"She's less weird when you get to know her though. Last night I felt so sorry for her. I could tell she was crushed by my dad hitting her, if that is indeed what happened, "said Phil.

"I bet your dad did hit her," said Ricki now leaning in toward Phil, "Last week I heard your dad just about self-combusted in clinic. I had no details other than it was something to do with Ava. The neurology fellow in the same work room said everybody in there saw him just about lose his shit in front of her before he stormed out. Did Ava ever think it could be your dad behind it all? He is threatening you and your career, and evidently me and mine too. He has an embarrassing mess on his hands if Ava is pregnant with his child. If that is the case, then what do you think your mom would do? What do you think the dean would do? Shit, Phil, your dad is absolutely hosed in every way if what Ava told you is true."

Phil was looking at Ricki as though he'd seen a ghost and after seconds spurted out, "Holy F'ing crap! This cannot be happening! No way, no way. There has got to be another explanation." The color drained from Phil's face.

"Phil, I didn't tell you this earlier, but you want to know the gossip in the OR today? The scrub and circulator heard that you and Ava had been dating secretly for over a year," said Ricki.

"Bullshit! Where the hell does that come from? You know that's not true!" exclaimed Phil, Jr.

"Phil, you know *I* do. But perception can be everything for others that don't *know* you like I do," said Ricki with a soft understanding tone as he reached out and touched Phil's hand. Ricki quickly withdrew his hand though as he spied Dr. Kleinwurst angrily stomping across the cafeteria floor toward them. Kleinwurst had clearly spotted them first.

"Sorry to interrupt your date, *doctors*, but Wozniak had to leave the operating room before we finished so he could go throw up," Dr. Kleinwurst said, then muttered, "Weak

Polish piece of shit," and continued, "I need somebody to write the post op orders and check on my patient when she is more awake. If I am interrupting a *moment* between you two lovebirds, just know, I am not sorry." He then turned before even allowing a reply and continued stomping crossing the cafeteria to the far exit door leading toward the neurosurgical offices. They could hear Kleinwurst talking to himself, "Ava and Junior! Right! What a crock of shit."

"What an asshole," said Phil.

"Yea, he is. I'm pretty much numb to him by now though," responded Ricki, "He's a brilliant surgeon, but something crawled up inside him, ate his soul, and died. I'll write the orders and check on his patient in a little while. You should get out of here. You've got call again tomorrow night. I don't know the source of the rumors concerning you and Ava, but I have my suspicions. And Phil, I'm sorry, but I think your dad has lost it. We both need to be careful, and probably more careful in public. Tell Ava my thoughts. She needs to be careful too."

"Will do, chief," Phil said as he winked and stood to leave.

As Phil walked toward the locker room, he passed one of the general surgery chief residents who smiled at Phil and said, "Lucky man, Moss. Ava Chelidon! She is a beauty!"

All Phil could do was smile politely and nod his head. How was he to have a discussion with somebody he barely knew in a hospital hallway about what is really happening with Ava?

When Phil arrived home, there were two large suitcases and a few boxes on the floor in front of the TV. One suitcase was open, half filled with clothes. Ava was busily taking clothes from the suitcases and hanging them in the foyer coat closet. "Oh, hello, Phil," she said as he entered his apartment. He looked mildly flummoxed. Realizing this, Ava continued, "the police told me I could collect my clothes and some things as it would be a while before I was allowed back into my home. I drove up today and retrieved what I could. I hope you don't mind. I'll have everything put away shortly."

"Whatever," Phil, Jr., said with no attempt to disguise his sense of futility with the situation. He began walking toward his bedroom when he stopped, turned, and asked, "Ava, have you spoken to anyone at the hospital since whatever happened at your place a few nights ago happened?"

"Only your father, and...your mother," Ava replied, "why do you ask?"

"My mom! When did you call my mom?" asked Phil, Jr.

"The morning after I tried calling Phillip, but he did not answer his Nokia. I was scared and panicked and called your parents' home hoping to find Phillip there, and your mom answered. She seemed quite surprised when I called. She was extremely sweet, too sweet, and begged me to come to their house, but I just could not because I thought she was the one who wanted me dead," answered Ava.

"Well, there are rumors throughout the hospital that you and I are dating and have been for a long time. Where would that bullshit come from?" said Phil, Jr.

"Phil, I have wanted to be with your father and be part of your family for years, but I have started no rumors!" responded Ava. "I did not even call in sick to the clinic. Phillip called work for me to say I would be out all week."

"Ricki thinks my dad is behind all this," said Phil, Jr. as he looked out the window into the darkness.

"Behind saying we are dating?" asked Ava.

"Behind *everything*," replied Phil, Jr.

"So not your mom," said Ava with a pondering look on her face, as Phil shook his head and looked at the floor.

"There is no way my mom would have somebody killed. She may rip somebody a new one if they piss her off, but no way on murder. Are you sure you saw bullet holes in your bed and floor?" queried Phil, Jr.

"Very much so. I'll take you there and show you!" said Ava.

"I'm on call tomorrow. Maybe if I can get out early the next day we can drive up and you can show me," said Phil, Jr.

"Let's plan on it. Screw the cops. It's my house. So, unless they've changed the locks, I still have a key. The day after tomorrow I will show you what I am talking about," said Ava.

"Maybe we should tell the police we are going to look," said Phil.

"I would not even know who to call. It was Phillip that told me the police said I could retrieve my clothes and any valuables. I say the fewer people that know, the better," Ava said confidently.

"You are probably right. Now please tell me there is still spaghetti left over from last night," Phil, Jr., said with a smile.

The next day in the hospital for Phil, Jr., was very typical regarding the clinical workload, but very atypical regarding how he was treated by others. He would hear his name spoken in hushed whispers that were not quite out of earshot as he went about performing his duties. He also would hear, "Ava", and "Dad's N.P." in those same hushed voices. Some people would simply come up and say how happy they were for him to have found someone. A few people went so far as to offer congratulations, which he found to be odd. One of the ENT residents who was an intern with Phil, Jr., and clearly had a crush on Ava from the day he first saw her was the only one to start a conversation about Ava. When Phil tried to explain that he and Ava were not dating, but simply living together, the ENT resident was incredulous in a good-natured way and just walked away laughing.

Phil, Jr., survived another night on call and had worked things out with Ricki so he could leave as early as possible on Friday. Friday remained under control in the operating rooms, emergency room, and intensive care units. Phil, Jr., was able to leave by an unprecedented three p.m. He and Ava were on the road by three-thirty to her home south of Butler, an approximate forty-five-minute drive.

About the same time as Ava and Phil, Jr., were on their journey, Ricki Bouba and the other residents on rounds crossed paths with Dr. Moss in the ICU. Dr. Moss was quick to notice his son was not within the group and asked Ricki regarding Phil, Jr.'s whereabouts. Ricki was truthful and in front of the resident staff told Dr. Moss that his son was driving with Ava back to her house. This truthfulness strengthened the perceived validity of the rumor about Phil, Jr., and Ava's relationship in both the skeptical and less skeptical minds alike. There was an awkward silence followed by Dr. Moss asking Ricki whose car they took. Ricki did his best to reply politely that he had no idea. Dr. Moss then curtly excused himself and rushed from the ICU.

As Phil was driving north on Highway 8 about five miles from Ava's house, he saw flashing lights approaching rapidly in his rearview mirror. He knew he had been rushing, but did not think that going five or six miles over the speed limit would garner him a traffic citation. He slowed down and pulled onto the shoulder and became somewhat distraught when he realized he had left his wallet in his book bag at the apartment. The flashing lights never slowed down, and a deputy flew by them at high speed in a Ford Crown Victoria. Phil pulled the car back out onto the highway, and within another minute he saw flashing lights again in his rearview mirror. Once again, he pulled over. This time a state trooper followed moments later by a fire engine roared past Phil and Ava. As they turned off the highway, they saw billows of black smoke ahead of them, about a mile away.

Phil remarked, "Something must be on fire. We've had enough rain and snow though...."

Ava interrupted him with a simple, "Oh shit," and put her head in her hands.

"What?" responded Phil, Jr., looking at Ava. She was speechless. Phil looked forward and saw the mailbox with Ava's address number. Down a long dirt and gravel drive to the right were numerous emergency vehicles and a structure ablaze in the distance completely engulfed in flames. "Oh, shit is right," Phil, Jr., muttered. Phil parked the Valiant away from the drive entrance so as not to be anywhere near the inevitable coming and going of emergency vehicles. He looked at Ava who was now bawling and had pulled her blouse up to absorb her tears and muffle her cries. "I'm going to go ask somebody what is going on. Do you want to stay here or come with me?" Ava gestured with her left hand for him to go alone without saying a word or lifting her face from her blouse.

Phil grabbed his jacket from the backseat, crossed the road, and headed down the long driveway pocketed with puddles and made worse by deep ruts created by the heavy engines that had just passed down it. He was hoping to speak with a firefighter but was stopped by the deputy who had passed them on route 8 earlier. "Sorry sir, but nobody beyond this point according to the fire chief," said the deputy politely.

"That's my, um, friend's house. She's back in the car. Do you know what happened?" Phil said as he turned and pointed toward Ava in his car parked back on the road.

"I'm no expert, but the firefighters said a neighbor called in after hearing an explosion, like a sonic boom. He then said he saw a mushroom cloud. The poor elderly man thought it was the Russians attacking. The fire chief says that description and how fast the house has collapsed is classic for a gas leak and explosion. Anybody else living there? I'm sure the chief will want to talk to your, um, friend at some point too," said the deputy.

"Of course. No, she was the only one living there. No pets either. I have nothing to write with. Can I give you her name and my phone number? She was staying with me, and now it looks like she'll be with me for a while," said Phil, Jr., with a defeated tone in his voice.

The deputy quickly produced a notepad and pen. He wrote down the information Phil provided and said, "I'll be sure to pass this along to the fire chief and ask him to call her as soon as possible with all the information he knows about the fire. And tell her we are all sorry she has lost her home."

"Thanks deputy. I appreciate the information and your help," responded Phil, Jr., before returning to his car and Ava.

Ava had stopped crying by the time Phil returned. "I guess I am not showing you any bullet holes today," she said trying to be funny more for herself than for Phil.

"Certainly not here," said Phil with a sympathetic smile. "The fire chief says it was a gas leak and explosion. He should call you at the apartment today hopefully with an update," Phil said with the smile disappearing from his face.

"How the hell does that happen?" Ava angrily asked.

"Maybe a bullet hit a pipe?" Phil, Jr., replied.

"Great idea, if the home had gas. Everything is, or was, electric or wood-burning in my home," responded Ava.

"Ava, then how does your house explode?" Phil said, asking himself more than her.

"I guess we will see what the fire chief says," a resigned Ava said looking down at her lap. "Phil, I'm scared," Ava said now looking at Phil, "I don't have a home, I think somebody is trying to kill me, your father hit me and is...," her words stopped as she began crying again.

"Ava, you have a place to stay with me for now. Let's just worry about keeping you safe. We will find you a new place when the time is right. You did have insurance on your home, correct?" said Phil, Jr. Ava nodded in the affirmative. "Let's get back to Pittsburgh," said Phil, as he started the car.

Shortly after they arrived back to Phil, Jr.'s apartment the county fire chief called. He explained that an old underground liquid propane tank must have been disconnected from the house during a renovation and addition many years ago, well before Ava purchased the home, when the electric range top and oven, water heater, and heating elements were installed. He explained that a tank can spontaneously explode but the two most common culprits are an errant electrical current or elevated temperature. Because of the minute but real risk, these buried tanks were to be situated a certain distance from any building. Evidently this particular tank was left in place, still containing fuel, and the addition that included Ava's bedroom was built right over top of it. No building permit had ever been pulled by the contractor some thirty years ago when the work was done. Hence, no county inspections ever occurred. While it was a plausible explanation, it was difficult to embrace it as fact after what she had been through. Then again, the alleged tank was underneath her bedroom where agent Maggio unwittingly fired three rounds. She did not know what to believe in her current state of mind, other than she knew she had no home.

Phillip Moss, Sr., meanwhile in a panic thinking his son was walking into a potential house fire, had contacted Agent Robinson regarding the status of the plan to make Ava's home inhospitable. Agent Robinson informed him the plan was far more successful than planned. The intended appearance of a simple electrical fire caused by "old faulty wiring" turned into an unanticipated explosion that destroyed the entire structure. Agent Robinson assured Dr. Moss his son did not arrive until well after the event, and nobody was harmed. Dr. Moss was relieved with the news, but also knew he needed to get *his* plan wrapped up soon.

Back in Shadyside that evening Phillip and Cammie Moss were seated at the kitchen table in silence enduring another dinner together. Cammie spoke first and informed her husband about the panicked call from Ava a few mornings ago. He replied acknowledging that he was aware of "something" going on with Ava, and that evidently her home had burned down too.

"Oh my God, is she well? Is she okay?" asked Cammie.

"How do you mean? She has not been in to work all week," Phillip, Sr., replied.

"I was genuinely worried about her when she called here. Either she was in real danger, or she is schizophrenic. I told her to come here. She pulled up out front but never left her car. She took off with her tires screeching after a minute or two. Now I don't *know her like you do*, but she has always come across as very odd," said Cammie with an accusatory tone sprinkled in.

"Well odd or not, it seems she is staying with our son now," Phillip, Sr., said trying to hold back a smile, "There are rumors around the hospital that they have been secretly dating since she was here for Thanksgiving."

"Our Phillip? Are you sure?" a flummoxed Cammie asked.

"Why don't we have them over for dinner this weekend. I think it would be nice to see Phil outside the hospital and for you to get to know Ava better," suggested Phillip, Sr.

Cammie did not know whether to be happy for her son or enraged that this woman had somehow ensnared the hearts, or maybe other anatomy, of both her husband and son. She quickly decided to take the high road and put her best smile on replying, "I think that would be lovely." In the back of her mind though, she felt as though something very odd was occurring, but she had no idea what.

Phil, Jr., was on call Sunday, so Saturday was the day for dinner at his parents' home. His mother called him Friday evening with the invitation. Her phone call afforded him the opportunity to ask about any animosity she had toward Ava. Once again, Cammie Moss swallowed her pride and told her son the past is the past and she just wanted him to be happy and hoped Ava was feeling better. She said Ava is most certainly welcome in the Moss home. He did not know what to make of her comments entirely but decided not to press for clarification. He clearly did not hear anything from his mother that implied she wanted Ava dead.

The next day Ava and Phil, Jr., pulled up in front of the Moss home. The real estate sign next door immediately caught Phil, Jr.'s attention. "That's so sad," he moaned.

"What's so sad?" asked Ava.

"The Corchran's, or more specifically, Mrs. Corchran must have decided to move out. God, I loved that house as a kid. Her daughters were great friends to me and my sisters growing up. It will feel weird knowing somebody else is in that house," confessed Phil, Jr.

"A house is a house," Ava flatly replied as they exited Phil's Plymouth and walked to the front door.

Cammie Moss warmly greeted Phil and Ava. Phil gave his mom an affectionate embrace. Ava chose to extend her hand and shake Mrs. Moss's hand after an awkward second as each considered hugging the other. "Your father said he was going for a walk, so he should be back soon. Please come in the kitchen and keep me company," Cammie Moss said with as much cheer in her voice as she could muster.

Mrs. Moss was nicely dressed in heels and a tightly fitted dress. She wore an apron in the kitchen. Ava and Phil, Jr., took seats at the kitchen table. "I'm sorry to hear about your house burning down," said Mrs. Moss to Ava as she kept her back turned toward Ava and her son while working at the kitchen counter.

Ava reflexively thanked Mrs. Moss for the condolences regarding her destroyed home. Phil, Jr., however, suddenly sat up straight and asked, "Mom, from whom did you hear about Ava's house?"

"Oh, your father told me it had burned down the other day," replied Cammie Moss keeping her back turned toward the kitchen table. "It's so nice that Ava is able to stay with you while, uh, everything gets sorted out," she continued.

"Of course, I forgot I had mentioned it to dad," said Phil, Jr., catching Ava's eyes and shaking his head side to side and lifting his eyebrows. Ava immediately understood that neither Phil, Jr., nor she had shared the news of her home exploding in flames with anyone. As they silently looked at each other trying to comprehend the meaning of the situation, the front door opened noisily, and claws could be heard on the hardwood floor making their way rapidly to the kitchen.

Dr. Phillip Moss entered the kitchen well behind Charlie who was already burying himself under Phil, Jr.'s legs trying to maximize body contact as much as possible and coaxing any dangling hand to pet him. "Hello, Ava…son. I'm glad you could join us tonight," said Dr. Phillip Moss stiffly as he walked over and gave his wife an emotionless kiss on the cheek. "I ran into the realtor for next door the other day. She told me the Corchran's are asking only four-hundred-twenty-five thousand dollars."

"I don't know if four-hundred-twenty-five thousand dollars qualifies for using the word, only!" remarked Phil, Jr.

"Well, it is a beautiful house with a pool, in a great neighborhood convenient to downtown," he said to no one in particular and then turned and looked at his son and Ava continuing, "and it would be a very *safe* place for a young family to live."

The words and the way they were delivered were not lost on either Ava or Phil, Jr. A chill went down Phil, Jr.'s spine as he digested the intent of his father's comments. Rage was boiling up inside of Ava as she wanted to tell her lover that she would gladly live in that home next door with *him*, if he only had the balls to leave his wife and marry her. Phil, Jr., sensed her rapidly growing ire and put his hand atop hers and looked at her with pleading eyes not to erupt. The last thing he wanted was to see his mother become collateral damage from whatever Ava wanted to say to his father. Ava swallowed hard and then excused herself to use the restroom, leaving the three Mosses to themselves for a moment.

While Dr. Moss poured himself a Scotch, Mrs. Moss broke the brief silence, while keeping her attention on the kitchen counter and asked her son, "I was a bit surprised to hear you and Ava were roommates. How long has *that* been going on?"

Phil, Jr., took a moment to find the correct words that would explain the bizarre intersection of his life with Ava's. As he opened his mouth to explain, Ava, who had been just outside the kitchen listening stepped in and said, "Well Cammie, I don't know what you mean by *that*, but your son and I have been friends for a long time. But I only moved in with him this week, and he has been a Godsend." She then leaned down, put her right arm around his neck and kissed Phil, Jr., on his left cheek before sitting down next to him. Mrs. Moss had turned at the sound of Ava's voice and witnessed it all. Dr. Moss, meanwhile, choked on his Scotch. After sitting Ava reached up and intertwined the fingers of her right hand with those of Phil, Jr.'s left hand that was resting on the table. Phil, Jr., turned beet red as both parents saw their son holding a woman's hand for the first time in a very long time.

As they all enjoyed a fine dinner in the dining room, Ava's small acts of affection continued in subtle and tasteful ways to anyone observing. Only the recipient of these affectionate acts seemed bothered by them. Phil, Jr., could sense, however, the tension among the three others at the table began to melt. Natural conversations were breaking out between Ava and his mother. His typically stoic father was sharing funny anecdotes regarding his first dates with his mother and from his residency. For the first time since returning to Pittsburgh Phil, Jr., witnessed happy parents that for all the world looked completely in love with each other.

At the end of the evening while Mrs. Moss and Ava were clearing the table, Dr. Moss told his son he had something to show him in his office. While in the office Dr. Moss told his son to have a seat. Dr. Moss pulled out a piece of canvas that had been wrapped around something about 9 inches long. "Here, go ahead and unwrap this," Phil, Sr., said.

Phil, Jr., quickly unrolled the loose canvas to find a simple surgical instrument. It was nothing more than a smooth flattened end with a cylindrical handle, all made from a single piece of metal. "Uh, thanks, dad."

"You do know what that is, right?" asked Dr. Moss.

"It looks like a number four," replied Phil, Jr.

"Yes. It is a Penfield four," said Dr. Moss, "but more importantly, it was Dr. Penfield's own number four. My fellowship mentor gave it to me. I want you to have it."

"Thanks dad. Wilder Penfield's own surgical instrument! This should be in a museum! But why now?" asked Phil, Jr.

"In gratitude for how happy you have made your mother, and in turn me. There are certain things in life we do for the sakes of others and not for ourselves directly. For instance, you want to be a neurosurgeon and to complete your training here at Pittsburgh. For that to occur, I need to not only remain chairman but also remain married to your mother. You saw how she transformed tonight. Few things would make her happier than to see you complete your training here and stay on as faculty. The thought of you raising a family nearby would be a dream come true for her," Dr. Moss concluded as he looked at photos of all his children and Cammie on his desk.

"But dad, I'm not sure I...," Phil, Jr., spoke before being interrupted by his father.

"No buts. We are not discussing choices here. We are discussing things that must be done for the sake of the family; actions that may seem irrational, but actions nonetheless we take to support and preserve our family. For instance, I know how much you loved the Corchran's home next door. I knew that Mrs. Corchran selling her home would make you unhappy for many nostalgic reasons that I fail to fully understand," stated Dr. Moss.

"Yes, but yea I was kind of sad when I saw they were selling it," said Phil, Jr.

"Well, they are not selling it. They have sold it," said Dr. Moss.

"Really? Already? How long was it on the market? To whom? The Corchran's were like family to me. I hope nice people move in. I kind of fantasized about living there one day. I could have been next door to you and mom," Phil, Jr., babbled with pressured speech and sadness in his eyes.

"Are you done?" Dr. Moss asked.

"Sorry. Yes, sir," replied Phil, Jr.

"If you want dreams to come true, then you must make sacrifices. You should know that by now given the career path you have taken. While many of your college buddies are working forty-hour weeks, attending each other's weddings, going to high school and college reunions, collecting nice paychecks, driving nice cars, living in nice homes, worrying about the scores of ball games, and planning poker nights, you chose to work one-hundred hour weeks, live each day worrying whether someone might live or die at your hands, neglecting your health, missing weddings, reunions, ball games, concerts, and poker, with a social life living in a suspended state of animation while you barely sleep and eat enough to make it through each day. Your nutrition is knowledge, information, and surgical experience. All so that one day you can call yourself a brain surgeon and do some good with the skills and knowledge you have amassed. I can tell you; it is worth it. But like a just war that ends in victory there will be casualties, scars, and ruin. So, at some point in your career you honor and recognize the fallen, be they lives, relationships, or opportunities, dress the scars, rebuild the ruins, and persist and keep doing good as best you can. I've caused casualties, scars, and ruin amongst the good done. While no son should bare the sins of his father, it is a situation that repeats itself throughout history," Dr. Moss concluded now looking directly into his son's eyes.

"Geez Dad, you make it sound like being a neurosurgeon is a Greek tragedy. You know I'd do anything for you and mom. You also know for how long I have wanted to become a neurosurgeon, to follow in your footsteps, and to be like you. But I feel I've gone above and beyond the call of duty already with how hard I have worked and now helping Ava. What else can I possibly do?" asked Phil, Jr.

"It's not what you can do, it is what you must do," Dr. Moss replied firmly as he bit his lower lip.

"How so?" Phil, Jr., replied with trepidation.

"I've not answered all your questions about the Corchran's house yet," said Dr. Moss.

"Damn it Dad, I don't care about that house now. Whoever bought it, bought it. What do you want from me?" Phil, Jr., pleaded.

"Maybe you should care," said Dr. Moss resolutely.

"Okay, I care. Please tell me about them," Phil, Jr., responded sarcastically and out of character for speaking to his father.

"We have bought the Corchran home," stated Dr. Moss.

"We? You and mom?" his perplexed son responded.

"Not exactly. Our family trust has purchased the home. A trust in which you are a beneficiary," replied Dr. Moss.

"So, I own the home?" an even more perplexed Phil, Jr., responded.

"No, the trust owns it. Consider it a house owned by your mother and me that automatically becomes yours and your sisters when we die. All you need to know is that you will have the opportunity to live in it soon. I've already spoken to your sisters about this. They think it's a great investment, but neither have any desire to return to Pittsburgh for their respective careers," said Dr. Moss.

"I can live in it?" a still perplexed Phil, Jr., asked.

"Not quite yet, but soon, and only under specific and enduring conditions," said Dr. Moss.

"Heck dad, I'll cut the grass. I'll keep it clean. I'll sweep the sidewalk. I'll learn to take care of the pool. I'll shovel the snow. I will take very good care of it!" exclaimed Phil excitedly.

"Yes. I am certain you will do all those basic tasks of home ownership. But you will need to do those things living there with Ava as your wife," a stone-faced Dr. Moss replied.

Phil, Jr., felt as though he could not breathe. At that moment, he knew why his father was telling him to marry Ava, but the only word that escaped his lips was, "Why?"

"Son, I am not going to explain the *why*. I will explain, however, the *if not*," Dr. Moss replied with an air of impatience. "For you, it would put your ability to remain in this residency in jeopardy, and in turn make it very difficult for you to join another program elsewhere. Dr. Kleinwurst has assured me that would be the case. For Dr. Bouba, Dr. Kleinwurst and I fear he may need more time abroad to sharpen his surgical independence before we can allow him to complete this residency. He would need to be very cautious back in Cameroon. If somehow people there were to become aware of his *proclivities*, then my understanding is he could be dealt with quite harshly by both the government and the Cameroonians. It would be a shame if he never returned. As well, other issues could become out of my control and may make it impossible for me to remain as chairman, or even on faculty. As for your mother, I suspect she would be devastated and distraught for her own reasons. I fear she would not have the will or strength to go on. The family trust would dissolve and the Corchran house placed back on the market. And finally, Ava. She is special to me and is a remarkable young woman. She needs a good man though in her life for stability and with which to raise a family. I cannot think of a better man than you. Our family benefits by inviting her to join it. I am certain I can count on you to do the right thing." With those final words Phillip Moss, Sr., walked out of the room and back toward the kitchen leaving his slack jawed son by himself. Phil, Jr., remained seated. The Penfield four slipped from his hands landing on the hardwood floor and he began to weep.

## Chapter Nineteen: The Best Man

As soon as the Sunday morning rounds were completed, Phil, Jr., signaled to Ricki that they needed to talk again. Phil, Jr., recounted line by line the very one-sided discussion he had with his father the night before. Ricki was appalled by what he heard, but a large part of him was not surprised. The chairman seemed to always get what he wanted. This, however, was on a whole different level. Arranged marriages did not happen with white boys from upper class families in America. The two of them brainstormed for a plan that would free Phil, Jr., from this mess, but all solutions had hypothetical and likely collateral damage that neither was willing to accept.

Phil, Jr., could not bear the thought of Ricki returning to Cameroon with the real possibility of Dr. Bouba never returning alive if the right words were whispered into the wrong ears. Thoughts of how happy his mother appeared that night at dinner filled his consciousness too. It had been so long since he had seen his mother behaving as he remembered her from before he left for college. He wondered if she was happy because she thought her son had a girlfriend, or that her husband no longer had his. Either scenario left him feeling as though a chunk of his soul was missing, as though he was betraying each parent to please the other.

Ricki saw the talent and brilliance in Phil, Jr. He knew that Phil, Jr., had the intelligence and hands to become a very accomplished neurosurgeon. He also knew that Phil,

Jr.'s dream and life goal was to become a prominent neurosurgeon, and in many respects follow his father's professional path after training under his father's tutelage. Ricki knew he had to let Phil, Jr., make the decisions as to how far he would bend in order to fulfill that dream and goal. Ricki could see their relationship being sacrificed upon the altar of neurosurgery with Dr. Phillip Moss, Sr., presiding as priest. While he and Phil, Jr., had developed a loving bond, he was always struck in conversation by how much Phil, Jr., idolized his father, even throughout all the recent drama. Seeking paternal approval seemed to always be the top priority for Phil, Jr. Ricki was rapidly realizing his relationship with Phil, Jr., and Phil, Jr.'s own identity were likely doomed. The power of son needing to please father was simply too great.

Toward the end of their conversation both of their moods turned somber as the new reality about to unfold sank into their consciousnesses. They tried to convince themselves they were not losing a war, but simply a battle. They would find a way forward together in the future. For now, the priorities needed to be professional success and personal safety. Love and happiness would need to be shelved.

"But what does Ava think about all this? I mean, shit, she doesn't love you," asked Ricki.

"I am unsure. Part of me thinks she is in on this whole twisted plot with my father. Another part of me thinks she sees me as an opportunity to be part of the Moss family, and yet another part of me thinks she is scared for her life and is seeking any port in a storm," replied Phil, Jr.

"Probably wise to ask her. Don't you think?" asked Ricki.

"Probably so, but I don't think her answer will change anything," Phil, Jr. replied with downcast eyes.

"Have you guys talked about this?" asked Ricki.

"Not really. I sense excitement on her part. I pretty much only feel dread," replied Phil, Jr.

"Jesus Phil, if you are going to fall on this sword, at least have an understanding with her first. You cannot let your true self be wiped from the face of the earth! Damn it man, it's difficult enough imagining you marrying Ava, but I still want *you* to remain *you*, for both our sakes!" exclaimed Ricki.

"I hear you, Ricki. I will, of course, speak with Ava. But one question for you, will you be my, uh, best man?" Phil, Jr., asked with a smile and a tear forming in his eye.

"Always," replied Ricki as they embraced.

"I guess I have to fucking ask her to marry me now," said Phil, Jr., with a tortured smile breaking out across his face.

## Chapter Twenty: The Wedding Party

"I need a drink, and I don't drink," said Kamal as he struggled to keep the phone pressed to his ear. "You are getting married? To a woman? And she is pregnant? Holy Lakshmi Phil! I knew a neurosurgical residency could change a person, but this is unprecedented."

"I'll save details for when I see you. I want you in the wedding. My apologies for the short notice. Can you be in Pittsburgh a week from Saturday? I've asked Ava to include Lisa in the bridal party too. Ava does not have family or many friends. You and Lisa could come together. It would be great to see you both again," said Phil.

"Lisa and I don't see each other that much anymore, given this residency thing we are both doing. Oh wait, speak of the devil, here she is just coming out of my shower," Kamal proclaimed.

Phil could then hear Lisa's irritated voice asking who was on the phone and why nobody needed to know she had just finished showering. There were some indiscernible words made by Kamal, followed by a shriek from Lisa. This was followed by sounds compatible with the phone being dropped, possibly kicked, then landing somewhere with a clang, all while muffled words between Lisa and Kamal continued. Eventually the mechanical sounds of a phone being picked up were followed by Lisa's confident voice saying, "What the fuck Phil! We haven't seen you for over two years and now you want us in Pittsburgh to be in your wedding in under two weeks! Damn straight we will be there you total asshole! I'm giving the phone back to this prick who is looking at me and drooling. I need to get dressed." Phil, Jr., never was able to say a word to Lisa.

Kamal and Phil, Jr., promised to talk more later. Phil, Jr., gave Kamal the skeleton details of the when, where, and what to wear. He also told Kamal that Ava would reach out to Lisa at some point as well. He thanked Kamal profusely for not asking too many questions and for being such a reliable friend.

Phil, Jr., through his sisters recruited Trey and Josh for his groomsmen in addition to Kamal. That gave him Ricki as his best man and three groomsmen. Ava, likewise, had Ella as her maid of honor and Phil, Jr.'s two sisters and Lisa as bridesmaids. The discussions Phil, Jr., had with his sisters were surprisingly brief. He sensed as though they had somehow been briefed on the "situation" and instructed not to "make waves." Every time he tried to begin to explain the situation to them, each immediately redirected the conversation. He desperately wanted to share his feelings and garner their opinions and guidance. He thought each sister almost sounded tearful at the conclusion of each phone conversation. They promised their unwavering support for him and hoped he and Ava would be happy together. He appreciated the unfiltered crass comments of Lisa much more.

As Phil, Jr., hung up the phone after speaking with his older sister, Anne, he looked over at Ava who was sitting at the kitchen table and asked, "What are we doing?"

"We are getting married. I will become Mrs. Phillip Moss, and you will be my husband. It's that simple," Ava said with little emotion.

"Will you be happy married to me?" asked Phil, Jr.

"Not if you always sound this pathetic. But otherwise, yes, I will be happy. We will live in the house of your dreams and raise beautiful children," replied Ava coolly.

"But what about my dad? You and he were…," Phil pondered searching for words.

"Fucking? Yes, quite regularly. I see no need for that to stop. Just as I see no need for you to refrain from what makes you happy," Ava replied with brutal honesty.

"So, this, us, whatever the hell it is, is all a charade?" responded Phil, Jr.

"Call it what you like, but I think this so-called charade is a beautiful arrangement for everyone," Ava spoke as she flipped pages in a bridal magazine.

"How so? This is completely fucked up!" Phil, Jr., responded with a hint of anger as he stood up from the couch.

"Sweetie, *you* asked me to marry you. Remember? Plus, you and I both would not want *our* child to be raised by a single parent. Would you?" Ava rhetorically responded while finally looking up from the magazine with a smirk. "Consider this darling; you are able to continue to pursue your dreams and goals and live in a fancy house next to your parents. Dr. Bouba, likewise, stays safely within the confines of the country and will move on to his fellowship. And just maybe he will return to Pittsburgh as faculty afterward. I am sure you would like that. Your mother is relieved by assuming there is no affair between Phillip and me, and gains grandchildren who will live next door in the process. Phillip keeps his precious reputation and marriage intact. He remains chair, while gaining his favorite N.P. as his daughter-in-law and continued *friend* and next-door neighbor. I am able to join a family headed by someone I love, become a mother, and most importantly, remain alive."

Phil, Jr.'s brain went numb with the cold logic of Ava's declaration. How could her assertions be so right, yet so wrong. Here she was preparing to marry him, and outwardly stating she was in love with his father and intending for that torrid affair to continue indefinitely. He felt the vortex he had been pulled into growing in strength and pulling him deeper toward its eye. At that moment the phone rang. He picked up the receiver. His mother had called to speak with Ava. Mrs. Moss was excitedly talking about the catering service she had secured for the wedding and needed to share the good news with Ava. As he handed the phone to Ava, he realized the walls of the vortex's eye had closed, heightened, and now surrounded him. Escape would require dramatic action on his part. Action that would cause harm to those he loved and respected.

That night Phil, Jr., had a tortured night of little sleep, made more difficult by Ava now sharing his bed with him. As he tossed and turned, his mind kept running through scenarios or solutions that he and Ricki may not have considered. The unthinkable kept rising to the forefront of his consciousness as the only solution. The elimination of one person would free him to complete his residency, live his life as he wished, marry whom he chose, and protect Ricki from harm. He silently wrestled with how and when he could accomplish such a task as he drifted in and out of sleep.

He saw Ava's smirking face as his hands wrapped around her neck. She gave no struggle as he looked at her smirking face. He squeezed harder and harder without effect. Finally, the color in her face became rubrous and plethoric, yet the smirk remained. She started to struggle as the color of her face became almost purple, then blue. Her feeble struggles stopped. He released his grip and found himself looking into the bulging dead eyes of his father. He heard sirens getting louder. He tried to run but could not. He tried to scream. Suddenly he felt a blow to his shoulder. The sound of wailing sirens was replaced by the sharp staccatos of his alarm clock. He opened his eyes in a panic and reached out for Ava in the darkness. As his hands found her shoulder in the darkness she simply said, "Time to get up, doctor. And please turn your alarm off." Phil, Jr., dragged his sweat-soaked body out of bed and took a quick shower before heading into the hospital. He was still shaking as he walked toward the bank of elevators in the hospital. He realized then, there was no way he could break out of the vortex that contained him.

**Chapter Twenty-One: I do**

The Pittsburgh Golf Club served as the venue for both the wedding and reception. Ava was predictably stunning, dressed in her white gown. She made no attempt to hide her early pregnancy, but it really did not matter. Phil, Jr., did his best to keep a forced smile plastered across his face. Dr. and Mrs. Moss proudly beamed throughout the ceremony. The wedding party seemed to mimic Phil, Jr., regarding facial expressions and emotions. The eye contact amongst the wedding party when the preacher asked for anyone to come forward and protest the impending union did not go unnoticed by Dr. Phillip Moss, Sr., as the smile on his face evaporated. After what seemed like an eternity, no one spoke. Vows were exchanged and the couple was joined officially in holy matrimony. The string quartet began playing Vivaldi and the congregation applauded as Dr. Phillip and Mrs. Ava Moss walked back down the aisle.

The reception soon followed in an adjoining ballroom. The quartet was substituted with a disc jockey, and the freshly betrothed took the dance floor to Aerosmith's "I Don't Want to Miss a Thing". There was not a dry eye in the wedding party apart from Josh who had already wandered over to the still covered buffet inspecting the food and stealing what he could before being shooed away. To the outsider Ava and Phil, Jr., dancing and the emotionally moved friends and family failing to hold back tears was a beautiful sight. To those aware of the atrocity, however, the tears were an expression of sadness and grief as they watched their friend or brother have a piece of him seemingly die before their eyes for unclear reasons. Only Ricki grasped the full and complete picture. One of the more uncomfortable moments was after the first dance when the bride and father of the groom danced, while Cammie danced with her son. Those paying attention could see the uncharacteristic awkwardness in Dr. Moss, Sr.'s posture. Ava seemed to be very much enjoying the moment and pressed herself up against him on more than one occasion. At the conclusion of Stevie Wonder's "Signed, Sealed, Delivered" Dr. Moss, Sr. could not return to his seat fast enough, forgetting his wife on the dance floor. The best man stayed by the groom's side during the festivities as situations allowed. Ricki took over dancing with Cammie Moss for the next song.

Ricki choked back tears as he gave the toast. His emotions touched almost everyone in attendance. After Dr. Bouba sat back down at the conclusion of the toast and subsequent salutations and applause, Dr. Phillip Moss, Sr., leaned back in his chair and looking behind his wife caught Ricki's attention and said with a wry smile, "The Cleveland Clinic will be fortunate to have you as a fellow. Well done." Ricki could only return a nod of acknowledgment and resisted the urge to communicate anything more. Dr. Moss, Sr., then turned to his wife, Cammie, and asked, "Where is Jack Moretti? We did invite him. Correct?"

Cammie replied, "Yes. He sent his regrets that he could not attend the wedding."

"Really?" Dr. Moss, Sr., responded with a hurt look on his face.

"Yes, dear. Don't look so wounded. This is your son's wedding, not ours. Eat, drink, and be merry," Cammie cheerfully replied.

The evening eventually wound down with the dance floor mainly occupied by drunk neurosurgical residents. The sendoff of the new couple had the appropriate celebratory mood. Ava and Phil, Jr., we're headed to Aruba for five days for their honeymoon. Cammie and her husband made their way into the darkness of the club parking lot when a dark figure suddenly stood before them, startling them both. "Good evening. Sorry to frighten you both. Ma'am, do you mind if your husband has a word with Mr. Moretti? It will just be a few minutes," said Joey Scarlucci. Dr. Moss was then directed toward a dark SUV parked at the end of the parking lot. He gave his wife the keys to his Jaguar and told her to wait in the car for him.

Joey opened the rear door and Dr. Moss climbed in to see Jack Moretti sitting on the other side, holding a wrapped gift. "Please give this to Phil, Jr., and let him know I am sorry I did not attend the wedding," said Jack without his usual smile and warm greeting.

"Jack, I will, but this is odd. If you couldn't make the wedding, you could have just mailed the gift," said Dr. Moss, Sr.

"All true. Some things I just need to deliver in person though. And I wanted to deliver this gift as well as this message: we are even. I will always remember what you did for me, but I will also always remember what you did to your son, and tried to do to his now bride, your concubine. I can't be part of that. At some point honor and principle outlasts loyalty and even friendship. I wish you well, Phillip," Jack stated solemnly. Almost on cue, Joey opened the door allowing Dr. Moss to exit. When Dr. Moss extended his hand to shake Jack's hand, he was met with Jack Moretti turning away and looking out the car window into the night, with Jack saying, "Time to go, Joey."

A crushed Phillip Moss walked numbly through the dark with his son's wedding gift held loosely at his side. He slid into the driver's seat with Cammie patiently waiting on the passenger side and tossed the gift upon the dashboard. Before she could ask why Jack had arrived late, let alone, at all, and been so secretive, he sternly stated he did not want to talk about it, and to not forget to give Phil, Jr., the gift. The short drive home was accomplished in silence.

Cammie was hoping that on such a night of celebration that maybe her husband would finally treat her as he had long ago. She fell asleep that night untouched and thinking about the new tennis pro, Robert, at the club that liked to flirt with her. He made her feel special. She promised herself to flirt back next time Robert flashed his killer smile and remarked on what she was wearing. With those thoughts she fell asleep and had dreams she had not had in a very long time.

## Chapter Twenty-Two: Phillip the Third

After returning from Aruba the new couple's focus turned to moving into the Corchran's house and preparing for the baby. Ava continued to work full time. By the time Ricki's residency completion celebration rolled around, Ava was about halfway through the pregnancy. The obstetrician, Dr. Rebecca Wepfer, calculated the date of conception to have been about Valentine's Day. "How romantic," she stated as the twenty-week ultrasound was being performed. Dr. Wepfer then asked if Ava would like to know the sex of her child. Ava nodded yes and was informed she was carrying a baby boy.

At the June twenty-eighth chief resident graduation party, Ava proudly told everyone she was having a boy. She assured the other nurse practitioners that she would continue working as long as she could and come back as soon as possible. While Ava beamed with pride and joy, Phil, Jr., was much more subdued and could barely muster a smile when congratulated about his impending parenthood. While the annual chief resident graduation was routinely a time of happiness for all residents, primarily because it was an open bar and free food, this year for Phil, Jr., it marked Ricki's departure. The last person in the world Phil, Jr., wanted to see or speak with, Dr. Kleinwurst, suddenly appeared at his side holding a Scotch. "You know I'm no idiot," said Dr. Kleinwurst looking out upon the gathering.

"Of course, sir," Phil, Jr., quickly responded.

"I know what's been going on, and why you are moping around tonight like your dog died," said Kleinwurst with an unexpected tinge of sympathy. "My younger son just came out, as your generation says."

"Oh, I did not know you had children, sir," responded Phil, Jr.

"Four. Two boys and two girls. I dearly love them all. My younger boy, Stephen, is a junior at NYU. Brilliant kid, thinking of med school. His older brother is in his last year of law school there. Damn, I think I'd be prouder of a gay physician son, than a straight attorney son. Anyway, the girls are older and married. From what my wife tells me I'll be a grandfather soon. Shit. That kind of news makes a parent feel old," said Kleinwurst as he took another sip of Scotch.

"My mom seems very excited about the baby and becoming a grandma," said Phil, Jr.

"Well, technically she won't be. How's your dad handling it?" asked Kleinwurst as he looked Phil, Jr. in the eye and took another sip.

"He doesn't ask much about the baby," responded Phil, Jr., breaking eye contact with Dr. Kleinwurst.

"I'm sure that doesn't surprise you," said Kleinwurst.

"No sir," said Phil, Jr. realizing the unspoken communication that was now taking place.

"I apologize for *most* of the shit, I've given you and Ricki," said Kleinwurst. "You both will be fine neurosurgeons, and more importantly are good people. I've asked your dad to bring Ricki back after fellowship to help with some of the functional and tumor work, we are doing. He would be a great asset to the department."

"Does Ricki know that sir?" Phil, Jr. excitedly asked.

"No. I thought you'd like to tell him. Now, holy Moses, would you enjoy this party! And best wishes for the baby. I hope he has your eyes," Dr. Kleinwurst said before slapping the back of Phil, Jr.'s shoulder, downing the last of his Scotch and heading to the bar for another.

Well, that was unexpected thought Phil, Jr. The "has your eyes" comment seemed overly complimentary to Phil, Jr. Both he and Ava had striking blue eyes, so why would it matter? A lot of people would comment that he looked just like his father *except for his blue eyes*. Then Kleinwurst's parting comment hit him like a freight train. Dr. Kleinwurst certainly was no idiot. Ava had blue eyes. Phil, Jr., had blue eyes. Cammie had blue eyes. Phillip Moss, Sr., had brown eyes. In the scientific discipline known as Mendelian genetics, if the baby had brown eyes, then Phil, Jr., could not be the biological father. There was a fifty percent chance, a coin toss, whether this baby would have brown eyes given Dr. Phiilip Moss, Sr., was the true father. Immersed in a medical community for every aspect of his professional, social, and family life, there would be no hiding the glaring reality of eye color in the child. The permanent eye color could take up to a year to develop, especially if brown. This would be one more source of anxiety to pile upon the mountain of anxiety already burdening his shoulders. He shook off this newly discovered burden and went to find Ricki. Kleinwurst better have told him the truth, because Phil, Jr., was going to share Kleinwurst's comments with Ricki as soon as he found him. He needed something positive to occupy his consciousness immediately.

Phil, Jr., found Ava first who was excitedly talking with Ella and another nurse practitioner. He let her know that he was looking for Ricki to share some good news. Ava grabbed his arm, pulled him toward her, and whispered in his ear, "I've done everything I could under the circumstances to convince your father to recruit Ricki back to the department. I hope I've succeeded and that's the good news you are telling Ricki." She gave a wink and a coy smile before waving him off and then returned to her animated conversation with Ella.

Phil, Jr., found Ricki gathered with the other two chief residents who were graduating. They were collectively discussing about what cars they would drive after they each had paid off their quarter million dollars in student debt. One of the chief residents proudly extolled the virtues of a well-maintained AMC Pacer. While the other proclaimed he was getting a new BMW M3 ordered as soon as he started his new job in Cincinnati. Phil, Jr., decided to share the news from Kleinwurst in front of all three. That way, he had witnesses should Kleinwurst renege on his earlier comments. Ricki stayed composed, but Phil, Jr., could tell he wanted to reach out and give him a heartfelt embrace. The other two sang Ricki's virtues as to how he would be a natural to fill that role on the faculty. There were smiles all around. Phil, Jr., told Ricki he was going to visit his friends, Kamal and Lisa in Cleveland, so might as well help Ricki move there for his fellowship. Phil, Jr., was starting a neuropathology rotation and would have some flexibility in his schedule for the first time in years. Ricki accepted the offer with a smile that grew even larger than when Phil, Jr., mentioned Kleinwurst's comments.

Summer turned to fall. Kamal had begun a research rotation in Cleveland, so Phil, Jr., made it a point to visit Kamal and Lisa monthly, or that's what he told everyone. While he did see Kamal and Lisa, he cherished his time with Ricki. As Ava's pregnancy progressed deeper into the third trimester, he felt guilty leaving for a weekend despite her insistence that he visit his friends. When Phil, Jr., returned late on an early November Sunday night, Ava was lying on the couch with his mother and Ella seated in chairs. Cammie Moss looked at her son somewhat disapprovingly and said, "I think you need to take your wife to the hospital. She's about to become a mother."

Phillip Joseph Moss III was born at four thirty-seven a.m. and weighed an even seven pounds. The neonate's eye color was deemed "indeterminate" by the pediatrician and obstetrician. Mother and baby were healthy with a planned discharge for the following day. Late that Monday afternoon Phil, Jr.'s mother and father came to visit Ava and the baby. Cammie was exploding with joy as she held Phillip Joseph. When she offered the baby to her husband to hold, he simply said, "I'm okay just feeling the fontanel," as he reached out and ran his thumb across the baby's soft spot.

"Absolutely precious," said Cammie as she handed Phillip Joseph back to Ava. After exchanging a few more pleasantries with the young couple, the new "grandparents" left Magee-Women's hospital and headed home. Ava remained completely comfortable with the visit, while Phil, Jr., did his best to absorb as much information from the Weather Channel playing on the wall mounted TV in Ava's maternity ward room until his parents departed.

After Phillip Joseph finished nursing Ava held him up and beckoned Phil, Jr., to hold him for a while. Phil, Jr., took the new life in his hands swaddled in a baby blanket and stood looking out the window trying to show the newborn as much of Pittsburgh as could be seen from the room's vantage point. He bent down, kissed the baby's forehead, and whispered, "Welcome to the world baby brother."

## Chapter Twenty-Three: Good Neighbors

    With Ava delivering Phillip Joseph in early November the holiday season made it quite easy for her to refrain from returning to work until after the new year. Phil, Jr., spent more time at home than he ever had after becoming a resident. His six months of time on neuropathology ended with the year however, and he would be back on the clinical service in January. With three human beings named Phillip Moss in the same immediate family, Ava struggled to find an appropriate nickname if she were to abandon "Phillip Joseph." She considered PJ, P-Three, PhilJo, Joey, and Joe. After looking at her newborn sleeping and saying each name aloud, she decided Phillip Joseph was most appropriate. Future friends, teachers, classmates, teammates, or coaches could use any of the other names. She was sticking with the given names.

    With the realization that both Ava and Phil, Jr., would be at home a lot less come the new year, a plan was needed to care for Phillip Joseph. "Grandma" Moss was more than happy to help out but made it very clear that she still needed her tennis time twice a week. Some of those days included late afternoon and early evening "tennis time" she said that were hard to predict. Phil, Jr., would be back to in-hospital call every third or every other night. Ava was home every night and weekends but worked ten to twelve-hour days. It became apparent that they would need to hire somebody to help look after Phillip Joseph. This need for childcare became a dinner table discussion item in both Moss houses. Dr. Phillip Moss, Sr., told his wife he would survey the department faculty and staff for anyone that may be interested in watching Phillip Joseph two days a week. Cammie had bravely but excitedly volunteered to watch her "grandchild" on her non-tennis days.

One of the secretaries, Angela Hawkins, in the neurosurgery department had a daughter who was finishing her undergraduate degree in English Literature at Pitt. Her daughter only needed six more credit hours, so she had only two classes on Monday, Wednesday, and Friday, leaving her Tuesday and Thursday for reading days. Her classes did not start until the third week in January, so she was more than ready to put in twenty to twenty-four hours per week, and get a jump start on the syllabus of her upcoming classes. She had babysat while in high school and college for many faculty and was universally loved by the children she watched. Some of the mothers were not too enthralled with her, however, and not because of any competence, reliability, or safety issues. These mothers preferred other less capable sitters because Amy Hawkins was beautiful, breathtakingly so. Fathers could not help reacting foolishly in her presence. These fathers' wives had front row seats to the display of awkward male stupidity every time Amy crossed the threshold into a home. The only father, a spine surgeon, that actually did something reprehensible when driving Amy home one evening, had to explain his limping gait and bloody broken nose to his wife when he returned. It was a painful and embarrassing way for him to learn that Amy had a black belt in Taekwondo. The residents learned of the event and called that particular attending, "Ap Chagi", behind his back for years afterward.

These stories were shared with Ava when she first spoke to Amy's mother. Ava assured her that Amy would never have to worry about anything if in Phil, Jr.'s presence alone or otherwise. Also, Phil, Jr., was always at the hospital. Ava then mentioned if Phil, Jr., were an attending he would be around a lot more, but that was years away. Her own comment gave her pause for some reason.

The new year progressed quickly. The alternating Grandma Cammie-Amy childcare system was working well. Amy had no trouble keeping up with her academic responsibilities while providing solid care for Phillip Joseph. During the infant's naps there was plenty of time to read. Cammie was as happy as she had been in years despite the long days caring for Phillip Joseph and seemingly rabid devotion to improving her tennis game with her markedly increased time spent "at the club" on some days. The grey and snowy winter yielded to a grey and damp spring. Ava and Phil, Jr.'s first wedding anniversary passed with little fanfare. In May Pittsburgh suddenly seemed beautiful. Flowering trees, comfortable temperatures, and some sunshine lifted the spirits of all but the most serious of Pirates' fans who were now perpetually disappointed with life. The announcement was made for the next chief resident graduation ceremony in June. Phillip Joseph was beginning to sit on his own. Amy shared this observation with Ava one evening upon Ava's return from work. Amy also mentioned that Dr. Moss from next door came by *again* in the afternoon to see if she needed anything.

The next day at work Ava was quick to confront her boss regarding his daytime visits to her home. She coolly told him that Amy does not *need* anything from him, but if he *needed* something then maybe he should visit in the evening when Phil, Jr., is on call. He commented how walking Charlie in the evening was taking longer as Charlie was old, and maybe a rest next door before completing their journey around the block would be a good idea, for Charlie's sake. Dr. Moss for the first time in years suddenly took great interest in the resident call schedule. Next Thursday his son was on call and Cammie was always playing tennis late on most Thursdays now. Ava agreed that it would be a perfect time for him to visit their son.

When the Venn diagram of Phil, Jr., taking call, tennis Thursdays, and Phil, Sr., not stuck at the hospital overlapped, Phillip Moss, Sr., and Ava were unleashing their respective coiled springs of libido after over a year of celibacy. They did not make love; they had pelvic pounding sex and used each other for their own carnal pleasures until exhausted. This ritual took on a rhythm of its own with no end in sight for the foreseeable future. The chairman knew the resident call schedule by heart.

## Chapter Twenty-Four: Growing Department and Growing Family, 1998

At the chief resident graduation party Phil, Jr., was surprised by an unexpected guest. Ricki was in town and had been invited by the chairman to the event. More importantly, however, Dr. Bouba was in town to find a place to live. He had been offered and accepted a faculty position as Assistant Professor in the Department of Neurological Surgery, as Dr. Kleinwurst alluded one year prior. Ricki was taking the month of July off before starting the first of August. He planned to see family in Cameroon for two of those weeks. He had been offered a position to stay at the Cleveland Clinic with a much higher salary, but despite his accumulated student debt he knew he would be happier back in Pittsburgh. Phil, Jr.'s mood was markedly improved compared to a year ago.

Amy was pulling a rare nighttime babysitting shift watching Phillip Joseph so the collective Moss family could attend the annual celebration. Several of the residents insisted on taking Ricki out on the town after the party as they were thrilled to welcome him back as junior faculty. Ava told her husband to certainly join them as Cammie and Phil, Sr., could give her a ride home. Ava also told her husband that he could come home in the morning if he liked. Phil, Jr., took full advantage of that opportunity.

Phil, Jr., began his fourth year of resident training on July first. Three years down and four to go he thought to himself as he walked in the early dawn light from the parking garage. At least now he was able to arrive between five thirty and six in the morning rather than at the four thirty a.m. of his earlier years. Seniority, if that's what you called it, had its perks he chuckled to himself. In one month, Ricki Bouba would be a faculty member and attending neurosurgeon. Ricki was flying to Cameroon from Cleveland tomorrow. Phil, Jr., was counting on Ricki to lay low and just hang out with family. His father's words regarding Cameroon and Ricki still echoed in his consciousness.

The summer and fall were some of Phil, Jr.'s most pleasant recent memories. In August Ricki was safely ensconced in Pittsburgh and in the attending call rotation. Ricki reminded him with a big smile to call him "Dr. Bouba" now. Only the second and third-year residents referred to him as such though. Everyone that worked with Ricki while he was a resident called him whatever they wanted. Back in Shadyside, Phil, Jr., could tell everyone was happy. His mother in particular had a near constant smile on her face. Ava was content in both her work and home life. His father was much more approachable and less intimidating. By Halloween Phillip Joseph was pulling himself to stand and independent walking was just weeks away. For Halloween the almost one-year old was dressed as a miniature Terry Bradshaw, while a nearby little girl about the same age rode in the same wagon dressed as figure skater Jojo Starbuck. Even though the real former couple had been divorced for fifteen years, the chuckles and accolades were overflowing as they did their door-to-door rounds trick or treating.

Phil, Jr., and Ricki were able to steal time away together. While they both wanted more, the current situation was enough to keep their relationship alive and growing. Ricki was even invited to Phillip Joseph's first birthday party in November. Ricki brought an authentic

Cameroon helmet mask as a gift, but counseled Ava and Phil, Jr., to use it for photos only and not let it become a giant teething ring, because the thousands of colored beads would not be a welcome sight in Phillip Joseph's dirty diapers.

    Soon Thanksgiving had arrived and the annual family celebration at the House of Moss was once again occurring. Both daughters, including Anne's husband, Josh, and Sarah's fiancé, Trey, were present. Sarah and Trey were to be married in early June. Much conversation amongst the women revolved around the impending nuptials. Anne, who noticeably had not been enjoying any wine or beer, then announced to the family that she and Josh had a due date exactly one month before the date of Sarah's wedding. Cammie Moss was becoming a puddle as tears of joy filled her face. After the clamber of excitement died down regarding Anne's pregnancy, Ava then spoke. She apologized at first, not knowing if this was the right time as she did not want to steal anything away from the joyful announcements and plans of her sisters-in-law, but she wanted everyone to know that she and Phil, Jr., would be welcoming a second child in July. Everyone in the room except for the three Phillips immediately broke out in big smiles offering heartfelt congratulations. Phillip, Sr., expelled beer through his nostrils which triggered a coughing fit. Phillip, Jr., who was animatedly playing with Phillip Joseph by bouncing him on his knee went stone faced and looked at his coughing father. Phillip Joseph who had been giggling and laughing went quiet at the change in Phillip, Jr.'s demeanor. The young boy tilted his head to one side and just gazed with his chestnut brown eyes at the man he considered his father wanting to ask what was wrong, if he only could.

Made in the USA
Columbia, SC
08 March 2025